*E*nduring *D*reams

# Enduring Dreams

Widow's Might Series

Book One

Sandra Ardoin

Corner Room Books

# SANDRA ARDOIN

ISBN: 978-1-7334630-2-7 (Print); 978-1-7334630-3-4 (E-book)

Library of Congress Control Number: 2020914845

Cover design by Evelyne Labelle, Carpe Librum Book Design.

Edited by Lynne Tagawa

# ENDURING DREAMS

## Widow's Might Series
*Enduring Dreams*, Book One
*Unwrapping Hope*, Novella

## Additional Novels and Novellas
*A Love Most Worthy*
*A Reluctant Melody*
*The Yuletide Angel*

Make no little plans; they have no magic to stir men's blood
and probably will themselves not be realized.

—Daniel Burnham, Architect

# Chapter One

"At long last, this is a reality." Mark Gregory stood in the center of the empty drafting room of his new architectural office. His gaze skimmed every corner, every square foot of the cool and empty room. He was three months late taking in this sight, and he intended to enjoy it.

There was nothing more stimulating, more capable of pumping the blood through a man's veins with vigor, than seeing something he'd dreamed about for months—years, even  come to fruition. His own business.

"Come see this, Mark."

He peered over his shoulder at Addison O'Keefe, the agent who leased him the office. "Tell me about it."

Addison stared out a window and chuckled. "We're only on the second floor. What harm could come to you?"

*Plenty.*

Mark reminded himself that his new friend spoke in innocence, ignorant of the circumstances surrounding the death of Stefen Grzegorczyk. Addison assumed fear held Mark back. In fact, heights recalled his father's suffering and the reason for it. He rubbed his left forearm, painful only in his memory.

He ambled to the open window and peered down at the people scurrying from one place to another. A steady stream of horse-drawn traffic moved up and down Commerce Street, the town's main thoroughfare. His nose wrinkled at catching a whiff of coal smoke and last night's trash—a mild stench compared to what he left behind in Chicago.

Addison pointed west. "What do you make of that?"

Thankful for the distraction, Mark concentrated on the half-finished, three-story structure a block away. He had passed the building numerous times since arriving in town a few days ago.

"It's hideous." The structure looked like a hodge-podge of various patterns with no common connection. And what good would that bell tower do? It was attached to an office building, not a church. A good architect would have stuck to one style and ensured that every element flowed together. "Clearly, the designer attempted to create something unique but only proved he has too little talent to realize his goal."

"I agree. However, that hasn't stopped me from contacting the owner to act as his leasing agent."

"I wish you luck." Mark chuckled. "Actually, the blight is an advantage. The people of Riverport now have access to an architect they can trust to provide sensible designs."

"And you will." Addison slapped Mark's back. He might have no financial interest in Mark's company beyond his work for the landlord, but in their communications and meetings, the two men had quickly become friends.

Mark turned to survey his rented space again, unable to get enough of it. His hands rested on his hips as he admired the large room. Two electric lamps hung from the ceiling and the wood floor had been buffed to a sheen. The only flaw was the small closet that blocked a window. It was soon to be torn out.

"This room is large enough to accommodate three or four additional draftsmen. I'll need them in the future." It was an audacious statement, but with the threat of a significant loan payment due in a few months, he must think audaciously. He hadn't the time to be timid or modest.

His father's words echoed in his mind. "A man's reputation is everything, son. Don't throw it away on debt."

In the past, Mark had agreed, but old age would have overtaken him by the time he'd saved the amount required to tide him over until the business began a profit. He had vowed years ago that he would not die young like his father without making a name for himself first. This venture gave him the opportunity.

Although he had budgeted for a less expensive rent payment, Mark had selected this suite because of the natural lighting coming from the triple bowed windows in the drafting room. More importantly, the limestone façade presented an appearance of the success he expected to achieve.

If not for his mother's illness, he would have opened the office in February, easing the strain on his timetable. But he couldn't—wouldn't—leave her alone in Chicago with no one to care for her. Now, he must work harder and faster to achieve his goal. He must. Failure was unacceptable.

The empty space amplified his *harrumph*. He would not fail. Not only would he lose everything, including the reputation he wished to build, but his mother would insist he tuck tail and rush them back to the old neighborhood.

From this moment on, the word "failure" was struck from his vocabulary.

Mark rubbed his hands together, eager to get started. "Tomorrow, the furniture is delivered." He had purchased everything from a retiring architect, impressed by the excellent condition of the pieces and swayed by the reasonable price.

Addison pointed to the turret area. "You've already said you'll position the drafting easel near these long windows to take advantage of the light. What else?"

"For the time being, the table for conferring with clients will go in the middle of the room. The bookcase and a smaller table there."

Mark pointed to the back wall. "I have a desk and chair for the outer office. Eventually, I'll hire an assistant for that room—a man to handle the visitors, billing, and correspondence."

"Marek?"

Mark stiffened at the voice that called his name—the one given to him at birth. He strode into the front room. "I wasn't expecting you here today, Mama."

She brandished a broom in one hand. A bucket filled with rags and scrub brushes hung from her other arm.

He took the items from her and set them on the floor. "What is all this?"

She tucked a stray lock of salt-and-pepper hair under her hat. "You must not move your furniture into a dirty office." Even after living in America for thirty years, she still spoke with a slight Polish accent, although her English was near perfect...when it suited her.

"The office isn't dirty. The janitor cleaned it the other day."

She expressed her disbelief with a sniff. "It will not take long."

As usual, he might as well speak to the wall. What did it matter? Moving here had uprooted her from the community in which she felt at home, so if cleaning the office pleased her, he would oblige.

His arm swept the air with a flourish. "Do what makes you happy, Mama." As soon as he said that dangerous phrase, he regretted it.

She set to work sweeping the floor and dusting windowsills, then smiled when he grabbed a rag and started on the other end of the room.

"How do you like the house, Mrs. Grzegorczyk?" Addison asked.

"It is too big, Mr. O'Keefe."

"It's not much bigger than your old house." Mark rented the new one for its three bedrooms as well as the separate dining room and large kitchen with a nice pantry. His mother could cook Polish dishes to her heart's content.

"Still, I have been thinking."

Mark caught himself before his inner cringe shivered into a visible one.

"I will look for a boarder for that extra room upstairs."

He paused in the middle of wiping down a wall, and his temple throbbed. "We don't need a boarder."

"We don't need an extra bedroom, either. Until you are a rich and famous architect, you could use the money. Perhaps you have a recommendation for someone, Mr. O'Keefe?"

Behind him, Addison snickered. Mark shot him a look. O'Keefe backed toward the room's entrance. "It was nice to see you, Mrs. Grzegorczyk, but I'm afraid I'll leave this subject for you and your son to discuss." He slipped out the door and into the hall. His laughter trailed behind him like a comet's tail.

"We don't need money from a boarder, Mama." Not once his business became known. "Also, I'm certain it's against the conditions of my lease."

She waved her hand, and her rag flew like a flag in a stiff wind. "All these new expenses to make you look like an important businessman. What do we need with three bedrooms?"

"What if *Ciotka* Gizela visits?"

"Then my sister can stay with me in my room, as she always does."

Mark fought to wipe exasperation from his voice and said, "No boarder, Mama. That's my final word on the subject."

"Marek, *mój słodki chłopcze*, we will discuss it later. For now, work."

Calling him her sweet boy meant trouble and an intention to finagle a way to get what she wanted. She also called him that whenever she bemoaned his offenses against his Polish heritage—among them, moving her out of their neighborhood, Americanizing his name, and refusing to marry Paulina, the woman she believed best suited him.

After his father died when he was twelve, Mark had assumed the responsibility of caring for his mother, a responsibility he'd gladly accepted as an only child. Those years taught him to be vigilant and as stubborn as the woman who bore him.

No, sir. He loved his mother, but in the matter of a boarder, he would dig in his heels. And when he married, it would be to a woman of *his* choosing, no one else's.

Mark's shoulders slumped. What a pretty speech. The truth was, when Anastazja Grzegorczyk chose to do something, only God could stop her, and Mark learned long ago that the Almighty rarely wished to intercede on his behalf.

Why should he ask God to intervene in his minor problems when God had refused to intervene in the matter of saving his father's life?

CLAIRE KINGSLEY'S JAW ached after nine hours of smiling. In the privacy of the employee salon, she stretched her arms, then released a groan.

After a full day of selling indecisive and sometimes peevish women everything from undergarments to evening gowns, she couldn't wait to leave behind the bustle and noise of S. F. Newland's Department Store. She couldn't wait to reach the quiet of her bedroom and...

And what? Retreat into the past, into a time when her imagination soared—into a world she once embraced but no longer called her own?

Claire took the elevator from the fourth floor down to the first and left the store through a rear door. She walked around the corner and down Commerce Street on her way to her parents' house, to the place she had called home for almost two years. She loved her family, but how she missed having her own house, her own things around her, her own right of possession.

Perhaps it was time to look for a room to rent. She had intended to live with her family for months, not years, only until she'd come to grips with her new circumstances and assuaged some of the grief.

She had intended to do many things with her life. That included spending the rest of it with Richard, designing buildings in an age when elevators carried people up ten or fifteen stories to the tops of skyscrapers. She'd intended a life with her husband that included children who might someday follow in their parents' professional footsteps.

If Claire had learned one thing in life, it was that intentions lasted only as long as the will and the courage to achieve them.

At the corner of Commerce and Henning, she paused to survey the building being constructed across the street. Whoever designed it had succeeded in creating the ugliest structure she had ever laid eyes on.

An older gentleman, short and stout, stopped on the sidewalk beside her. One hand gripped a black walking stick with a carved ivory top while the other stroked a full gray beard. His attention never wavered from the monstrosity on the other side of the street. "That's quite something, isn't it?"

"Yes. It is something."

He turned to her. "You aren't impressed?"

For all Claire knew, the man could be the architect or owner. While she hesitated to insult him, she wouldn't lie. Instead, she implemented the diplomacy she had perfected while dealing with customers at the store. "It is an interesting choice of style."

The man pursed his lips as he studied the building again. "It does look as if the designer couldn't make up his mind and preferred, therefore, to use everything in his creative arsenal in a single building."

She laughed at the disgust in his tone, which freed her to give her true opinion. "I see a hint of Georgian in the pattern and form of the windows, a little Romanesque in that corner tower, and...heaven only knows what that flat roof line with the extended eaves is supposed to represent. Architecture should welcome the onlooker, not repel him. What I see instills nothing more than confusion."

"You're well-informed about architecture."

"For a woman?" Claire flashed her practiced smile, hoping to take the sting from the words that sprang from her mouth, even if she couldn't hide the bitterness.

"I cannot deny my surprise. Although I assure you, no offense was intended."

Defending her work in the profession of architecture was a battle she had fought too often, with her parents, and especially with her husband's partner, George Brant. That man hadn't waited until Richard was cold in the ground before informing her that her services were no longer needed at Kingsley and Brant Architects.

True, she'd had no formal education, but she'd had something better. She'd had her husband's expertise to guide and teach her...superior to any classroom study.

She sighed. "I owe you an apology, sir. Sometimes, I'm too passionate in my own defense. But my being female doesn't mean I have no imagination or skills."

"I agree with your viewpoint, ma'am." The gentleman beside her arched an eyebrow. "Then you are an architect?"

As it had so often, the truth stabbed her like the point of a drawing compass to the heart. According to the firm's contract, the business went to George as the surviving partner. Claire, the surviving partner in life, was stripped of any official role in the company and the ability to carry on the profession she'd shared with Richard. "Not anymore. Before my husband passed away, we often worked together."

The man shifted the walking stick he carried to his other hand.

"I'm sorry to learn of your loss. However, if God has given you a pursuit, never apologize for being passionate about it or for a commitment to it."

Surely, God did not instill dreams in one person to destroy the life of another. That had been her doing.

"May I ask why you work in a department store these days, ma'am, rather than in an architectural office?" Her curiosity in learning how he knew where she worked must have shown on her face, because he pointed to her gray suit. "The other women in Newland's dress in similar clothing."

"You are perceptive, Mr...."

"Dover, ma'am. Charles Dover."

"It's nice to meet you, Mr. Dover. I'm Claire Kingsley."

He dipped his head in acknowledgment. "You were about to tell me why you're no longer an architect."

This man would not be sidetracked. Never would she tell him that, because of that passion they discussed, her precious Richard perished, or that, because she feared another miscarriage, he died without an heir.

"We have no architectural office in Riverport, though if we did, I doubt they would hire me. Not all men are as open-minded as you, Mr. Dover."

Though she had never admitted it to others, the truth was that resuming work in the profession terrified her, even as it called to her with a thunderous voice.

"A pity." Once more, he arched an eyebrow, the other one this time. "It has always taken pioneers to blaze the way through new territory, you know."

At one time, she had believed she possessed the pluck to be a pioneer. She had been young and naïve. Society had its role for women, one that didn't include working in a man's world. Even her parents had pleaded for her to remain where a woman belonged and not venture into uncharted territory. She had ignored them and the other naysayers...until she let the fantasy exact too high a price.

"Are you an architect, sir?"

"No. I'm simply someone who recognizes what he likes when he sees it." He raised the stick and pointed it at the building. "That is not it."

"We agree." Curiosity gained a foothold. "May I ask why you support the idea of professional women?"

His brow crinkled. "My niece fought long and hard to become a respected physician, to gain patients who trusted her ability and advice. Many of her loudest detractors were colleagues."

"Did she succeed?"

"Eventually." He tapped the brim of his hat. "I have enjoyed speaking with you, Mrs. Kingsley. Perhaps, one day, we'll meet in front of another new building and stop to compare opinions."

"I would like that, sir."

Claire stared after him as he walked away. What an understanding, modern thinker.

She studied the building once more. Such a waste of an expensive piece of property. Richard could have created something inspiring on that lot. They could have created it together.

Because of her, he would never create anything again. Because of her, the Kingsley name would never grace another blueprint of a well-received design.

# Chapter Two

I f Mark's mother ever admitted to a vice, it would be a love for hats—seeing them, trying them on, examining every little adornment.

Mark had little time or money to spare, but if a new hat helped her to feel better about their move to Riverport, he would devote a few minutes of his day and a portion of the coins in his pocket to escort her on a shopping excursion. Though why she desired a new hat, he couldn't say. Not when she crafted them herself like another woman might crochet lace or embroider a pillow covering. What had she done with them all?

As he followed her through the elaborate front door of S. F. Newland's, he pulled out his father's silver pocket watch etched with a simple leaf design on the back. Thirty minutes should give her time to find something nice.

He slipped the watch back in his pocket and surveyed the first floor of the department store. Just as Riverport was nothing to rival Chicago, this store was nothing to rival Marshall Fields in size or style. Still, at four stories, it was the tallest and most impressive building in town, a building designed with both luxury and functionality in mind. Even during a workday, the place buzzed with customers. People must come from miles around to shop its merchandise.

He approached the marble-topped counter in the center of the first floor and asked the male concierge manning it, "Where will we find ladies' hats?"

"All women's fashions are on the third floor, sir. Ask for Mrs. Kingsley."

The young man's enthusiastic grin was infectious, and Mark responded in kind. "Thank you."

He led his mother to the elevator next to a wide staircase, prepared to escort her up the steps. She balked. "I am not so feeble that I cannot climb stairs, Marek, and you have no business in a ladies department. Who knows what you will see."

After almost twenty-nine years of watching her unmentionables flying from the clothesline, he doubted he'd see anything to shock him.

"You're not feeble, Mama—" far from it—"but it hasn't been long since your bout with influenza."

"I am well. Now go."

"Fine. I'll look around down here. Remember to ask for Mrs. Kingsley."

She gripped the wrought iron handrail and nodded. "I will not be long."

Mark wandered through the departments on the first floor—from the perfumes to the kitchen supplies. He stopped at a display of linens, pulled out a white damask tablecloth, and held it out to examine the fruit design and scrollwork border. Perhaps his mother would like it for the dining room table.

Probably, but she would only tell him he couldn't afford it, and she'd be right. Not even three months before the bank expected a large payment on his loan.

When Mark decided on a location for his office, he looked for a growing town with little competition. Not that he lacked the self-assurance to succeed. Quite the contrary. However, Chicago already ran rife with some of the century's most amazing architects: Lewis Sullivan, Daniel Burnham, and Dankmar Adler, to name a few. He wanted somewhere ready for his business but not overwhelmed with talent.

A fellow draftsman at D. H. Burnham and Company suggested Riverport near his hometown in Indiana. More than a farming community, Riverport had experienced strong growth in the past two decades, both in population and wealth. New buildings. New homes. New department store. It was a splendid place for a new beginning.

Mark refolded the linen and put it back on the shelf. All he needed was one important project between now and the end of July.

After wandering some more, he stopped near the concierge counter for the second time. The young man asked, "Did your mother find what she was looking for, sir?"

"She's still up there."

"Well, if she met Mrs. Kingsley as I suggested, she might be a while. My sister is quite the saleswoman."

And the brother was adept at promoting his sister. "I hope she's not too much of a saleswoman. We'll need to eat the rest of the month." It was a half-hearted joke, but perhaps he should make sure the clerk didn't take advantage of his mother. He pulled out the watch and checked the time again. "I think I'll hurry them along."

He stopped at the staircase of white marble treads and walnut risers and looked up at two floors with nothing but a slim, waist-high wrought iron barrier to prevent a customer from tumbling and falling to the first floor. Foolishness.

Mark wrapped his fingers around the handrail of the staircase and climbed to the second-floor landing. He looked up and craned his neck, trying to locate his mother above him. Naturally, she was nowhere in his line of sight.

Halfway to the third floor, a child of seven or eight bumped into him as he raced down the stairs without a second thought to his safety.

"Be careful that you don't fall." Mark imagined the boy tripping and lunging headfirst in a tumble to rest in a broken heap on the landing. The rascal reached the second floor, never having looked back. Mark shook his head.

The first thing he saw on the third floor was a display of women's hats. He searched the area for his mother with no success.

A straw boater snagged his attention. Thick, black feather plumes stuck straight up, held by folds of some type of orange-gold material that matched one of her suits. He thumped a feather and watched it wave back and forth.

"That's a beautiful choice, sir, though you may prefer a style that better matches your suit."

He looked up to find a mesmerizing blonde with expressive blue eyes grinning at him. Her light gray suit with a white shirtwaist matched the uniforms of other women who worked in the store.

Without permitting himself a second thought over his absurd response, Mark picked up the hat and placed it on his head. "Are you sure? I think it adds a certain flair to my wardrobe, don't you?"

She crossed her arms and studied it from various angles, a twitch of her well-formed lips the only sign of humor on her fair, angelic face. "I will admit, it does accentuate the amber in your eyes." Pink tinted her cheeks. Then she masked her delightful sense of humor with the starched formality of an ordinary sales clerk. "I'm with a customer, sir. May I find someone else to help you?"

He opened his mouth to ask about his mother when Mama appeared, sporting a hat she hadn't worn into the store. "Marek?" She glanced between him and the clerk, a scowl marring her face. "I would suggest you walk down one flight and try on a felt derby. Brown is more your color."

Heat scorched his face and, no doubt, stained it the same shade as the clerk's. He yanked off the hat and handed it to the blonde. "I apologize for my ridiculous behavior, Miss...?"

The clerk's smile was a remnant of what he'd seen a moment earlier. "Mrs. Kingsley."

So this was the expert saleswoman. Her coloring did reflect her brother's.

Mark's buoyant mood had lasted less than two minutes. *Mrs.* He'd flirted with a married woman. Now, he really did feel ridiculous...and disappointed. "I beg your pardon, ma'am."

"No harm done." She turned to his mother, the smile back in place. She held out the hat. "Your son has good taste in choosing this lovely piece for you, Mrs. She... Shegor..."

"It is pronounced Zhi-gor-chek." Mama removed the hat on her head and shoved it at Mrs. Kingsley. She swiped her own hat from a nearby shelf and started for the staircase. "I am no longer interested in buying anything, madam."

Mark's jaw fell slack. What had gotten into his mother?

The wide-eyed clerk turned to Mark. "I'm sorry, I didn't mean to offend her, Mr. Grzegorczyk."

She pronounced it perfectly this time, but he didn't have the heart to ask her to call him Mr. Gregory. "It wasn't your fault, Mrs. Kingsley. Thank you for your assistance."

He followed his mother as she stomped down each stair. Once they reached the first floor, he asked, "Why didn't you buy a hat? It was what you came here to do." Why waste time looking only to change her mind and not purchase anything?

"I will not buy from that woman."

"Why not? She seemed friendly."

"Too friendly for someone who is married. *If* you understand my meaning." His mother marched to the door. "And she could not pronounce our name."

"You insist on holding that against the woman?" For the sake of his career, he had legally changed his name to save clients from the same discomfort he had seen on Mrs. Kingsley's face. "You were rude to her, Mama."

"She flirted with you."

"We were laughing over the hat. Besides, you misunderstood." He opened the door and they stepped onto the sidewalk. "I flirted with her."

His mother stopped and stared at him. "Marek."

"That was before I learned she was married." He might not live the most devout Christian life, but he knew right from wrong. He knew of the practical and spiritual hazards brought on by an attraction to a married woman.

"Married and not Polish."

"Please don't start that. Whether you like it or not, Mama, you're in America. You've lived here for thirty years. Don't you think it's time you stopped acting as though Father kidnapped you and brought you here against your will?"

"You're *tata*—"

Mark raised both hands to stop her. "My father wanted a better life for his family, which didn't include his children living under a Prussian thumb."

His mother stiffened. "At least Paulina can pronounce our name. You need a wife who understands your background."

"Paulina Kowalski is a wonderful woman, a friend, but I will marry someone I love be she Polish, English, or Tasmanian." Tired of the familiar argument, he clutched his mother's elbow and urged her on. "Let's go home. It's getting late, and I have a big day tomorrow."

On the walk to their new house, Mark tried to concentrate on the list of tasks still to complete with the move into the new office. But time after time, his mind returned to the image of a blue-eyed blonde with a flawless face, a ready smile, and a quick wit.

What kind of man had she married? For her sake, he hoped her husband enjoyed laughter.

Mark quickened his pace. Thinking of married women meant

trouble, and that kind of trouble was the last thing he sought.

"IS SOMETHING TROUBLING you?"

Claire looked up from the book on her lap. "Why do you ask, Ma?"

"You look tired and worried."

Not worried. Conflicted. Embarrassed. Foolish. Lonely.

Speaking with Mr. Dover on Wednesday and then today's disastrous encounter at the store with the Grzegorczyks had worn on her.

"It's nothing. I upset a customer this afternoon. She was Polish or Russian, probably, with a difficult name. As a result, Newland's lost a sale."

Though the story was true, what really bothered Claire about the incident was how she had made a fool of herself in front of the woman's son. It was unbecoming, unprofessional, and...and completely unacceptable on every level. She was fortunate neither mother nor son had complained to her employers about her behavior—not yet, anyway.

Her mother dropped her paintbrush in the old jar. It hit the side of the glass with a soft *clink*. A talented amateur china painter, she'd almost finished the colorful bouquet of red roses, orange zinnias, and pink hollyhocks decorating the vase on the small table in front of her. Claire assumed she'd received her artistic gift from her mother, since her father couldn't draw a straight line with a ruler.

"I'm sorry you lost the sale."

Claire produced her brightest smile. "Don't worry. There will be others." Other sales, not flirtations.

Until today, the only man she had ever flirted with was Richard. Nevertheless, she had taken one look at a strong chin and an amber twinkle in the eyes of a stranger and lost all sense of propriety. Even now, she fought a smile. He'd looked bizarre wearing that hat. Somehow, though, the comedic lark took nothing away from his dignity and air of self-confidence.

No man had ever affected her that way upon first glance. If she were truthful, not even her husband.

Mr. Grzegorczyk's antics had prompted her to act frivolous and impulsive in return. That, too, was unacceptable. For all she knew, he was a married man.

Regardless, she wasn't ready for romance and would not be ready for marriage again until she was safely past childbearing age.

She slapped the cover closed on the novel. Mark Twain had been Richard's favorite author, but after giving in to the urge to dig his book, *A Connecticut Yankee in King Arthur's Court*, out of the trunk in her room, she hadn't turned a page in the last twenty minutes. "You're right. I am a bit tired. I think I'll go upstairs. Good night, Ma."

Her mother studied her a moment, and she nearly withered and confessed all under the concerned and questioning stare. "Good night, Claire."

Once in her bedroom, she lifted the rounded lid of her grandmother's Jenny Lind trunk and laid the book inside. Her attention snagged on another book half-buried under a woolen skirt she'd packed away for the summer. She must have exposed it when removing the novel.

She pulled it from the trunk. Her heart hammered as she ran a finger over the black linen cover. The sketchbook contained drawings of building elevations, interior rooms, even the landscapes on which her imagined homes sat. As modest or as extravagant as she desired, they represented a shadow of the dream she'd once had the will to reach for, the one that filled her with joy.

These days, she kept the book to herself, hidden in the chest as though the drawings amounted to a collection of naughty sketches created by a debauched hand. She hadn't opened it since—

Claire stuffed the sketchbook back under the skirt and slammed the trunk's curved lid shut.

# Chapter Three

M ark's goals were on the verge of being met. He controlled his own success, his destiny. He felt it in every breath of the office air he inhaled and every client he imagined.

If only those clients would walk through the door in front of him, the one his stare bore a hole through.

Maybe he'd expected too much, too soon.

The article in the *Riverport Times* came out a week ago, seven days after he'd stopped in at the newspaper office. Short and impersonal, it left out much of the information he had given the bored clerk, who had blocked him from speaking with a journalist.

The original had been a fine paragraph, too. He'd spent an hour writing it and remembered every word.

*As a draftsman and designer under the supervision and tutelage of architect Daniel Burnham of D. H. Burnham in Chicago, Mark Gregory gained the experience and respect required to establish his own firm in the fine city of Riverport.*

*The designs of Mark Gregory Architecture shine with individuality yet never stray from the practicality essential to his clients. Mr. Gregory is a forward-thinker who brings unique beauty to a building and showcases the latest and safest innovations in construction materials and methods.*

*You may call upon him at Mark Gregory Architecture, 245 Commerce Street, Suite 2-B.*

Unfortunately, the information printed was less than stellar and cost him the price of an advertisement.

*As a draftsman and designer under the supervision and tutelage of architect Daniel Burnham of D. H. Burnham and Company in Chicago, Mark Gregory has established his own firm in the fine city of Riverport.*

*Call upon him at Mark Gregory Architecture, 245 Commerce Street, Suite 2-B.*

Settled in the chair behind the used desk, Mark placed his palms on the clean, paperless surface and ran a hand over the silky wood. Within the next six months, the top of this desk would teem with orders, invoices, and correspondence.

No, within two months. Addison repeatedly said that if he was to dream, it was a sin to dream small.

The rumor that Harris Lefler planned to build in Riverport presented Mark with his best opportunity for a quick and notable start. So far, he'd received no response to his letter of introduction. Although his chance of gaining the wealthy businessman's attention was slim, he refused to dream small.

He tapped his fingers on the wood. Where was the sign man? Seeing the firm's name painted on the glass would symbolize the official start to the business. The man was an hour later than anticipated today and two weeks later than when Mark had needed him.

He had no right to complain. By the time he'd contacted the painter, his schedule was full.

It did little good to sit around bemoaning a lack of business or the tardiness of the painter, so he went to the storage area off the drafting room. As he rearranged the architectural supplies and tools on the shelves, the outer door to the office opened, alerting him to a visitor.

*At last!*

Mark returned to the front office to find a rail-thin older man dressed in paint-splattered clothing standing near the desk. He smelled of turpentine and some type of strong cheese. "I hope you're here to letter the door."

"Yes, sir. Sorry I'm late. My last customer kept changing his order." He frowned at Mark as if expecting his current customer to be every bit as ambivalent. He gestured behind him. "This the door?"

"Yes. You have what I require?"

The man pulled out a sheet of paper, and they went over the details. "Seems clear enough. I'll get right to work."

"Good."

"By the way, you are Mr. Gregory, aren't you?"

"Yes."

He tapped an envelope on the desk. "A messenger boy came in with me and left this for you."

Mark snatched the envelope and slit the seal with his finger. "Why didn't he call out?"

"Said he had another delivery to make and asked me to be sure you saw it."

Mark read the message. "Are you familiar with a gentleman by the name of Dover?"

The man's mouth twisted in a sign of deep thought. "No, sir. Don't think so."

Whoever this Dover was, he'd seen the article in the newspaper and wanted to meet with Mark on Friday to discuss a project. He refolded the letter and stuffed it in the envelope. A possible client.

On his way back to the drafting room, he paused to admire the *M* and *A* already outlined on the glass. What a day. What a start to the future.

Addison was right. Why should he dream small?

"DO WE STILL HAVE LAST week's newspaper?" Why wasn't it

in the pile as usual, and why even look for it? There it was. "Never mind, Ma, I found it."

Claire's friend, Roslyn Malone, had told her of an article announcing the opening of an architectural office in Riverport. *"It's high time you left this store and gave others the opportunity to realize your talent."* Roslyn's words echoed in her mind.

Claire had tried to ignore the longing to find the article, but here she stood, shuffling through a stack of old newspapers kept in the mudroom to light the stove.

"What is so interesting?" Her mother's voice had risen higher than normal. She paused while peeling potatoes for their supper, which included baked chicken, according to Claire's nose. "Is Newland's having a sale?"

"They're always having a sale, Ma, but it's not what I'm looking for."

"Then why are you tearing through those pages?"

If she admitted the goal of her search, her mother would tell her father. Unlike Roslyn, her parents hadn't approved of her working in Richard's office. They had wanted her to stay home and give them grandchildren. A pain twisted inside her, crushing her lungs. She had tried...for a while.

"You heard, didn't you?" At the somber note in her mother's voice, Claire stopped turning pages. "Your pa thought if he hid the newspaper..."

"He thought if he hid it, I wouldn't find out about the new architect in town?"

Ma nodded. "We don't want you hurt again."

"I appreciate your concern for me. I really do. But you're not responsible for my decisions." Their parental smothering was another reason to find her own place. "I simply want to see who it is. Maybe I know him."

Claire sped through the tiny bit of information in the article and absorbed the salient points before she balled the paper up and tossed it into the stove's firebox. "See? That's all I wanted. Now, let me help you peel those potatoes."

She may as well have tattooed the address of the firm on her palm with newsprint. She doubted she would forget it soon. But what would she do with it?

"Ma, how would you feel if I said I planned to look for a room to let?"

Her mother's hands paused. "Why would you do that, Claire? You have a perfectly good room here."

"I do, but I can't live here forever."

She took her mother's prolonged silence as her answer.

Her brother, Wallace, walked into the kitchen. "This letter came for you, Claire."

She set the paring knife and half-peeled potato on the counter, wiped her hands on her apron, and took the envelope from him. Printed on the flap were monogrammed initials—a *D* flanked by a *C* and *M*.

"CMD. CD." She shook her head. "I can't think of anyone with those initials."

Wallace nodded toward the envelope. "Seems to me there's a way to identify the sender."

Claire grinned. She ripped the envelope open and pulled out a sheet of notepaper with a handwritten message. "It's an invitation to meet with Mr. Dover."

Her mother peered over her shoulder at the paper. "Who is Mr. Dover?"

"I met him on my walk home from the store two weeks ago."

"And he wants to meet with you? Why?"

She reread the short message, a suspicion niggling at the back of her mind, but it wasn't a suspicion she cared to share with her family. "It doesn't exactly say. He writes that it's an important matter."

Ma clucked her tongue. "Sounds inappropriate to me."

"It's at his office on Friday afternoon. How inappropriate could it be?"

Her mother's eyes widened. "Claire Ellen, you are no child. You know very well—"

"Ma, I'll be fine. He was a nice man. Besides, he must be at least Pa's age."

"Men are men no matter the age."

Her mother had a point. Still, Claire couldn't imagine the gentleman she met having a wicked intent. Though he made no mention of it, instinct told her the invitation involved their previous conversation.

What did he want? Perhaps he'd found another building to discuss with her. Or, perhaps, he had also read about the new architectural firm. If so, what plan did he have up his sleeve?

"You'll go, won't you?"

Claire hated hearing the concern mingled with resignation in her mother's voice. With no children of her own, she was left to imagine what it was like for a parent to see a child make a decision deemed to be unwise—no matter the child's age. "I don't know yet."

She could convince herself she only wanted to see a kindly gentleman again, but she knew better. The curiosity had already weaved its way under her skin.

Along with it, she felt the rise of an old passion and the familiar fear it instilled.

CLAIRE PAUSED ON THE sidewalk on Commerce Street and lowered her umbrella. Had she not learned her lesson two years ago?

Perhaps she'd jumped to conclusions. In his invitation, Mr. Dover had been coy in stating his purpose. It might have nothing to do with the profession of architecture.

The morning rain had stopped, leaving a damp and fresh scent in the air...along with mud on her shoes and splotches of it on the hem of her gray skirt. A fine impression to leave with a man who had struck her as fastidious in his dress.

She shook the raindrops off the umbrella. After going round and round since Tuesday, she could only say that her midnight conversations with God brought her a tentative peace only after she had agreed to meet with Mr. Dover. It made no sense. God knew her weakness. Why put her in this position once more?

If she hadn't already sent word to Mr. Dover accepting his invitation, she would turn around and walk back to the store—peace or no peace.

She glanced up at the smoky clouds and bemoaned their presence, wishing for a bright, cheery afternoon to calm her nerves. At least, she'd finished with tramping across another muddy street.

People strolled up and down the walk on both sides of Commerce. Some had lowered their umbrellas as she had done. Others held the instrument high, seemingly oblivious to the fact it no longer rained.

Although she hadn't reached her destination, Claire scraped thick, heavy clumps of dark soil off the soles of her shoes by running them across the edge of the curb. Her brain taunted the futile effort as one of procrastination.

As soon as she turned the corner onto Riverside Avenue, she spotted a child of about four, not much younger than her first child would be today.

A woman, who Claire assumed was the girl's mother, plodded ahead with her back to the child, shoulders slumped and head down, while the girl hopscotched down the walkway behind her.

Prior to the first miscarriage, Claire had helped Richard and George at the office on occasion. After the second, she grew ever more involved in the business and the design work. Starting a family had been a goal for their future, but she had never imagined it would bring such pain, or that their future had a limited time frame.

If she and Richard had tried again for children—if she had been willing—would they eventually have become parents to girls, boys, or a mix of genders? She kicked the question to the street, along with another clump of mud. What good did it do to ponder something impossible to answer?

Without the busyness and impediments of a street such as Commerce, Riverside Avenue's traffic often tended to travel with more speed than prudence. A sense of danger shouted at her to increase her pace as the child wandered ever closer to the street.

Behind her, the rattle of a vehicle caught her ear. At the same moment, the girl danced off the curb and splashed through a series of mud puddles, progressing farther into the street, and soiling her stockings as well as the faded blue calico dress she wore.

Claire increased her pace, glancing over her shoulder at the fast-approaching beer wagon from Schroeder's Brewery. Its forest-green body swayed with the fast trot of the team of draft horses pulling it through the mud. The driver appeared focused on the mutt lying across his lap.

She latched onto her skirt, lifting it to run. "Stop!"

The girl splashed once more, then halted in the middle of a puddle to stare at her—right in a path to be trampled.

With her heart striking an insane rhythm, Claire tossed aside the umbrella and jumped off the curb. Out of the corner of her eye, she noticed the mother turn around. Claire lunged and wrapped her right arm around the girl's waist, scooping her up and leaping for the curb as the right lead horse brushed past.

She twisted, placing her back to the wagon to protect the girl. As she did so, her foot slipped in the slick mud. Her left arm flailed as she struggled to stay on her feet, but the weight of the child pulled her off-balance. They both tumbled sideways to the ground. She thanked the Lord that the little girl fell on top of her rather than the other way around.

Fortunately, the wagon passed them, the driver oblivious to what happened, but the dog barked with excitement.

Before Claire could catch her breath, someone pulled the girl away, then clutched her upper arm. "Are you hurt, Mrs. Kingsley?"

Her mind worked to identify the familiar voice. Claire looked into the face of her rescuer. *Of course, it would be him.*

How she wished to hide her face in the mud and pretend Mr. Grzegorczyk hadn't witnessed her fall.

# Chapter Four

B etween their previous meeting and this one, Mr. Grzegorczyk must believe Claire to be a complete lunatic.

Since he held tight to her arm, she allowed him to help her to her feet and over to the sidewalk before she pulled away from his hold.

"Are you hurt?"

Despite a muscle that pinched from twisting her body and the remnants of panic that left her trembling, she answered his repeated question. "No. How is the girl? She wasn't injured when we fell?"

The child hid her face in the folds of her mother's skirt. Her little shoulders quaked.

"Other than being scared and covered in mud, she seems fine." The admiration in his smile sent heat rushing through Claire. "Thanks to you."

Claire released a nervous chuckle and joked, "She did a fine job of getting dirty before I got involved. I simply finished the work." Glancing down, she noticed only a smidgen of mud on the lower leg of his trousers. How had he stepped into the street and kept so clean?

"You're a brave woman, Mrs. Kingsley. You saved that child's life."

After lifting the still-sobbing girl into her arms, the young mother approached Claire. "I can't thank you enough, ma'am. If you hadn't been here to see the danger, my Cissy would be..." She covered her mouth and her shoulders heaved with a cry not quite as loud as her daughter's. "I should have paid more attention, but my mind was on other matters."

SANDRA ARDOIN

"We all become distracted at times." How well Claire knew.

"I don't want you to think I'm not a good mother, and it's no excuse, but I've lost my job at Madame Marie's, and I was pondering the future."

"You worked for the dressmaker?"

The woman nodded. "She's closing soon."

"I'm sorry." Claire had heard the business was having financial difficulties but not to that extent. "I'm Claire Kingsley."

"Louisa Gruhn. My girl is Cecilia, but we...I call her Cissy."

"Hello, Cissy." Realizing it was covered in mud, Claire removed her glove and rubbed the child's back. She received a shy smile in return.

Mr. Grzegorczyk asked, "I don't mean to sound rude, Mrs. Gruhn, but your husband is employed, isn't he?"

The young mother didn't appear to take offense, probably due to the concern in his soft voice. "It's just me and her. My husband died several months ago."

"I'm terribly sorry."

Memories of being alone without employment after Richard died assaulted Claire. Her heart ached for the woman who had the added responsibility of raising a child. It seemed whenever Claire began to feel sorry for her own circumstances, God introduced her to someone less fortunate.

Though Newland's wasn't the sole source of the custom dressmaker's decline, Claire hesitated to admit her association with the department store. But if this woman were as astute as Mr. Dover, she would know by the outfit Claire wore. "Mrs. Gruhn, if you're interested, I've heard that Newland's is hiring. I would be happy to recommend you for a position."

"Newland's? I'd feel a traitor. That store is responsible for the failure of Marie's business."

Mr. Grzegorczyk handed Claire her umbrella. "Or, ma'am, it

34

could fill your daughter's empty belly."

Mrs. Gruhn's mouth drooped. "You're right, sir. Thank you, Mrs. Kingsley. I would appreciate the recommendation."

Claire shot Mr. Grzegorczyk a grateful smile before he stepped back and retrieved the derby and a leather case lying on the sidewalk. The hat reminded her of their first meeting.

"If you'll excuse me, ladies, I have an appointment." He bobbed his chin and walked away.

"We should go, too. Say thank you and goodbye, Cissy."

A tug on Claire's skirt took her attention off the figure of the retreating man in the crisp, brown suit. Cissy stared up at her. Without saying anything, the girl wrapped her little arms around Claire's legs.

Mrs. Gruhn picked up her daughter and hugged her close. Claire grinned at the brown splotch that painted the side of the child's face, a remnant of their tumble in the mud. She had the face of a cherub. Would the faces of Claire's children have shown the same sweetness?

When she looked again, Mr. Grzegorczyk had disappeared. The incident must have made him late.

She gasped. Her appointment. She frowned at her skirt and shirtwaist. She couldn't meet with Mr. Dover covered in mud from her shoes to her neck.

Mrs. Gruhn asked, "Is something wrong?"

"I also have an appointment soon, but I can't go like this."

The woman eyed her from head to toe, motioned for Claire to follow, and started down the sidewalk at a brisk clip.

Claire tried to keep up without trotting. "Where are we going, Mrs. Gruhn?"

"Call me Louisa. I don't live far. You're about my size, so I'm sure I have something you can wear. It's the least I can do."

After a short walk into a drab neighborhood of small homes, they entered the yard of a house that reminded Claire of the one in which her friend Phoebe Crain lived. A one-story, unadorned box. She dodged several dubious-looking porch boards and removed her muddy shoes before stepping inside. Regardless of the dingy wallpaper and worn carpets, the place was as neat as a pin.

While Claire cleaned the mud from her shoes and skin, Louisa laid a peach and white-striped day dress across her bed, then added a pair of white gloves. "These should fit."

"The dress is lovely."

"My employer insisted we reflect well on her while at the shop." Louisa fingered the silky material. "She's letting me keep it."

The dress fit lengthwise but was slightly loose in the waist. Under the circumstances, Claire had no complaints. "Thank you. I'll return it tomorrow and pick up my things."

She hurried back to Riverside Street and into the building at the address Mr. Dover had given her. After climbing the stairs to the third floor, she stopped a moment to catch her breath before finding the right office. She was almost fifteen minutes late.

Claire gave the secretary her name and told him of her appointment with Mr. Dover.

Instead of a polite scolding for her tardiness, he opened the door behind him and said, "In here, ma'am."

"Thank you."

Mr. Dover sat behind a large, heavy desk in an office fit for someone of importance. He rose, his grin as friendly as the last time she saw him.

"I'm sorry I'm late, sir. I—" She'd started to cross the room, then drew up at seeing another gentleman staring at her from a chair across from Mr. Dover.

Mr. Grzegorczyk? Again?

DOVER STOOD FOR HIS latest guest. "Welcome Mrs. Kingsley.

I'm glad you've joined us."

Mark waffled between scowling and grinning like a fool. Mrs. Kingsley was the other guest whose arrival Charles Dover had insisted they await?

He needed the work. However, he didn't need further temptation in the form of an unattainable beauty. Yet, this added an unexpected mystery to the man's summons.

He leapt to his feet like the gentleman his mother raised him to be and kept his expression as neutral as possible.

Mrs. Kingsley turned her attention from him back to their host. "I'm sorry for being late. I had a slight accident on the way and needed to change my muddy clothes."

The pale orange color suited her better than the gray, but he could picture her in burlap and still be impressed. Not even seeing her lying in an unflattering position in the street and covered with mud had dampened the draw he felt toward her, which told him it had nothing to do with her appearance.

Even more reason to keep his distance. He could control a lustful attraction, but one of the heart would consume him.

Mr. Dover's eyebrows dipped, creating more creases in his middle-aged brow. "I trust you weren't hurt."

"No, sir."

She was being far too modest, so Mark decided to give her the credit due her. "As a matter of fact, Mrs. Kingsley is quite the heroine, sir."

A slight smile tipped the older man's lips. "How so?"

She shook her head. "I—"

"On her way here, she pulled a child from the path of an oncoming beer wagon."

"It wasn't as dramatic as all that, Mr. Dover."

"As a witness to the event, ma'am, it was even more dramatic."

Mark had thought his heart would stop at the sight of the child in the street and a wagon loaded with barrels bearing down on her. Then, when Mrs. Kingsley rushed to the rescue, beating him there, it had nearly stopped again.

"I didn't thank you for your role in the matter, Mr. Grzegorczyk."

"Grzegorczyk?" Mr. Dover's gaze jerked to Mark. "I invited Mr. Gregory."

"My name is Mark Gregory, sir."

Mrs. Kingsley straightened. "But I thought..."

This wasn't a conversation he'd expected or longed to have in front of a potential client. "A natural assumption and not altogether wrong. Grzegorczyk is my family name. For business purposes, I changed it years ago."

"I can understand why." That familiar ruddy hue blossomed on her fair skin, and she grimaced. "It's not that your last name isn't lovely...both of them. It's just that...I mean..."

"I'm not ashamed of my Polish heritage. It's just simpler this way." In the past, Mrs. Kingsley's remark would have offended him, but how could he claim outrage for an unintended insult after his mother's intentional fuss? At least, Mrs. Kingsley didn't appear to hold a grudge against him for his own, more egregious conduct at the store.

"I wasn't aware you two had met." Mr. Dover leaned over his desk. "Good. It makes my request easier."

His request? "I was under the impression you called me here to discuss a new design project."

Mrs. Kingsley's gaze hit Dover a glancing blow before it landed on Mark. "You're the Gregory in Mark Gregory Architecture."

"Yes."

He'd barely gotten the word out when she sighed. "Mr. Dover, I assume you intend to discuss blazing that path we talked about the last time we met, but I don't believe it's fair to involve this gentleman."

"What's not fair to me? What path blazing?"

Dover raised a hand. "Please, take a seat, Mrs. Kingsley, and I'll explain."

Once she was seated, he and Mark reclaimed their chairs.

"It isn't my intention to demand anything of either of you. Once you hear me out, you'll each be free to accept or decline my offer."

"What offer?" The question came from both Mark's and Mrs. Kingsley's mouths at the same time.

The man chuckled. "I can see the two of you are not as fond of a mystery as I am."

Mysteries were for books, not architects in search of work.

Dover leaned back in his chair and crossed his arms over his ample middle. "My wife and I moved to Riverport several months ago. At that time, we rented a nice house with the intention of eventually settling into a place of our own. So far, we've found nothing that pleases us. When I read of the opening of your firm in the newspaper, Mr. Gregory, I made some inquiries into your professional background. I was quite impressed to learn you had been employed by Daniel Burnham."

"Thank you, sir."

Mrs. Kingsley turned sideways in the chair to stare at him with wide, interested eyes. "You were associated with Mr. Burnham's firm?"

"Yes, ma'am, from '92 through earlier this year."

"Oh."

The awe in that one little word piqued Mark's interest, but before he could ask what she knew of the firm, Mr. Dover said, "I'd like you to prepare some ideas for a new residence for Mrs. Dover and myself."

"I'd be happy to do that." Mark leaned over the chair arm and grasped his notebook, ready to get down to business and make notes about the man's needs.

"There is a proviso."

He straightened at the warning in the man's voice. "A proviso, sir?"

"Yes."

Mark followed Dover's gaze to the woman beside him. She ducked her head, evidently more informed as to what was to come.

"Should she accept, Mrs. Kingsley is to work with you in preparing the design."

An apology darkened the pale eyes that normally held a sparkle, but she said nothing.

Mark's mind scrambled for a response that wouldn't risk the opportunity he'd been presented. "With all due respect, sir, I'm not sure what you expect her to do." He faced Mrs. Kingsley. "Please don't consider me impertinent, ma'am, but architecture is a serious undertaking. It isn't just a matter of making drawings on a sheet of paper. It takes precision, knowledge of materials and engineering, artistic thinking."

She opened her mouth, but whatever words she'd intended to speak were replaced by a bright smile that unraveled his thoughts. He'd had his share of attractions to females and didn't believe in falling in love after one meeting, but why must the only woman he'd fancied in some time be married?

Mark looked to Mr. Dover for help or, at a minimum, input from an arbiter. The man merely smiled as if he were watching a Gilbert and Sullivan production.

"Please understand me." Mark attempted to appeal to Mrs. Kingsley's good sense. "With your lack of experience as an architect, it would do neither of us any good to work together and could lead to harm for this gentleman and his wife. I won't put someone's life at risk through poor design."

"I appreciate your position, Mr. Gregory." Mr. Dover grinned. "I've already discussed it with my wife. We will take that chance."

"Why are you so certain I have no experience, Mr. Gregory?"

He'd thought it obvious. "You work in a department store, ma'am."

"And your office has been open only a few weeks. How do I know your work is up to my standards?"

Dover choked on his laughter, breaking what was turning into a contentious stare between Mark and Claire Kingsley. "I'm only asking that you give her an opportunity to prove herself. If you find you have no confidence in her ability, then I'll release you from our agreement. As long as you give her a fair trial, it will not affect your work for me. Is that acceptable?"

He'd been given a way out. Still... "I'll need to consider it, sir, as I'm sure is the case for Mrs. Kingsley." Maybe he'd angered her enough that she would decline.

When she nodded her agreement, Mr. Dover said, "Take a few days and let me know of your decisions next week. I'm in no hurry for a design. My wife and I have rented our current house for the next ten months. As for your assumption that Mrs. Kingsley has no experience, Mr. Gregory, it's true that she has no formal education. However, I have it on good authority that, when her husband was alive, they worked together in his Indianapolis architectural firm. I've been told she participated in a number of important projects, but since his passing, she's been given no occasion to practice the trade."

She breathed a wry laugh. "You have been busy since we last met."

As Dover's words sank deeper in his mind, Mark sank deeper into his seat. This bolt of shock that ran through him...was it a result of learning Claire Kingsley, a store clerk, once apprenticed as an architect? Or had it come from the startling news that she was a widow?

# Chapter Five

E very middle-of-the-night creak of the house shouted out Claire's solitude. Each one mocked her anxiety.

*Why God? Why put this temptation in my path? It caused only grief last time.*

She sat on her bed with her knees drawn to her chin. Though the night was cool, beads of moisture slid from her hairline down the sides of her face. She denied herself the warmth of slipping under the covers and shutting her eyes.

The scent of impending rain invaded the bedroom through the open window. Shadows blanketed the moon and dampened its glow, reflecting the way the shadows in her past dampened her life in the present.

A low rumble rolled in the distance. Perhaps thunder had awakened her.

On the other hand, nightmares often invaded her sleep with no rhyme or reason—nightmares that caused her to relive the truth.

In the dark, she saw and sensed and felt everything involved with the day her husband died. It started as a glorious and romantic time, a picnic in celebration of four years together. A celebration she ruined through her persistent demands.

Sitting in the grass, Claire sketched a design that pleaded for a life of its own, a sketch that helped calm her resentment. After their argument, Richard left to swim the White River alone. Rather, he had gone off alone when she refused to join him.

Lost in the composition on the page, time passed in a fog of solitude until a dog's bark broke through her concentration.

She dropped the sketch pad onto the quilt and stood, searching for her husband in the water and seeing nothing but a series of circles on the surface several yards from the bank. They rippled outward from the center, tiny wakes spreading into larger and larger rings, yet growing ever gentler until they merged with the normal flow of the river and vanished.

Vanished like her husband?

"Richard? Richard!" She found her voice, rasping as it was.

Where was he?

Not a soul waited for her in the grass or among the trees on the slightly sloping ground. Nothing but a scruffy dog that barked incessantly, casting blame on her for being unaware of her husband's absence.

"Richard!"

Already clothed in her bathing costume, Claire jumped into the moss-colored river and dove under the water's surface. After spotting nothing in the depths but shadowy tree limbs and rocks, she broke through to fill her lungs with fresh air. She spun in a circle, surveying the landscape across the river and along each bank.

Plunging back underwater, her search through the murky depths resumed with both sight and touch. It carried her farther downriver than she would have expected Richard to go.

Her fingers brushed fabric before she saw the weightless form of her husband at her side. With an inner cry that threatened to burst from her throat, she tugged to release him from tree branches clutching his suit like demonic claws.

After the third try, the material tore and broke free. With his arms secured in her iron grip, she shot upward, breached the surface, and swam toward the nearest bank. She towed him with a strength borne of desperation.

Claire collapsed in the gritty soil beside her husband, unable to look into his face. With time the enemy, she forced herself to her knees and felt his chest for a heartbeat, a breath, anything that proved her fears were only grim imaginings.

Nothing.

"Wake up!" She beat his chest. Prayed and beat. Repeating the actions until there were no more words and her fist ached.

River water dripped from her hair and down her cheeks—fresh water that merged with salty tears to sprinkle Richard's already sodden bathing suit.

A whine broke the stillness. She shivered. Had the sound come from her or the dog sitting on its haunches nearby?

She gripped Richard's wet hand as if doing so could infuse the limp fingers with her own heartbeat, the warmth of her blood.

Then she knew. The whine was hers, and it turned into a bloodcurdling scream.

Claire scrambled off the bed, her bare feet cool on floorboards smoothed by years of use. She shook her head as if doing so would rid her of the images her consciousness failed to chase away. She covered her mouth with her hands, and hot breaths warmed her skin. Why? Why hadn't she kept a better eye on Richard? Unlike him, she'd always been a strong swimmer. Why had she let a senseless argument distract her? Why had she allowed petty anger and ambition to steal the precious last moments between her and her husband?

Why couldn't her conscience leave the past alone, leave the dead alone?

She had sought God's forgiveness for that day by the river. Why must she relive the heartbreak over and over?

More than likely tonight's trip back in time was a consequence of her meeting with Mr. Dover and the outlandish offer he had presented to her and Mr. Gregory.

Claire walked to the window and leaned a shoulder against the frame. No lamplight illuminated the homes of the neighbors. No movement attracted her attention on the street. Everyone was tucked safely in bed. Everyone sleeping with no sense of loss and self-reproach.

The same breeze that ruffled the young leaves on the newly planted maple tree below her window floated through the screen to ruffle her nightdress. The tepid air and ring around a full moon half-hidden by thick, slate-gray clouds predicted a growing storm. Another soft rumble of thunder added its warning of the stormy weather to come.

Tonight's memory wreaked its own storm in her heart.

With her eyes adjusted to the darkness in the house, Claire left her room and tiptoed down the hall, past her brother's bedroom and down the stairs to the kitchen. She lit a lamp and placed a kettle on the stove to heat water for tea, all the while moving as quietly as possible to keep from disturbing the rest of the family.

It seemed ages since she'd slept through the night. When she was married, if she awoke, she'd been in her own home with only one person to worry about waking. It wasn't much of a worry. Richard usually slept like a hibernating bear. She never thought she would miss those roaring snores or the tossing and turning her husband did in his sleep when concerned about a project.

A streak of lightning lit the room, and the thunder grew closer. She prepared her tea and carried the cup to the table.

Wallace shuffled into the kitchen. His hair—the color of wet sand—stood on end, and he wore a striped robe that hung crooked on his ever-maturing frame. Her brother had grown into a man before her eyes.

"What are you doing down here?"

He pulled out a chair, flopped onto it, and yawned. "I heard you up."

"I tried not to wake anyone."

"It didn't work." His mouth angled into a tired, lazy grin.

People complimented Wallace on his sunny disposition, saying he brightened their days. It came naturally to him. Claire worked hard to present a happy face to the world. It was easier than dealing with questions and the well-meaning encouragement of others.

Steam rose from her cup to moisten her face. "Would you like some tea?"

"No. I only came down here hoping to convince you to return to bed."

From the drawing room, the grandfather clock struck twice, a hollow, hopeless sound.

"Hear that? It's late, Claire."

"I'm not sleepy."

"You have too many nights when you're not sleepy. What's wrong?"

"There's nothing—"

"Don't try to fool me, sis. I've heard the boards creak as you pace back and forth in your bedroom or sneak down the stairs. I've seen you curled up in a parlor chair in the middle of the night, dead to the world."

She winced at his choice of words. "I never realized you knew of my occasional nighttime habits." She'd always managed to go back to her room before morning.

"We are *all* aware of your occasional nighttime habits, and we're all worried about you. We know you miss Richard, but don't you think it's time you..." He raised a shoulder.

"Forget him? Forget what happened? How am I supposed to do that, Wallace? I should have saved my husband." She shouldn't have contributed to the danger he faced to begin with.

Claire sucked in a deep breath to calm herself before her strident voice woke her parents. She had told her family of her argument with Richard before his death. They'd tried to convince her she wasn't at fault, that she shouldn't be ashamed of her pettiness and be afraid of what others would think of her. But that didn't make her innocent.

Mr. Gregory had called her a heroine for pulling Cissy Gruhn from the path of the beer wagon. How little he knew of her.

Drops of tea sloshed onto her hand when her trembling fingers picked up the cup. "Sometimes I wonder why it wasn't me."

Wallace leaned over the table and grabbed her hand. "Don't talk that way. Do you think Richard would have wanted that for you? Do you think this family would want to lose you? We all liked him, sis, and we all miss him. No, you shouldn't forget, but focus on the good things, the good days. Don't let the worst day devour your happiness."

Claire reminded herself that her brother meant well, just as everyone who tried to console someone in their loss meant well.

At twenty-eight, she was nine years older than Wallace. Some people considered him rather scatterbrained. They didn't understand that he was a young man with a sharp mind and aspirations for the future that now and again swelled into wild dreams. They didn't understand the depth of his sentiments. Even she rarely heard him speak as he just had. But in this case, Wallace was the one who didn't understand. No one understood.

She finished the tea. "We should go back upstairs. We're both expected at the store early tomorrow."

Wallace stood and pushed in his chair. His mouth drew down in mock seriousness. "Newland's can't get by without us."

Claire set the cup in the sink, turned down the lamp, and joked as they walked out of the room, "Of course not. We're the department store's best assets."

She only wished she had been her husband's best asset.

CLAIRE FOLLOWED ROSLYN Malone up the steps to the roof

of the department store building. They settled in a corner facing Commerce Street. Shaded by the low parapet wall, they could talk and relax before returning to jobs that required them to stand for hours.

With a quick glance over the edge of the wall, Claire scanned the foot and carriage traffic that moved up and down the street, noisy and restless.

Roslyn spread the blanket Claire kept in the fourth-floor room everyone referred to as the employee salon. It wasn't much more than a large cloakroom. On sunny and temperate days, they carried their lunches to the roof and ate in the fresh air. On this day, a breeze carried the faint smell of pigs from a farm on the western edge of town, a reminder that the ever-growing Riverport hadn't outgrown its agricultural history.

Roslyn sat opposite Claire and tucked her legs under her. "I've wanted to say something to you for quite a while."

"What is it?"

She reached out and squeezed Claire's arm. "Thank you."

"For what?"

"For this. For being my friend."

Claire unfolded the napkin that held her sandwich. She had once considered the pretty, young blonde to be silly and somewhat childish, but an embezzlement scandal involving the department store and Roslyn's missing husband seemed to have matured her. It also left her feeling ostracized at times.

Although another employer might have quietly fired Roslyn, the Newland family retained her, and Claire had made a point of befriending her, even if she couldn't have said why at first. In the end, she did not regret the decision.

"I hope it isn't because you feel sorry for me."

Claire laughed. "Me, feel sorry for you? Absolutely not. Do you feel sorry for yourself?"

Roslyn grinned. "Absolutely not."

Maybe that was the reason Claire had befriended the woman. She possessed a can-do spirit—a strength Claire wished she hadn't lost. "Steel and silk."

Roslyn cocked her head. "I beg your pardon?"

"It's how I see you. Steel. You're strong and don't let anyone push you around, yet there's vulnerability that surrounds you. Silk."

"You make me sound like a heroine in a tragic novel. I wish it were true, but I let Gil push me around too often. I thought..."

When Roslyn didn't finish, Claire said, "For your sake, I hope they find him soon."

"Would you ever consider...?" Roslyn bent her head, an odd reservation coming from a woman who was generally anything but reserved.

"Consider what?"

Roslyn looked up. "Have you ever thought about moving out of your parents' house?"

"Off and on. Why?"

"To tell you the truth, I've never lived alone and am a little frightened by it."

Claire had raised her sandwich to take a bite but paused and lowered it to the cloth on her lap. "Frightened? Why?"

"Before going to bed the other night, I went to the kitchen for a drink of water. When I looked out the window, I saw someone in the yard."

"Who?"

"I don't know. It was too dark to see him clearly, and he knelt next to a tree. He must have seen me, because he disappeared like a ghost."

"Are you sure nighttime shadows didn't play a trick on you?"

"No. I saw a man."

"Your husband?"

"I don't know. I think Gil would have come inside, if for no other reason than to torment me."

"You've had no word from him?"

"No. It's been five months since he ran off. The police have lost his trail...if they ever had it. There are times when I wonder if he's dead."

After associating with Roslyn over the past months, it was clear the woman hadn't enjoyed her marriage. Claire felt all the more blessed for having experienced her years of marital happiness.

Everyone knew Gil Malone had had an accomplice. Claire asked, "Still no idea of the identity of Gil's partner?"

"No." Roslyn pushed a stray hair away from her face. "Most people are convinced I was Gil's partner in the embezzlement. If I'd had an inkling that he was taking money from Newland's, I would have done something. Confronted him, even turned him in. You know that, don't you?"

"I do. Did you tell the police about seeing someone at the house?"

"No."

"Roslyn—"

"I don't want to talk about it anymore, Claire, or I'll give myself nightmares." She chuckled, a nervous sound. "I'm sure you're right, and it was a matter of shifting shadows."

Claire hoped so.

"Anyway, I wondered if you'd consider moving in with me."

Move in with Roslyn? "What if Gil comes back home?"

"We both know he's deserted me. Besides, he wouldn't be home long. He would be in jail where he belongs. You and I would make good roommates, don't you think?"

Would they? "I'll admit, it isn't something that occurred to me. I'd like time to think about it."

"I hope you'll say yes." Roslyn finished eating the cookie she'd broken into pieces as she talked, then she dusted the crumbs from her hands. "You've been hard at work in your department again."

"I can't help but tinker sometimes. Thankfully, Mr. Newland doesn't mind."

Claire often advised the Newlands on the locations of display cases that would instill interest and take advantage of the store's electric lamplight and large windows. It wasn't exactly what she had done when working with Richard, but she could pretend.

The design of interior spaces had often been Claire's gift. Richard said she had an instinct for locations of windows and lights, fireplaces, and interior walls. It was what made her fit hand-in-glove with him, professionally.

"Mrs. Newland might be responsible for ordering the fashions that appeal to women, but you give them the treatment they deserve, and you're so clever at it." Roslyn sighed. "There's not much to be done in the perfume department other than placing the bottles on the shelves or leaving a few out on the counter."

"In the afternoon, a certain amount of sunlight shines through the front window nearest your station. I wonder if Mr. Newland would be willing to move the perfume counter closer to that window. You could arrange the bottles so the light shines on and through them, making them sparkle like colored jewels so they attract the attention of customers."

Roslyn sat straight. "What a wonderful idea. Do you mind if I bring it to Spence's attention?"

"Not at all." Claire finished her sandwich and closed her lunch pail.

On occasion, she caught herself referring to her employer as simply The Third. Most people did. It was easier than trying to differentiate between three generations of Spencer Fanning Newlands. However, she could never get accustomed to a fellow employee calling the store's owner by his first name, even though

Roslyn's husband had been a friend of The Third's since college. That friendship made Gil Malone's treacherous betrayal even harder for everyone to stomach.

"A customer came into the store a few days ago to buy his wife a new fragrance. We started chatting, and guess what?" Roslyn folded her napkin in half, then half again, as she talked. "He's in town because he plans to build a new office building on that vacant lot over on Webster Street. He said it would be the biggest in Riverport."

"Do you know the name of this man?"

Roslyn drummed her fingers on her knee. "It was Lester or Ledler or—"

Claire's pulse jumped. "Lefler? Was his name Harris Lefler?"

"You know him?"

"I know of him." Richard and George would have paid the wealthy businessman for the chance to design his buildings, the first one, anyway. After that, they would expect him to pay...exceptionally well.

Roslyn's smug look put Claire on edge. "So?"

"So what?"

"Are you going to contact him about preparing his design?"

"No." Neither would she tell Roslyn about Mr. Dover's offer. Still, a part of her couldn't let go of the possibility of working with Mr. Gregory, especially when it both alarmed her and made her feel more alive than she had in two years. "Mr. Lefler has an architect."

"Evidently not. He said he was looking for a new one."

"Then, I'm sure he'll find the right one." Perhaps Mr. Gregory. Was he aware of the opportunity? Had he met with Lefler?

Roslyn pinned her with a hard stare. "Where is your spirit, Claire Kingsley? Where is your"—her chin jutted upward—"*your* steel?"

Claire laughed. "It's in my corset."

# Chapter Six

C laire set the plate on Verbenia's kitchen counter. When she had volunteered to prepare a dessert for this week's Widow's Might meeting, she hadn't realized how thankful she would be for the distraction.

Verbenia Jensen's skirt brushed Claire's. "Those look delicious. I know it's early and not all the ladies are present, but may I try one?"

About Claire's mother's age, Verbenia, the founder of the Widow's Might circle, brought her personal experience, empathy, and mentorship to some of Riverport's young widows.

"Help yourself."

The woman bit into the square of cake and shut her eyes. "Mmm... What is this?"

"I found the recipe in Fannie Farmer's *The Boston Cooking School Cookbook.* She calls it a brownie." It was a simple recipe, a blessing given her scattered thoughts during the past few days.

"You and Miss Farmer are clever girls."

Yes, so clever she hadn't settled on a response to Mr. Dover's offer yet. Or Roslyn's.

Together, Claire and Richard had discussed their hopes, dreams, problems, and choices. Discussing either subject with her parents would prove prickly. She'd already sought her mother's thoughts on a move and received nothing but silence and a frown.

"You seem preoccupied, Claire. Is there something troubling you?"

The older widow's words had often provided a balm to Claire's wounded spirit. Yes, she had her mother to rely on for counsel, but her mother had never walked in Claire's shoes. Then again, in this situation, neither had Verbenia. Still, it might not hurt to seek wisdom where it was offered.

"There's a new architect in town named Mark Gregory. Another gentleman I met recently requested that I work with Mr. Gregory to design a house plan for him."

"That's wonderful news." Verbenia eyed her and frowned. "But I can see you aren't happy about it. What is the problem?"

"I'm not sure I should."

Verbenia brushed the sand-colored brownie crumbs clinging to her hands into the sink. "What do you know about this new architect? Is he competent?"

After meeting with him in Mr. Dover's office, Claire suspected Mr. Gregory was quite competent, and Mr. Burnham would not have employed him otherwise. "He has an impressive background and came here from one of the most respected firms in Chicago."

"It sounds promising. Why hesitate?"

Claire shrugged. She'd never told Verbenia or any of the Widow's Might women everything about her life in Indianapolis. She hadn't the courage. "It won't be the same as working with Richard."

"No, it won't. Our lives don't remain constant, and that part of yours is over."

Claire took a step back at the blunt statement. This woman, who always seemed to understand her charges' needs, clearly missed the mark this time. It wasn't her fault. She'd been given a partial account of Claire's history.

"I'm sorry to sound harsh, but you aren't the first woman I've counseled who held onto the past because of fear of the future." Verbenia laid a gentle hand on Claire's wrist. "When the time is right, God often introduces us to people and events that take us in a new direction, one that fits His plan. It's up to us to recognize that opportunity and seize it, not look back like Lot's wife because we're afraid to leave the security of the familiar."

Was Claire ready for a new direction at this time in her life? "Not every opportunity leads to a path we should follow. Not every introduction is one from God."

"I agree." Verbenia released her. "Have you prayed about this opportunity?"

Claire huffed. "Since the moment it was first presented to me."

"And?"

"And I have no clear answer."

After a period in which Verbenia studied her like a horticulturist would study a leaf under a microscope, she said, "Is it possible you have no clear answer because you don't want to know the answer?"

Had she drowned out God's voice through her anxiety over what it might mean for her future? Perhaps her friend hadn't missed the mark after all.

Verbenia picked up the plate with the brownies. "I'll take this to the dining room. The rest of the ladies will be here soon."

Claire followed at a sedate pace, her mind as foggy as ever.

Until she'd lost her babies, she'd been sure of herself, of the things she wanted from life—a happy marriage, motherhood, the occasional opportunity to assist in creating something beautiful for others.

Afterward, she replaced the dread of added heartache with more and more work. Then Richard died. Now...

Now the idea of resuming a portion of her past life tickled a tiny spot inside she'd fought to numb.

What would it be like to work alongside the new architect? Surely, not the same as working with Richard.

While watching Mr. Gregory during their discussion of Mr.

Dover's requirements, he had struck her as solid in his knowledge, driven, and not a man to suffer fools gladly or accept an assistant unable to do the job. She could do the job…if she wanted to.

As she walked into the foyer, someone knocked on the front door. Claire peeked inside the parlor to see three women already seated and talking. The sound of laughter coming from outside told her more than one of the remaining three members of their group stood on the porch.

She cast off her concerns and opened the door to find Phoebe Crain and Mavis Lipp chattering like magpies. Though a fellow member of the Widow's Might group, poor Phoebe wasn't a widow in the strictest sense of the word. She had been tricked into a sham marriage that produced a daughter. Once the truth came out—no thanks to the spite of a jealous woman—the other members had rallied around her.

Phoebe had conquered her fears. Would Claire ever find the courage to conquer hers?

Edythe Westin stood behind the others, a placid smile on her regal face. The tall and lithe brunette came from a family of wealth and power, yet she was one of the most reticent people Claire had ever met.

"The three of you are late."

Phoebe shook her head. "We're right on time, because you know you couldn't start without us."

Claire laughed. "She thinks much of herself."

Soon, the Widow's Might ladies anticipated losing Phoebe's participation in these Sunday afternoon fellowship gatherings. They all knew Spence Newland, heir to his family's business interests, had fallen in love with Phoebe last Christmas. Any day, the ladies expected news of a formal announcement.

Claire would miss her friend's presence, but she enjoyed hearing Phoebe laugh. For too long the former concert pianist had worried over what people would say about the scandal in her past, until the Newlands—one of the most influential families in Riverport—had accepted her. As far as Claire was concerned, no one else's opinion mattered.

God had taken Phoebe's life in a direction she'd never expected, and it turned out to be good for her and for her young daughter.

How could Claire expect the same result if she rejected the path God would have her take?

CLAIRE LEFT THE WIDOW'S Might meeting, her mood heavier than when she'd entered it. She hadn't been honest with Verbenia, even after the woman suggested Claire's prayers might have resulted in an answer she couldn't accept.

Why would God lead Claire to walk a new path toward something that made her heart sing when she didn't deserve the second chance the opportunity presented?

Of course, all her hand-wringing might prove to be a moot point if Mr. Gregory rejected the plan Mr. Dover presented him.

On her way home, Claire approached the Patton Place Hotel. A recent addition to the town, the hotel's brick pavers led to the two-story portico at the front of the building built of the same red brick. An arched doorway and urns of greenery welcomed the hotel's guests. Its restaurant drew patrons from all over the county to sample the cuisine of its French-trained chef. Claire had never dined there, but an article in the newspaper had claimed that every drop of the Béarnaise sauce was more enjoyable than the perfection of the steak it covered.

She scooted into the grass to let a small hack from the railroad station pass by. The horses clip-clopped down the hotel's drive to stop under the portico in front of the entrance. The door to the cab opened, and a gentleman descended. "Please take my suitcase inside.

I'll be there shortly."

Claire froze, recognizing a voice she hadn't heard in close to two years. She looked down, hoping her hat brim provided a cover for much of her face. At the same time, she slid her gaze sideways, raised only high enough to catch a glimpse of the man from behind.

Medium size. Brown hair. A broad build, though not portly. A stylish dresser in a black suit, the material expertly altered. Her heart dropped to her stomach. She wouldn't know for sure it was George Brant unless he turned around. In which case, if she could help it, he would not see her.

Trotting past the hotel would only bring attention to her, but there was nowhere to hide, except...

Claire crept toward an outer column of the portico and halted behind it, fully aware it wasn't wide enough to completely conceal her. Thankfully, the carriage blocked part of the column, so she scooted forward.

Standing motionless, with her eyes closed, she fooled herself into thinking if she saw no one, no one saw her. For added insurance, she prayed the carriage wouldn't move and expose her until after George had entered the hotel.

"Claire Kingsley? Is that you?"

She jumped at the soft voice at her shoulder. After drawing a deep breath for the purpose of patience and calm, she opened her eyes and turned around. "Why, George."

*Why, George? Why are you here?*

"I thought I saw you from the carriage. What a surprise that you're the first person I meet on my arrival in Riverport." He eyed the brick column. His crocodile smile, amid the perfectly trimmed beard, grated on her. "You weren't hiding from me, were you?"

"Don't be silly." She glanced at the ground to cover the heat that rose with her lie. Seeing a coin on the ground, she bent and picked it up. Adding to her deception, she said, "I found a penny."

His laughing eyes said she hadn't fooled him. "Then it was well worth the pause in your walk."

He had no idea how hard she worked for her pennies. "What are you doing in Riverport, George?"

"I'm here on business."

Surely, Mr. Dover hadn't requested George's services, too.

Then the truth occurred to her. "You're after Mr. Lefler's project and came to look over the property."

"He's planning an office building on Webster Street. Four stories and over thirty thousand square feet."

Roslyn had said it was to be special. Claire had not imagined something that large. "That's quite a feather in some architect's hat. Of course, we have our own architectural office in town now." Why antagonize him?

He frowned. "You're working for another architect?"

She hadn't meant to suggest such an association with Mr. Gregory. "I..."

This was the man who had refused to let her become a permanent member of Kingsley and Brant—the man whose dictate was behind the argument with her husband the day he died. There was no reason to give him the satisfaction of learning she sold women's fashions in a department store.

It wasn't a lie to say, "I've been requested to work on a single project—a house design with another architect. Perhaps you've heard of Mark Gregory? Before opening his office in Riverport, he was employed by Daniel Burnham in Chicago."

George might well have yawned for the impression that last statement made on him. "I don't believe I know anything of the man."

"I'm sure you'll hear much about him in the future." She smiled, even as words of retribution took hold of her tongue. "It wouldn't surprise me to learn he's sought Lefler's project too. It's possible you'll have some strong competition."

"You should know by now that I'm not afraid of competition, Claire. Besides, the opportunity to submit is by invitation only. If he's new, I doubt he's received one, no matter who employed him in the past." George returned her smile. "After that train ride from Indianapolis, I could use some refreshment. Would you like to join me in the hotel restaurant? It will give us a chance to talk further."

Not even the temptation of sipping tea in a luxurious restaurant could sway her to spend more time with him. "I'm afraid I can't. It's getting late and I have a busy day tomorrow."

If she didn't know better, she would say the loss of his grin indicated disappointment. He straightened his already straight tie. "There is one thing I want to discuss before you go."

What could he possibly say that would interest her? "I really should—"

"I've taken on a new partner and renamed the company."

Claire ran his rushed words back through her mind. Her stomach dropped as though she stood at the edge of a cliff looking down into a canyon littered with knife-edged rocks. "You've replaced Richard now? You've erased his name as though he never existed?"

"I needed another partner." George fumbled with the hat he held in his hands, twisting the brim and twirling the headpiece. "You know that I'm fully capable of creating a practical design, but Richard had vision. He possessed the ingenuity to create something to be remembered. When I found someone whose talent matched his, I offered him a partnership. He insisted on the name change. I couldn't afford to deny him the request, and it wasn't fair for me to do so."

"But it was fair to deny me an opportunity to keep the Kingsley name alive in the business?"

"I'm not the one who let Richard's name die with him." A tick flickered in George's cheek, then he touched her arm. "I'm sorry to upset you, and I understand it was difficult for you to lose your children, but Richard felt that loss, too."

Richard had talked to his partner about the intimate details of their personal life? "We planned—"

"No, darling, you planned. He went along with it, because you needed time to grieve, and he didn't want to hurt you."

"You're saying he placated me? That he chose to put up with my work until I came to my senses?" She pulled away from George's venomous touch. "You know nothing about our life."

"Claire—"

"No." She held up a hand to silence him and began to back away, not wanting to hear another word from him.

It was one thing to bring someone else into the company her husband helped found, but to make him a partner and remove the name Kingsley—Richard's name—from the business... Hearing that was like living through her husband's death a second time. And George had no right to bring up the subject of the losses she and Richard suffered, a subject that continued to haunt her.

"Good day, George."

She walked away, the path before her blurry from her tears.

"I hope to see you again before I leave town, Claire."

He could hope until Judgment Day.

Each footstep crushed a bit more of her sorrow, leaving deeper and deeper imprints of anger, resentment, and regret in its place. George's previous dismissal of her had stung, would always sting, but now he'd cast aside Richard's memory, his name, as if it didn't matter that her husband had helped him become the architect he was today. As if Richard were yesterday's trash!

If only she could best George in securing an important commission such as Harris Lefler's. The Kingsley name would remain known in the architectural field. Richard's name would live on regardless of George's search for success and despite her failure as a wife.

If only.

Her march forward slowed. Telling George that Mark Gregory might be his competition had been idle talk. But what if Mr. Gregory did go after the Lefler prize? And what if, in a small way, the Kingsley name was associated with the architect who beat George and his new partner for the commission?

Vindictiveness was an ugly word. But was it vindictive to honor someone's memory—someone who had been wronged? Was it indefensible to want to atone for her own wrong against that person?

*Lord, I know I failed last time. I failed You and I failed Richard. I don't deserve a second chance to prove myself, but I am asking for it. I am asking for a morsel of Your grace...for Richard's memory.*

She couldn't give her husband children. She couldn't give him back his life. But if God granted that grace, she could give his name to one more architectural project.

# Chapter Seven

Had Mark really imagined clients would break down the door of his office and demand he fit them into his busy schedule? Truthfully, yes.

The image had taken over his daydreams more than once since before he opened the office in Riverport. On occasion, the expectation invaded his nighttime dreams.

Mark bent over the dining room table and rubbed a pencil across a portion of a drawing, shading the front lawn of a two-story house. The place didn't exist, nor would it, unless he found the right client with the right land on which to build it. He simply enjoyed passing the time in the evenings by creating new elevations and floor plans. They might come to good use one day.

Evidently, no time soon. Two full weeks had passed since he opened his office—two lost weeks.

Not that there wasn't hope. Last Tuesday, Mark met with a man wanting to discuss a design for a small guesthouse to coordinate with the main residence. A good start, but that wasn't the large project Mark needed to satisfy the loan payment.

He lowered the pencil and propped his elbows on the table, his chin in his hands. Dover's project would help but he needed more. And the condition the man put on him left him in a tenuous position.

The timing of the situation couldn't be worse for someone who struggled to begin a new company. Though Mrs. Kingsley wasn't the first of her gender in the profession, women architects were rare, and he was being asked to work with someone without a degree in architecture. Of course, that wasn't a fair comment on her skill when his former employer had only received honorary degrees, yet he'd risen to be President of the American Institute of Architects.

The odds of Mrs. Kingsley being another Daniel Burnham were not in his favor. What if she wasn't up to doing the job? He couldn't afford to link himself to someone with inadequate skills and ruin the reputation of his company before he'd even built one.

For that reason alone, he should say no to Dover. Instead, his brain repeatedly reminded him of the fact that Claire Kingsley—a woman he'd thought unavailable—was widowed. Now that he knew about her husband's passing? He'd rather spend time with her socially than professionally.

Surely, it was folly to snatch at the chance to work alongside a woman solely to satisfy a desire to get to know her better. There was no guarantee of something more personal forming between them, or that they would even get along.

He'd glanced at her ring finger on Friday, something he should have done before acting like a fool the first time he met her. Seeing the raised outline of a band under her glove told him she was a woman whose dedication to her marriage continued to this day.

Yet, how often would he call himself an imbecile if he didn't take advantage of this opportunity when it had fallen in his lap?

"Are you still drawing?" His mother walked into the dining room, carrying a cup of coffee. She placed it in front of him, pulled out a chair on the other side of the table, and sat with a tiny grunt.

"You sound tired, Mama. You should rest more." He gulped down a third of the coffee loaded with cream. She knew he preferred it that way in the evenings—more white than black. When he overlooked her single-minded tenacity, he could admit to some advantages to living with her, with someone who knew him well.

"It has been years since I moved to a new place, and I am not as young I was then."

Which was a not-so-subtle reminder of his sin in uprooting her from the neighborhood. He knew her well, too.

"You should not work on a Sunday, Marek. It is a day of rest."

"I'm not working." Not officially. Besides, he'd attended Mass this morning. What more did God want from him?

She gestured to the drawing. "This is not for a new client?"

"No. As I've said before, it doesn't hurt to have an inventory of ideas to draw from should I find the right client and property." In fact, he could imagine the elevation in front of him as a potential fit for a vacant lot he'd seen while driving his mother around yesterday, acquainting them both with some of Riverport's neighborhoods.

"It also would not hurt to be paid for your lovely drawings, *mój słodki chłopcze,* so we may keep this lovely house that is too big for our lovely selves."

He laughed. "True." Then, as the idea struck him, the laughter ended with a quiet groan. "No, Mama."

"No what?"

"No boarder."

She focused on her finger as it traced a slight scratch in the table's surface. "You have already ordered me to put that notion out of my head."

And Mark could count on one hand the number of times she had listened to him. No more than she had listened to her husband when he was alive. His father had shown more patience with her than he could muster.

Mama rose and walked toward the hall. "I am going to my bedroom. I will need my rest for the day we move back to Chicago."

Any day now, he would arrive home to find a stranger encamped in his spare bedroom or seated at this dining table. The idea of it gave him even more incentive to see that he succeeded in his plans for his business.

Someone knocked on the front door, and he rose from his seat. Who visited them on a Sunday evening? Other than Addison, who should be home with his family, they'd met few people in town.

Mark reached the hall in time to hear a feminine voice, too soft to recognize. His mother turned away from the door. The lines around her mouth deepened with a scowl. "You have a visitor, Marek. Mrs. Kingsley is here."

Here? That could only mean one thing. She had decided.

What would he tell her when he hadn't made his decision yet? Would he let her down easy or turn into a lap dog with one look at that angelic face?

MARK GREGORY STOOD in the center of the entry hall, no tie, shirt unbuttoned at the neck, and his sleeves rolled to his elbows. One side of his mouth contorted into a guarded smile. It left Claire with the impression that part of him welcomed her and the other part was sorry she'd come.

In spying the stray lock of dark hair falling over his forehead—giving him the tussled look of a youth—she almost regretted it herself.

*This is business, Claire, nothing personal. Men want children—heirs. Remember that.*

"I'm sorry to bother you at home, Mr. Gregory, but I thought we might talk."

Although her conversation with George prompted this visit, Mr. Gregory needn't learn the details. He would either welcome the opportunity to work with her or tell her to leave. If the latter, then what?

He nodded some unspoken message to his mother and turned back to Claire. "Please come in, Mrs. Kingsley."

Mrs. Grzegorczyk crossed the hall. "I will be upstairs where I belong."

Not too proud to acknowledge that the woman intimidated her, Claire waited until she'd retreated up the steps to the second floor before she stepped into the front hall. "Your mother really doesn't like me, does she?"

He led her into the drawing room and asked her to be seated. "It isn't you...exactly."

What did that mean?

He plopped into a chair and sighed. "It's a long story, Mrs. Kingsley, but I owe you an apology." His abashed grin set Claire's heart pounding with apprehension. "My behavior in the store the first day we met was reprehensible. I don't know what got into me, but I am sorry."

It was a nice attempt to make her feel better about that day, but it failed. The confession brought back her own feelings of culpability over the incident. "I wouldn't call it reprehensible, especially when my foolishness encouraged it."

"Then let's say we were both in a frivolous mood that day and leave it alone."

"We'll forget all about it." She'd try. She'd try hard.

"Good. Now, you wanted to speak to me about something."

How to begin? Claire gathered her thoughts.

"I assume it relates to our meeting with Mr. Dover."

She nodded. "It's my turn to apologize. I had no idea he would involve you in his scheme."

"And if you had?"

Would she have accepted the invitation?

Mr. Gregory eased back in the chair and crossed his legs, his gaze never leaving her face. "You suspected what Dover had in mind."

"I suspected the subject of the meeting based on our conversation a week earlier. I had no idea you would be included or that he would propose such a...a peculiar deal."

"Why do you call it peculiar? People collaborate in various businesses."

"You don't think it's strange that he would force two strangers to work together to satisfy a desire to help one of them?"

"Truthfully, I do. I would like to design the man's house, but I'm not certain it's a good idea to..." His voice faded.

"Let me save you the trouble of struggling to find words that won't offend me, Mr. Gregory. What you mean to say is that you're not certain you want to work with a woman."

The casual pose he had displayed gave way to an expression that could cut steel. "No, Mrs. Kingsley. What I meant to say was I am not certain I want to work with someone whose training is doubtful."

"Doubtful?" That was worse than thinking his hesitation was due to her gender, because it not only reflected on her but on Richard. "My husband was a highly competent architect, and my apprenticeship under him was not a matter of whimsy and half-hearted teaching."

"I didn't mean to cast aspersions on Mr. Kingsley. I'm only saying that an apprenticeship might have worked a decade or two ago, but that's not good enough these days, not for me. The practice of architecture is changing. In the not-too-distant future, those who practice it will be expected to have earned a degree. And you only need look as far as the lawmakers in Illinois who want to require architects to be licensed. It won't be long before other states follow suit."

"A degree and a license do not guarantee skill."

"No, but they do indicate a responsibility to the profession."

"And if I had the formal education? Would you be willing to hire a woman?"

"Even if that were the case, I'm afraid I am in no position at the moment to hire anyone—male or female."

"I see."

She wasn't ignorant about the expenses of a business. After all, she had worked for Kingsley and Brant as their office clerk before she married Richard.

With Mr. Gregory's business being new, he must be careful to keep his costs to those that were necessary. He could design a house on his own and didn't need her.

"I don't understand Mr. Dover's intent." Mr. Gregory leaned forward in the chair, his gaze fixed on her as if expecting for her to clarify the man's reasoning. "Frankly, I'm bewildered by the situation."

And clearly feeling backed into a corner. "He thinks he's giving me a chance to be a pioneer."

Mr. Gregory's attempt to smooth the lines in his forehead with the tips of his fingers failed. "You used that term before. What does that mean?"

"I'm to prove my ability to you, to prove that females are as talented in the area of architecture as males."

"This is a social statement? At the expense of my business?" He shook his head. "I can't allow that, Mrs. Kingsley."

"I don't believe Mr. Dover means for you to endanger your business on my account, Mr. Gregory." Claire snapped her mouth shut. Confrontation would not get her what she wanted. "Being a sales clerk was never how I saw my future."

"Then what did you see?"

She recalled moments she and Richard shared in designing the house of their dreams and her joy in creating the little touches that made the rooms both practical and charming. "At one time, it was my desire to specialize in interior architectural design."

"Why?"

"Why interior—"

"No, ma'am. Why architecture? Why not teaching or engineering or accounting?"

She hadn't anticipated that question and took a moment to gather her thoughts, ones that led back to her childhood. "When I was nine, my parents sent me to stay with my grandmother for a month—the month of January. She'd been ill, and I was to help care for her, cook meals and clean or run errands."

Claire paused to gain control of her voice until she believed she could go on without the hoarseness. "The house was smaller than this one and poorly built. The entry hall was drafty and the fireplaces too small to emit much heat. I'd always enjoyed drawing, so we would spend the cold evenings curled up in her bed under a pile of quilts where I would draw the interiors of various houses. I told her she would live in one like them someday."

His expression softened. "Did she?"

She lowered her chin. "No. She didn't make it through that winter."

"I'm sorry."

If Claire didn't ignore the soothing tone in his voice and the sad smile, she wouldn't be able to finish her response to his question. "I enjoyed the creativity behind those drawings. There's a gratification in watching a fresh design go from a concept in the mind to a drawing on paper, and then to the physical reality of a beautiful structure. I'm sure you feel it, too."

"I do." He sank back in the chair. "You never pursued an education?"

"My parents objected to anything other than marriage and family, so I sought office employment with an architect. That's how I met my husband. We married in Indianapolis where he and a partner had formed their own company. He taught me a great deal. I studied his textbooks and devoured everything else I found on the subject. Perhaps I never went to school, but I received an education."

Mr. Gregory's expression tightened once more, evidently determined to use whatever weapon he could find to fight against working with her. "If architecture was your goal, why aren't you still in the office he founded?"

Claire gritted her teeth. "Richard's partner never approved of me working with them. He felt a female was a hindrance to their success. He wasn't the first to express to me the theories about women working in what was considered a man's profession. We haven't the imagination. We haven't the intelligence. We're deemed less feminine. Many men feel threatened by working with a woman." Claire especially believed it to be the case with George Brant.

Perhaps her husband hadn't minded working with a female, but according to George, he'd preferred she not be his wife.

Mr. Gregory focused on the front window behind her. What was he thinking while he sat with his brow twisted in a knot and as the seconds ticked by in silence?

Claire folded her hands in her lap, hoping to appear as serene as she pretended, and waited for his reply. Inside, her nerves hummed with tension. What part of what she'd said would weigh heavily in his decision?

He must say something soon or she'd jump out of her skin. "Mr. Gregory?"

Her voice roused him, and the tucks in his brow smoothed. "You said you've had experience as a clerk in an architectural office."

"Yes."

"You know basic accounting and can compose correspondence?"

"Yes." She tried to remain patient, but that patience was running thin.

"I've already told you I can't hire an architect."

Disappointment squeezed her lungs.

"However..."

Claire's toe tapped the carpet.

"I'm offering you an opportunity to clerk in my office, handling correspondence and accounting."

Her toe stopped tapping. A clerk? He wanted her to send out letters and record his debits and credits?

"While you're in the office, I'll determine the extent of your skill as you contribute to the design of the Dover house. The best I can do at this point is a couple of hours of clerical work, twice a week." He suggested a minimal wage.

A slow smile tugged at her mood but stopped at her lips. It wasn't what she'd anticipated, but he hadn't dismissed the idea of allowing her to work on Mr. Dover's house. If Spence Newland agreed to reduce her hours at the store, she wouldn't lose much pay.

"I'm afraid I can't promise you anything more than what I've stated, along with a draftsman's pay for the Dover project. As for the design, you'll follow my instructions and never forget that I am the architect. Nothing gets done without my say-so." He pinned her with a no-nonsense stare. "Are those terms satisfactory to you?"

If he wanted no-nonsense, she would give it to him. "I have one more request."

The wariness returned. "What is it?"

"The plan can't simply say 'Mark Gregory Architect.' It must also have the Kingsley name."

"I'm giving you a chance to join an architectural office again. If your desire is to become that pioneer you spoke of, Mrs. Kingsley, you'll take it."

"With that one condition." She refused to melt under his intense study. No matter what Mr. Dover said, Mr. Gregory's refusal to work with her would not look good to him.

In a flash, those amber accents in his eyes beamed with amusement. For the first time in their acquaintance, he laughed—deep and genuine and...masculine. "Provided you pull your weight, I'm not so proud that I can't share credit when it's deserved."

Claire controlled the impulse to jump to her feet and shout. Their association was only for one project, and hers was a minor role, but she'd gotten what she came for. He'd agreed to add the Kingsley name to the Dover blueprint.

She could accept his offer and pray it didn't lead to a repeat of past mistakes. An unnecessary concern. She could control the way her heart sped at seeing his smile, at hearing his laughter, at...well, everything about him.

He was nothing more than an employer and temporary colleague. This was business and nothing personal.

Claire stood. He did the same. She held out her hand, muscles taut to keep it from trembling with a lack of confidence in her decision. "In that case, I find your terms satisfactory, Mr. Gregory."

"My associates call me Mark."

Unprepared for the sharing of first names, she said nothing.

Rather than shake on their agreement as Claire had expected, he clasped her fingers, giving her the ridiculous notion that he might bend forward and kiss her hand. "When will you be available to begin work?"

She hadn't thought that far ahead. "I'll ask that my hours at the store be reduced. Will Tuesday and Thursday afternoons suit you? Of course, Mr. Newland must agree. I'll try to speak with him tomorrow."

"I'll contact Mr. Dover in the morning and inform him of our decision."

He'd held her fingers far too long. She slid them from his hold. "Thank you."

Mr. Gregory escorted her to the door and opened it. Was now the time to bring up Lefler? If she waited too long, there would be no point. "Are you aware that a man by the name of Harris Lefler has purchased property in Riverport with the intention of constructing an office building?"

"I've heard rumors. He owns property from Chicago to Indianapolis to Cincinnati and various towns in between. He has an uncanny knack for knowing where to buy and a mind for making money from that purchase. He must have faith in Riverport as a worthwhile investment."

She told him about the Webster Street purchase and the size building the man had proposed.

Mr. Gregory's low whistle pierced the air. "I hadn't heard what he had in mind."

"It's my understanding that Mr. Lefler cut ties with his latest architect."

"That I did know. I've already contacted him but haven't had a response."

Claire shook her head. "That isn't how he's planned this project. It's by invitation only."

The light of his excitement dimmed. "That's a disappointment."

Clearly, like George, he'd had high hopes for working with the man. "Only if you don't seek an invitation."

His eyebrows dipped. "Where are you getting your information?"

"George Brant is in Riverport. I ran into him today."

"Brant?"

"He was my husband's partner. George has wanted to work with Lefler for years. Now, he has a chance and is not one to be underestimated. He's a very good architect and won't make gaining the project easy for anyone."

Under the circumstances, Mark Gregory might never receive an opportunity to compete against him, but one could hope, and it was encouraging that he'd already contacted Lefler.

"Your Mr. Brant shouldn't underestimate me." Mr. Gregory stopped short of winking at her. Nonetheless, for some reason her imagination added the playful gesture. "If I'm given an opportunity to compete, I can assure you I won't make it easy for others, either, but thank you for the warning."

Claire admired his self-assurance but considered his self-satisfied grin a sign that he didn't take her admonition seriously. He didn't know George as she did.

"It's getting dark. If you'd like, I'll see you home, Claire."

There it was. His use of her given name. *Business, Claire. No escort home.* And how would she explain him to her parents? "No, thank you. It isn't far."

As she walked away from the house, she listened for the closing of the front door, but the silence led her to envision Mark Gregory watching from the doorway. Oddly, it was both comforting and unsettling.

She had arrived at his home expecting him to turn her away. Instead, she was leaving with a job as an office clerk and designer...albeit temporarily.

Now, if she could keep her mind on those tasks and not her employer, she'd add no more regrets to those of the past.

# Chapter Eight

Shortly after Mark arrived at the office on Monday morning, the outer door opened, then closed with a bang. Addison burst into the drafting room. Excitement poured from him like water from a well-primed hand pump. "I have good news."

"Let's hear it."

"I've learned about an office building planned for a lot on Webster Street and—this is where it concerns you—the owner is looking for an architect." Mark simply smiled, and Addison's enthusiasm dropped into a frown. "This isn't news to you."

"No. However, I only received the details last night."

"You realize what this means, don't you?"

"A possible job for me?"

"Exactly." Addison tossed a small square of paper on the table. "The seller gave me the new owner's address."

Mark picked up the paper. "I appreciate your work on my behalf, but I was told the project will be awarded through an invitation-only competition."

"Invitation?"

"Certain architectural companies are invited to submit a design. The architect is chosen from among the designs submitted. Given my lack of references, the chance of being invited is remote."

"Don't be a Negative Ned. Of course, you have references. You have your experience in Chicago." Addison's eyes narrowed with sternness. "You want that commission, don't you, Gregory?"

"Yes, I do." His friend had no idea of its importance to Mark.

"Then you have nothing to lose by asking for an opportunity."

"Which I was about to do when you burst in." Mark strode to the storage closet and opened the box of newly printed letterhead. He grabbed the top sheet, fresh and crisp, along with a piece of notepaper for drafting the letter, a pen, and an envelope, then carried everything to the table.

"I'll get the typewriter." Addison bounded into the front office and lugged the heavy Remington back to the drafting room.

Mark had tossed and turned last night, thinking about what he might say in a letter to gain entry into Lefler's competition. Together, the men perfected the wording until Mark grinned, confident he had a compelling communication. He rolled the letterhead into the typewriter. "I'll take this to the post office when I'm finished."

As he typed, Addison stood across the table. "Has Mama Grzegorczyk found a boarder yet?" His lips ticked up with enjoyment.

"I don't know what got into her, but rest assured, there will be no boarder." After his conversation with her last night, Mark said those words with more conviction than they deserved.

"We'll see." Addison laughed. "I wish I'd had a mirror to show you your face when she brought it up." His mouth fell open and eyes bulged, trying to imitate Mark's surprise.

When he crossed his eyes to add exaggeration to absurdity, Mark laughed. "I love my mother and want her to be happy, but I can't deny you've captured my expression when dealing with her odd notions."

"I like your mother's spirit."

"I like it, too, as long as it doesn't adversely involve me." For some reason, talking about his mother reminded Mark of Claire's visit last night. "Do you remember the appointment I mentioned with a Mr. Dover?"

"On Friday."

"I have my first confirmed job."

Addison slapped his knee. "Good work! What is it?"

"A house design. But there's a condition."

"What kind of condition?"

Mark went into the details of Mr. Dover's proviso. "He wants me to work with a woman by the name of Claire Kingsley. Do you know her?"

"I don't think so. A woman architect, huh? It sounds like nepotism. Who is she? A daughter? Cousin?"

"As far as I'm aware, there is no relation. They're almost strangers."

"But he's willing to risk your business reputation on a woman he doesn't know?"

Addison had a point. Why would Dover go out of his way to see that Claire returned to the architectural profession?

Provided that she followed Mark's instructions, he didn't care. In fact, he looked forward to their time together. More than he should.

Addison shook his head. "There must be something going on between them that you weren't told."

Mark bristled at the implication. "Mrs. Kingsley worked with her husband and has experience in design. I'll allow her input regarding the house plan but monitor her skills. We're in agreement that nothing is to be done without my approval. With bills to pay, I can't afford to turn down Charles Dover's business."

"I suppose you know what you're doing."

Mark typed Lefler's address on the envelope. A couple of years ago, he'd heard idle talk that the businessman held a low opinion of women architects—of women in any profession, but Mark's working relationship with Claire was for a single project. She would have nothing to do with Lefler's design—that is, if Mark won an invitation.

He folded the letter and stuffed it in the envelope. "Don't worry. It will all work out."

It must.

MARK STARED AT THE figures in front of him, seeing little more than squiggles. For half an hour, he'd attempted to review the estimated costs for refurbishing a small stable into a house for his client's aging parents.

His concentration failed him, and his thoughts slipped sideways. How had he, a practical man of business, let his attraction to Claire sway him into hiring her as an office clerk? He had little for her to do and even less money to pay her.

Truthfully, he should have denied Claire the opportunity to work on the Dover house. But when she related the difficulties of a woman seeking work in a man's world, he'd asked himself how he'd feel if placed in her position. What if he were denied the chance to do a job that appealed to him, solely because he was man?

*"Many men feel threatened by working with a woman."*

But not her Richard.

If Mark explored his decision in depth, he'd probably admit that the reference to her late husband's willingness to work with her tipped his resolve in her favor. If he refused her, she would see him as narrow-minded by comparison. The offhand thought gave him pause. How rational was it to attempt to compete with a dead man?

The office door opened and the subject of his lack of concentration drifted into the room like a whimsical vision. "I hope I'm not disturbing you."

Those eyes, the shade of a summer sky, had done nothing but disturb him each time he saw her. Her sense of humor brought out his own. Her bravery when saving a small child drew his respect. The story of drawing for her grandmother...

*Don't get carried away, Gregory. You're working with her, not courting her.*

Not yet.

He rose, grabbed his suit coat from the back of the chair, and put it on. "Not at all. Come in, Claire."

She smiled, and he was lost. Oh, he was in such trouble.

"I was on my way home from the store and wanted to let you know I spoke with Mr. Newland."

"What did he say?"

"He's a generous man, but he's also a businessman."

Perhaps offering her a job was a mistake. What if he had cost her more lucrative employment?

"Fortunately, one of the other ladies in my department had asked to work more hours, but they weren't available."

Relief buckled through him. "She'll replace you during those times when you're here."

"Yes. Mr. Newland agreed to reducing my hours starting Thursday." She inspected the small office with the same earnestness he'd expect to see from someone wishing to lease it. Then she turned her attention back to him. "How did Mr. Dover react?"

"He was pleased to know we'd be working together in some capacity, even though it wasn't what he'd had in mind." Mark's doubts flew like pigeons out the turret windows. "I told him I'd walk the lot boundary tomorrow. Would you like to come with me?"

Her eyes lit. "What time?"

"Six-thirty. If you'll be home from work by then, I'll pick you up, and we'll drive out there together." At Claire's puckered brow and the quiet seconds that ticked by, Mark braced himself to hear she had another engagement.

"If you don't mind, I'd rather meet you here."

The taut muscles in the back of his neck relaxed. "Whatever is most convenient."

She peered around him toward the drafting room. Curiosity practically exploded from her.

"Would you like to see the rest of the office?"

"May I?"

"This is where you'll sit in your role as office clerk." He tapped the back of the chair behind the desk, then led her into the large room in the rear of the suite.

Claire ran a hand over the table and turned in a circle to survey the whole room. He recognized that look of longing, as if she'd found Excalibur or the Fountain of Youth. He'd worn it, too, his first day employed in an architectural office. Beneath the longing had lain dread —the dread of failing. He saw something similar in Claire's stiff bearing.

"It's a fine space. The turret's triple windows provide much-needed natural lighting." She pointed to the tiny and worthless closet installed by a previous tenant. "May I?"

"Of course."

She opened the door. "I thought I saw light peeking under the door. This closet blocks another window. I'm sure you've considered removing it and opening up the room to even more light."

"I'm waiting on the landlord. He's promised it will be done in the next couple of days." Long past Mark's original expectation.

"That will make a difference in this area." She shut the door and returned to the table. "You chose your office well."

He fought to restrain the puff of his chest. "Thank you."

Claire started toward the front office. "I'm sure you're busy."

When she reached the desk, she stopped and nodded at the drawing on top. "A current project?"

"Yes. I'm drafting a possible floor plan to show the client." If he could concentrate long enough to finish.

"It's nice."

The compliment was as enthusiastic as his mother's response to laundry day. "But?"

"No buts." She chewed her bottom lip a moment, then flashed a shy grin. "Well, perhaps one small one?"

"Yes?"

Inhibition tossed aside, along with her purse, she leaned over the surface of the desk, filling the space between them with a sweet and flowery scent. It threatened to drive Mark to the greatest distraction he'd experienced all day—in months, really.

"See this door?" She pointed to the one off the western side elevation, in the middle of what would be a small sitting room.

Mark had left the door in its current location, but now that she pointed it out, he saw a better place for it. Did she have the same idea? "What about it?"

She pressed a rounded fingernail to a spot on the southern exterior wall of the room that jutted out four feet from the main structure. "If you move it here, you could turn the current door into a window that would brighten the room considerably, while not losing important wall space."

Her breath had ruffled the hair on the top of his head, calling attention to how near they stood to one another. On Thursday, he would use the pomade, not only to keep it in place but to keep his mind on his work.

As for the door... "I agree. Adding a small side porch"—he pointed to the new location—"will allow the residents to relax in the evening and look out on the open space adjoining the property."

"I like that idea."

"And I like yours." Rather than be embarrassed that she'd recommended something better, his trust in her ability grew.

She gathered her purse. "Now, I really am going."

Claire reached for the doorknob, evidently oblivious to the shadow of a figure on the other side of the glass. Mark pulled her out of the way of the door hitting her in the face as it was pushed open.

She let out a slight squeak and fell back against him.

Addison entered the office and his eyes narrowed at seeing the two of them nailed together like a pair of two-by-fours. "What's going on here?"

Mark glared at him. "You almost hit this woman."

His friend's eyes expanded. "I beg your pardon, ma'am. I didn't hurt you, did I?"

"No. I'm fine." Claire relaxed in Mark's hold, until she gazed at his arm encircling her waist. She glanced up at him and stiffened, her cheeks the color of a ripe crab apple.

He cleared his throat and released her. "Mrs. Kingsley, I'd like you to meet my friend Addison O'Keefe."

She planted that sales clerk smile on her face. "It's a pleasure to meet you, Mr. O'Keefe."

"And you, ma'am. I understand you'll be working with Mark."

"Starting Thursday." Claire moved toward the door. "I'll let you two visit and will see you tomorrow evening, Mr. Gregory."

Before Mark could get out a goodbye, she strode into the hall, leaving nothing behind but the sound of quick footsteps and her flowery scent. The former faded in seconds. The latter remained to taunt him.

Addison closed the door, then crossed his arms, feet apart in a stance that demanded attention. "Now I know."

"You know what?"

"The reason you seized Mr. Dover's deal."

"What are you talking about? I hardly seized it."

Addison's bearing eased and his lips twitched. "You looked at Mrs. Kingsley, and the truth popped out in bright red hearts all over your face."

Mark's laugh sputtered. "That's ludicrous."

He'd tried to hide his interest in Claire, but everything about her intrigued him. As she'd fit perfectly in his arms a minute ago, something deep inside—something he'd never felt before—convinced him that she would fit as perfectly into his life.

"I know what it is to be attracted to a woman, Mark. I felt the same way when I first met Lizzie...still do. But don't risk your future on a pretty face."

"She isn't merely a pretty face." Still, Addison's warning served as reminder of Mark's own concerns.

He glanced at the guesthouse drawing on the desk. She had noticed his error right away. Though awkward for him, her pointing it out gave him reason to look upon her as an asset rather than a burden.

Addison shrugged. "I can see that nothing will deter you. Far be it from me to stand in the way of a lovesick calf."

Mark opened his mouth to refute the claim, but no words made it past his lips.

# Chapter Nine

Claire sat next to Mark in the carriage on the way to the Dover lot. She tried to relax her hands as she clutched the small notebook in her lap, but the tension in her fingers remained. Her pulse thrummed in her ears, diminishing the sounds of children playing and traffic passing.

They were driving down several streets toward the southern end of town, which meant crossing the Wabash. Whenever possible, Claire avoided the river for the memories it conjured. Today, she had no choice.

The horse's clip-clop echoed across the wooden bridge as she sat stiff on the seat, not looking left or right. Once they reached the other side, her body relaxed.

They turned onto a side street where the lots grew bigger, as did the homes, although these structures were nothing compared to those in the area east of downtown—the area where people lived who possessed the same ample resources as the Newlands.

Claire had almost canceled this trip after the incident in Mark's office yesterday. She could thank him for saving her from being hit by the door. He'd been a gentleman. She couldn't forgive herself for sinking into a moment of pleasure when he wrapped his arm around her waist. That moment reminded her of what it felt like to be held by a man—warm, safe, secure in love.

But that was the problem, wasn't it? Mark was just another man, not her husband. Yes, a surge of excitement had swept through her,

SANDRA ARDOIN

but no love was involved in the embrace. Not even a wish for such intimacy and feeling—none she'd ever acknowledge. She couldn't say the same for him when a gleam of interest had flashed from his eyes as he'd looked down on her.

Why had she given him the wrong idea that day at the store? *Foolish, foolish, foolish woman.*

Mark reined the horse alongside the curb, behind another buggy and in front of a heavily wooded property. A break in the trees revealed a slight downward slope where a tiny creek meandered along the rear property line. She judged the lot to be a little more than an acre, bordered on both sides and across the street by established residences.

Mr. Dover stood with his back against the trunk of a hickory tree near the street, one ankle crossed over the other and his hands on the top of the cane he'd carried the first time she met him. He looked up and ambled toward them. "Welcome."

Mark helped Claire from the carriage. As soon as she hit the ground, she tugged her hand free from his, shook out her skirts to cover the abrupt action, and strolled to meet their client, leaving him to follow. "What lovely land."

Mr. Dover's cheeks puffed with his smile. "Leora took one look and demanded we buy it."

Claire laughed. "I see no injury to your arm as a result of her twisting it."

"None at all." He shook his arm to prove it. "Depending on the way the wind blows, there are days when we hear the river flowing. It isn't far beyond our property."

She listened. Today was not one of those days.

Mr. Dover shook Mark's hand. "Well, young man, what do you think you can do with this?"

Mark studied what could be seen of the land from front to back and side to side. "How many of the trees do you want to save?"

86

"As many as possible. It's what drew us to the property. We'd like to preserve the view from front and rear."

Claire glanced at Mark and gauged that the same question occurred to him. Many of the trees were on the upper portion of the lot. To keep them, where would the house go?

"My wife wants a small gazebo built at the bottom of the slope where the land overlooks the creek. She imagines us spending our elder years relaxing there." The feigned scowl gave way to a chuckle, exposing the respect and admiration Mr. Dover had for his wife. He wanted to please her, and in doing so, it pleased him. In that, he was much like Richard.

They discussed their client's preferences and budget. Claire jotted down copious notes in the little book, while Mark asked intelligent questions and made a few suggestions.

"I must go. I've kept Leora waiting supper. When may I expect to see a preliminary drawing?"

Mark turned back to eye the lot. "We'll need to review the city's building regulations. In the meantime, I'll prepare a written summary of the project requirements we've discussed for you to approve. Taking into consideration our schedules, we should be able to provide you with something preliminary a couple of weeks after that."

"As I said, there's no hurry. However, I will look forward to seeing it."

Once Mr. Dover had driven away, Claire cast a last look around, then hiked through the stand of trees toward the street. "That gives us a start." When she received no answer, she spun around. Mark was headed in the opposite direction, on his way to the back of the property. "Aren't we leaving?"

He glanced over his shoulder. "In a minute."

She studied Mark's movements and suspected he would examine each blade of grass on the Dover property and a bucket of soil if it meant the difference between constructing a generic and mediocre building or one that fit the lot like no other. And rightly so.

Rather than let him think she had no interest in what was on his mind, she traipsed back the way she'd come, lifting her skirts as she navigated through the trees and brush. Her dress snagged on a branch that had fallen from an oak tree. She carefully freed the claw-like piece from the material and tossed it aside, then continued to trail Mark.

Mark? Despite his request that she use his given name, she was only an employee.

He stopped near the point where the land sloped toward the creek in a gradual gradient. When she reached his side, somewhat winded, she followed his every glance, every stare, every narrowed gaze, preparing to share an opinion or idea he might request of her.

"We have our work ahead of us, Claire." He gestured to the wooded area she'd tramped through. "Dover wants to keep as many of those trees as possible, yet the land they sit on is the most level and suitable place for the size house he wishes to build."

"You did tell him, and he's an intelligent man. Are you thinking most of the trees will need to come down?"

"Probably more than he would like."

"That's a shame. They add character to the land."

"Let's see if we can come up with a better idea."

*We.* She liked the way Mark included her in the project...as long as their relationship remained strictly professional.

MARK SCANNED THE PROPERTY one more time, mainly to avoid focusing on Claire. As long as he concentrated on the Dover project, he could put her out of his mind. It was when his concentration lagged that he fought to keep his interest to himself.

In various little ways, she had let him know anything personal

ENDURING DREAMS

between them was not appreciated—everything from the posture of a yardstick to snatching her hand from his when he'd tried to help her from the carriage. At the same time, she kept that light smile on her face, one he suspected was more for show than heartfelt feeling. It made him more determined to get to know the real Claire Kingsley.

In good time.

He turned without a glance in her direction. "I've seen everything I need to see right now. Are you ready to leave?"

"Yes."

Keeping a respectable distance between them, he led Claire to her side of the buggy but let her climb aboard under her own power. Once he'd taken up the reins and guided the horse toward town, they delved into various subjects. He kept her talking as they traversed the bridge. For some reason, she'd barely breathed while crossing the river earlier. Fear of water or heights, he supposed.

"Living in Chicago during the time of the World's Columbian Exposition must have been exciting." The animation in Claire's voice parroted her statement. "It's a shame Mr. Root never lived to see the joy it brought to people from all over the country and beyond. He was such a force behind the planning and development of the fair."

The city of Chicago owed much to John Root, Mr. Burnham's late partner. "Did you know he sketched out his original ideas for the layout on a large sheet of brown paper?"

"I'd heard that."

Mark reined the horse around a stopped buggy on Commerce. "My one regret was never having had the chance to meet and learn from John Root. That said, I won't discount what I learned from Mr. Burnham, another man of vision."

"I understand they added bronze plaques to the Fine Arts Building in memory of Mr. Root and Mr. Olmsted's partner, Mr. Codman."

"True. Codman was my age. He accomplished much in his short life." Much more than Mark. But that would change. Perhaps the Lefler commission was the first step toward receiving his own important project in the style of a Columbian Exposition. "John Root was only a dozen years older than Codman when he succumbed to pneumonia. It isn't right that men die in their prime when they should have years to contribute to society."

"'For my thoughts are not your thoughts, neither are your ways my ways.'"

"What is that?"

"It's from the book of Isaiah. An early death may not seem right to those of us left behind, but we don't see the whole story, do we? We don't see God's purpose for an individual's life."

Mark's jaw clenched at being preached to. What did she know of it? Did God even care enough to have a plan for people's lives?

Then, it occurred to him that she had been one of those left behind, as had he when his father died. Unlike him, she showed no anger at losing her husband so young.

As though she wished to end the somber discussion, Claire twisted toward him and changed the subject. "Would I be treading on treacherous ground if I asked again about the situation with your mother?"

What she really asked was why his mother shunned her. "To be blunt, she's adamant that my future wife will have a Polish ancestry."

"I see."

At the dismay in her soft response, he regretted using the word wife and did his best to bury the memory with further explanation. "After my parents arrived in the United States, my father saw that she learned English and the ways of this country, but she protested every step. In moving her to Riverport, I took her out of another comfortable world, one occupied by fellow Poles."

Claire seemed to ponder the situation. "Your mother is afraid she'll lose more of her heritage, because she won't have others around to remind her of it?"

"An astute observation. It's been hard for her to adjust to leaving our Polish neighborhood in Chicago. I had assumed Mama would eventually come to like living here, but I might have made a mistake. Maybe I've only succeeded in ensuring her misery."

"I doubt that. If it helps, Riverport is my childhood home. When I moved to Indianapolis, it took time to make friends in a new place and to feel welcome. I'm sure she'll come around."

"Possibly." Even to his own ears, he didn't sound convinced. She hadn't changed in thirty years. Why should he expect her to change now? "I understand and can sympathize with her, but I'd like Mama to discover that accepting a new way of life isn't the same as abandoning the past. It's my hope that she'll make the most of her present life and find joy in it."

A wry smile graced Claire's face. "That is a noble goal."

As they neared the northern area of town, he leaned forward and slowed the horse, his attention on suspicious activity down the street.

"What's wrong?"

Mark's hands clenched the reins. "I don't like what I'm seeing up ahead."

He studied the two boys standing alongside the street. The one he judged to be about twelve kicked at something in the grass—something alive based on its flinch. The other one, younger, spat on it. Their jeers were loud enough to reach his ears.

Claire leaned forward in the seat. "What are those boys up to?"

"Nothing good, I'm sure."

Mark urged the horse into a trot, eager to prove himself wrong about what he saw. Once they neared the children, he drew back on the reins and jumped from the carriage, certain now of their activity.

"What do you two think you're doing?" He marched to the boys, who backed a few steps away from the trembling dog on the ground.

The older boy stood taller and sneered at Mark. "This mongrel's been hanging around the neighborhood all week. Pa don't want it here no more."

"That's no excuse for cruelty." The dog whimpered at the volume and tone of Mark's voice, something that failed to make an impact on the older boy. Not according to that malicious glint he aimed at Mark.

Years ago, Mark had seen that same look in another boy's eyes. In that instance, his father had come to his defense against a bully, as Mark now defended the dog. This time, the result of the encounter would be different.

The boy waved a hand through the air. "Go on. Get it outta here before Pa sees it again, 'cause he won't be near as nice to it as us."

Mark couldn't dispute the boy's statement. Surely, the apples hadn't fallen far from the twisted limbs of that family tree.

"It's nothin' but a bony old cur, anyway." The older delinquent slapped his brother on the arm. "Let's go to the pond and find us some tadpoles."

The brothers ran off and disappeared amid the trees, leaving Mark feeling sorry for any tadpoles they found.

He dug into a bag sitting in the carriage and removed the cookies his mother sent with him to the office that morning. He had eaten all but three. Cookies weren't the most suitable meal for an underfed dog, but he had nothing else to give it.

"What am I to do with you?" He couldn't leave an obvious stray here to starve or be mistreated again by those boys or their father.

He crouched a few feet from the animal—an unsightly thing with its nondescript coloring and clumps of dirt that clung to the ends of a wiry coat. Sad eyes, shimmering like brown silk, melted his anger.

"Come here." Mark whispered the words and held out a hand, palm down, for the dog—a female—to sniff. Mangy and thin, shoulders and hipbones protruding, she crept closer and stopped. He waited until she made up her mind to trust him.

It required more soft words and patience before he was rewarded with a crawl across the dirt on a hefty belly. With the stretch of her neck, her damp nose touched his fingertips. He laid a light hand on the dog's head and scratched her behind the ears.

Claire joined him and knelt in the grass, encouraging the dog's approach with soft words and coos. The animal licked her hand. "Poor thing. She looks hungry."

He held out one of the cookies. The dog sniffed it, snatched it, and ate it in one gulp. "I think I'll take her home with me." He turned to Claire. "Unless you would like to do so."

"I couldn't impose an animal on my family, not under these circumstances."

"These circumstances?"

Claire rose from the crouch. Those light eyes twinkled. "It won't be long before your cookie eater produces little crumbs."

Little crumbs? What did she mean by...? Mark studied the dog's enlarged middle. His face burned. How had he missed recognizing the stray's condition? "Well, I'll be."

"Congratulations."

He reconsidered his plan to take the dog with him. It took all of ten seconds. "I can't drive off and leave her here with those hooligans around."

"Maybe you'll find another home for her."

"If not, what will I do with puppies?"

"Give them away. As precious as their mother is, I'm sure it won't be hard."

"Let's hope not." He urged the animal into the buggy. She jumped on the seat, flopped down where Claire had sat, and sprawled across the leather with a canine sigh.

Claire laughed. "I'll walk from here."

"No, I'll put her on the floor and take you home."

"Don't bother. It isn't far. Goodnight." She quick-stepped down the street before he could argue.

When she turned a corner, Mark turned to the dog. "I looked forward to taking Claire home, you know." At a solemn whimper from the brown and gray lump on the seat, he said, "Let's get you something proper to eat."

Puppies? He shook his head and turned the horse toward home.

Maybe a pet would give his mother something to think about other than moving back to Chicago...if Mama accepted her.

# Chapter Ten

C laire whipped the paper out of the typewriter and reread it, looking for mistakes. It had been a while since she'd done any typing and the process had taken her longer than she'd expected. To keep this job, she must become faster.

When satisfied there were no errors, she carried the project summary into the drafting room where Mark sat on a stool in front of the easel. She handed him the paper. "This is ready for Mr. Dover's signature."

Mark perused the general list of expectations and estimated costs for his services and handed it back to her. "This looks good. Will you put it in an envelope and hand-carry it to Mr. Dover's office this afternoon?"

"Of course." Claire peered around him at the paper tacked to the board, her hands clenched behind her back as she studied a sketch for the Dover house. He had an eye for proportion and confident lines.

Should she show him some of her old drawings? Last night, she'd finally dredged up the nerve to dig out her sketchbook from the trunk. So far, she hadn't opened it.

"Have you settled on a plan to keep the trees?"

"I'm considering various concepts, but until the Dovers approve that list, we won't go too far."

"This one is nice."

"It's wrong." He ripped the paper from the board, wadded it, and dropped it on the floor. "A house should blend into the nature around it, but it should never be obvious. We want a design that complements its surroundings, not overwhelms it. Every segment of the structure should be in proportion to its setting."

Claire picked up the discarded paper and the other two rejected balls on the floor. "You sound like my husband. He would say, 'We want everyone who stops to observe the building to realize its beauty without being able to rationalize why it's beautiful. It must be an immediate and positive reaction.'"

"Hmm." The response was unenthusiastic at best.

Claire shifted to his other side. "Perhaps if we discuss it, we might draw ideas from one another."

"A pun?"

"If you think so."

He chuckled, obviously grasping that she fully intended him to see it that way. "So far, all of my ideas would require too many of the trees to be removed."

"Have you considered that you're thinking too precisely?"

"In what way?"

"Building the Dover house requires losing more trees than the couple would like, so what if we brought them into the house?"

"Trees in the house?"

Claire could see by his expression that he'd already rejected the image her words provoked. "I don't mean literally. What if they were given a sense of being in a wooded area within their own home?"

"Are you talking about something in a horseshoe shape around a cluster of trees?" He pointed to the paper balls in her hand. "If so, you'll already find that idea in one of those."

She crushed the rejected drawings into smaller spheres. "No, but it does have merit."

Her mood jumped between nervousness and excitement, resting somewhere along unease. Would he dismiss her idea as outrageous?

"Come, Claire, you want to tell me. What is it?"

His question broke through her hesitation. "What if the house contained characteristics of the outdoors?"

"In what ways?"

"Wood forms the floors and stairways of a house and is used to panel walls. That wood is cut and molded into civilized shapes, planed until silk wouldn't catch on it, and then stained or painted an unnatural color. Mr. Gregory, I think you should give that wood back its natural form and texture."

Grooves creased his brow. "You're talking about building a log-style house? I don't think that's what Dover has in mind."

"No logs on the exterior. I'm referring to little interior touches that bring the setting inside. Ceilings with rough-hewn beams. A staircase of natural wood treads." Claire's hand waved past her face as she talked, seeing everything she described. "A stone fireplace with carved side beams and mantel. Paint colors and wallpaper that reflect the outdoors."

The more she talked, the more she could see that he pictured the overall design. "We don't want to carry the concept too far."

"No, of course not."

"Why don't you sketch some ideas and I'll see if I can work with them?" Mark pointed to the table. "You'll find a sketch pad on the table over there."

Sketch her ideas? How did she do that when she couldn't bring herself to open the book at home? She should have kept quiet.

Then again, she was here because Mr. Dover requested her services. What had she thought would happen?

"Is there a problem?"

"No." She walked to the table. Her fingers crept toward the sketch pad, stopping before she reached it. "I have some work to do at my desk before I leave. I'll wait until tonight when I'm at home." If she could summon the courage to open the sketchbook and transfer the images in her head to paper.

Did she even belong in an architectural office, even temporarily, if she failed to draw a single line on paper?

MARK GRABBED HIS COAT from a hook on the wall. "We've accomplished all we can today. I'll walk you home."

"I can—"

"I'll walk you home, Claire."

She looked about to argue with him, then seemed to think better of it and gathered her hat and purse. "All right."

Her ideas for the Dover house and the excitement with which she'd presented them had intrigued him. He wanted to see more. What bothered him was the clear hesitation she'd shown when asked to draw those ideas. It was almost as though she was afraid of the sketchbook, the one she'd left behind.

He picked it up and held it out to her. "Don't forget this."

She paused, and he expected her to take it with the tips of her thumb and forefinger, holding it away from her body as if afraid it would bite. She fooled him and snatched it from his hand, then tucked it to her body in a tight hold, almost burying it within her arms.

Earlier, Mark had considered asking to take her to supper, but given her hesitancy to treat him as anything other than an employer, he doubted she would accept. She still insisted on calling him Mr. Gregory.

No, this was not the time to ask her to supper. This was a time to get to know her better in a more formal setting. If or when she gave him any indication of a wish for more—and he remained interested in her—he would ask.

What if she had a suitor? Why hadn't he thought of that before?

His gaze moved to the ring on her finger. If that were the case, she'd have removed her wedding band, right?

They strolled along the streets, remarking off and on about one building or another. She gave him a short history of the town and what she liked about it—the opportunities, the people, the nearby farms with cornstalks that rose higher than a man's head in years of good rainfall. Her enthusiasm and the pleasantness of her voice made it an enjoyable stroll.

"How is the stray?"

"Cookie."

Claire spit out a laugh. "You named her Cookie?"

Mark raised his hands in defense. "It wasn't my idea."

"What did your mother say when you arrived home with her?"

"To be honest, I expected her to ban the dog from the house, especially knowing she'd soon give birth. Instead, my mother shed tears at the poor animal's condition." At that moment, Mark knew he had done well in taking the dog home.

"I'm glad Cookie has a good, protected place to live. I'm also glad you confronted those awful boys."

"I saw the words 'reformatory school' when looking at them."

They neared Mark's street and Claire stopped. "There's no sense in you walking me home and having to come back here. I'll go the rest of the way alone."

He wasn't ready to say goodbye. "I used to play on a neighborhood baseball team, but since moving here, I've gotten little exercise. The extra walk will be good for me."

Her face lit. "You like baseball?"

"Is there a more exciting sport?"

"None. My husband never understood my interest in the game." A point in Mark's favor?

"Richard enjoyed chess. We played together on occasion." Perhaps not.

"Did you know we have an amateur team, the Riverport Pilots?"

"I'd heard."

"Steamboats are part of the river's history."

"And every steamboat needs a pilot."

"Correct." She continued walking. "My friend Mrs. Malone lives on your street a few houses down from you."

Malone? Where had he heard that name? He remembered. Though he didn't know the details, his mother spoke about some scandal involving someone in the neighborhood named Malone—another of her black marks against living here. As if scandal never invaded their old neighborhood.

Her joy, sparked by their conversation over baseball, turned grim. "It's probably good to have a dog around. Roslyn had some trouble not long ago."

"What kind of trouble?"

"She saw someone skulking around her yard late at night."

"A thief?" He'd make sure they locked the doors in the evenings. What was the world coming to when a homeowner must take such measures to guard his own property?

"She didn't recognize him but said he was watching the house. He disappeared when he saw her at the window."

"I'm sure her husband is taking precautions to keep his family safe." As would Mark.

"She lives alone. Her husband, Gil Malone, oversaw Newland's accounting department until they discovered he'd embezzled money from the store. It caused quite a stir last Christmas."

"He's in jail?"

Claire grimaced. "The police have looked for him since December, but he's disappeared."

"I hope he's found soon. I'm sure not knowing what happened to him is a burden on your friend." Sadness pervaded Claire's demeanor, and he sought a different topic. "You told me you live with your parents."

She nodded. "I'm sure we all thought my stay would be temporary but..."

"You miss not being on your own." She darted a glance in his direction as though trying to perceive the reasoning behind his deduction. "It was the resignation in your voice."

"I miss having my own home. It isn't that I don't appreciate all my family has done for me, but I'm mulling over the idea of renting a room somewhere."

Mark understood her need for independence. "Until we moved to Riverport, I lived a few blocks from the house in which I'd grown up—not far from my mother, so I could care for her, but far enough for some autonomy. When we came here, I decided we would move into one place in the beginning, until she grew accustomed to her new surroundings. I'll admit, I miss the freedom of my own space. At the same time, it is nice to have someone to come home to."

"I suppose."

But not the same as coming home to a beloved husband? *Very intelligent, Mark. Anymore dazzling statements to shine a light on Claire's loss?*

Now that he'd ventured into forbidden territory he might as well go the full distance. "Your parents aren't aware that you're working for me, are they?"

Her step stuttered, then resumed. "How did you know?"

"Your reluctance to let me near their house." He frowned. "Why haven't you told them?"

"It's a complicated situation." Her head tilted as she looked at him. "Do you tell your mother everything?"

If she knew all he had done in his youth and beyond—what he'd done to start his business—Mama would take to her bed. "I tell her what's important."

"Have you told her you're working with me?" At his hesitation, Claire smiled. "I didn't think so."

Since Mama never brought up Claire's visit to the house, he'd left well enough alone and hadn't provided an explanation. Maybe it was time to tell his mother, to get her used to Claire's presence, because every moment spent with this woman—witnessing her sense of humor, her concern over her friends, her joy over the game of baseball—motivated a desire for more.

He took a risk. "Perhaps, you'd like to attend a baseball game with me some time."

And with the snap of a finger, the smile disappeared. "Our time together is best spent working."

He'd pushed too hard and lost the gamble.

"May I ask you a question, Mr. Gregory?"

He'd hoped they were beyond the formality. "Whatever you want to ask sounds serious."

"I think the answer is important to our ability to work together."

Now, it sounded plain ominous. "Go ahead."

"Did your decision not to tell your mother have anything to do with me not being Polish?"

Her perception surpassed the credit he'd given her on their return from the Dover lot. "And if it did?"

"Then I think you should take her advice and find that Polish girl she wants for you."

As surely as a bucket of water poured over a campfire, her words doused the flame of hope that had sparked inside him during their walk. "You feel no attraction to me?"

"Finding someone else is for you own good, because I'll never remarry."

Before he could fully absorb her words, she said, "This is my street. Thank you for seeing me home."

Claire turned a corner, stopped, and looked back at him. Her half-smile signaled more regret than happiness.

On the heels of disappointment over her aversion to remarriage, a pleasant thought occurred. Claire Kingsley hadn't denied an attraction to him.

Long ago, Mark had learned to compete with honor for what he wanted. Just as he was determined to succeed in his business, he would succeed in winning Claire's affection. He would change her mind. First, he must move her past her resolve not to remarry.

Why would a young woman decline the prospect of being loved by a husband and children?

At least he could erase the idea that she had another suitor.

Mark thought of the ring on Claire's hand. No, there was no suitor. In all likelihood, his competition had nothing to do with someone of flesh and blood.

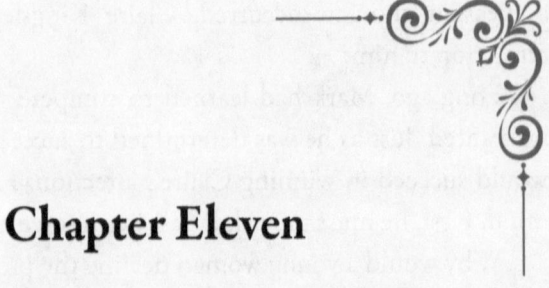

# Chapter Eleven

Claire shifted the pound cake she'd baked for Louisa Gruhn and Cissy from one hand to the other. Today, a busy body was better than a busy mind.

Her attempt failed, and her mind worked as hard as ever. Why bring up to Mark her intention of never remarrying?

The way he looked at her. The way he tried not to look at her. The hope in his invitation to accompany him to a baseball game. It wasn't vanity that whispered his attraction in her ear.

*"You feel no attraction to me?"*

Claire shifted the cake once more. She had sidestepped Mark's question, not wishing to say she was drawn to him with an intensity she hadn't felt since the early years of her marriage. That draw brought reflections of domestic bliss, even as warning bells reminded her of the selfishness of it.

Fear of another pregnancy had destroyed her future with Richard. After over a year of employing methods to control the possibility, they both realized the truth. She was too much a coward to bury another baby.

Whether Mark wanted children or not didn't matter. She could bear the physical pain of losing another child over and over. She would not bear the emotional pain a third time. She was not destined to be a mother. And she couldn't take the opportunity to be a father away from another man.

Mark would succeed at his business. She felt certain of it. He wouldn't succeed in wooing her. No one would, not for many years. Not when it meant the probability of heartbreak for both of them.

As Claire climbed the steps to Louisa Gruhn's porch, a board under her foot groaned and dipped. She held her breath and tested the next one before putting her full weight on it. Only then did she breathe again.

Louisa and Cissy had been on Claire's mind for several days, the memory of the widow's helpfulness begging her to pay a visit, and she hadn't come empty-handed. She sniffed the sweet-smelling pound cake, then cradled it on one arm and knocked on the front door.

While she waited for Louisa to answer, her gaze explored the outside of the house. It was as orderly and neat as she remembered from her last visit. But a closer look revealed several necessary repairs. The steps were the first thing she noticed, of course. Also, a few of the porch planks were cracked and warped. A windowsill sagged and the paint on the frame was chipped. Small things that could get out of hand and cause more damage if not repaired.

Claire raised her hand to knock again at the same time the door swung open. She looked down and nodded at the child on the other side. "Good evening, Cissy. Is your mother home?"

"Cissy, please don't answer the door without me." Louisa picked up her daughter. When she finally looked up, the worry lines on her face smoothed into a smile. "Claire, how nice to see you. Come in."

Claire stepped into the small front hall and held out her gift. "I hope you two like pound cake."

Cissy drew in a breath. "With sugar icing?"

"With lots of sugar icing." She tickled the girl, who squirmed in her mother's arms.

Louisa set the child down and closed the front door. "What a nice surprise. Cissy, show our guest to the parlor while I take this to the kitchen."

"I can't stay long." The sun was already on a downward slide to the horizon.

Once Claire was seated on the worn tapestry sofa, Cissy climbed onto her lap and snuggled up against her. The move sent an emotional jolt through Claire and tightened her chest. She forced herself to relax and wrap her arm around the little girl.

She had laughed with and teased Phoebe's daughter often, but her interactions with other small children had been few and far between. Holding this child prompted visions of a future in which it was a daily occurrence, visions she'd packed away long ago. Odd that such a simple act brought them back with a force that conveyed both sorrow and expectancy at the same time.

When Louisa returned with two plates of cake, she smiled at her daughter. "Yours is in the kitchen."

The four-year-old scrambled off Claire's lap and ran out of the room, sparking laughter from the women who watched her enthusiasm.

Claire cut off a small piece of the cake with her fork. "I understand you'll start work at Newland's soon."

"Yes, in the alterations department. I can't thank you enough for recommending me."

"I did nothing but mention your name and experience. You made the impression on the department manager."

"Still, if you and the gentleman hadn't convinced me to look into it that day you saved Cissy from... Well, I don't know if my pride would have allowed me to do so." Louisa paused. "The gentleman rushed off to his appointment before I got his name."

"It's Mark Gregory. He's new in town." She chose not to elaborate on their work together.

Claire steered the conversation away from the architect. They chatted and laughed until the mantel clock chimed, reminding her of the passing of time. She set her empty plate on a nearby table. "I want to be home before dark."

Louisa stepped outside with her, Cissy by her side. "Thank you for the cake and the visit."

"I enjoyed it." Claire descended the porch steps, careful to avoid the soft spot in the wood. Surely, Louisa was aware of the danger and possible injury to someone.

Before she could turn to mention it, the sound of cracking wood and a high-pitched screech whipped her around. Louisa stood on the porch, a grimace on her face and one leg lower than the other.

Claire rushed up the stairs to Louisa's side. "Let me help you." She wrapped an arm around the woman's waist. "Can you lift your leg?"

"I think so." Louisa winced and with a cautious movement lifted her leg from the hole created by the broken board. After putting weight on her foot, she yanked it back up and sucked air through her teeth. "I think I sprained my ankle."

Cissy began to sob. "Ma?"

"I'm fine, sweetheart. Go into the house, please."

Once Cissy obeyed, Claire helped Louisa to the door. "Let's get you inside, too."

With Claire's support, they made it to the parlor. She helped Louisa to the sofa, gently elevated the woman's foot, and removed her shoe to examine the ankle. Blood soaked part of Louisa's torn stocking, so Claire removed it, also. "You cut your leg, but it isn't deep. Shall I get a doctor for your ankle?"

"No!" Louisa waved her foot back and forth three times in a slow motion. Her gasping breaths belied her bravado. "It isn't broken. In fact, it already feels better. It scared me more than anything. I don't need a doctor."

Since Louisa could move it without excruciating pain, Claire didn't argue. "Would you like me to stay tonight and take care of Cissy while you rest your foot?" It shouldn't be too hard with the mother here to tell her what to do.

Louisa grasped her hand and squeezed. "That's thoughtful of you, but you go on home. Once I'm over the embarrassment, I'll be fine."

"There's no reason to be embarrassed."

"I should have fixed those boards long ago, but money has been scarce. That might have been you who fell through the rotted wood."

"It wasn't, so don't chastise yourself."

The tip of Claire's tongue tingled with the urge to tell Louisa of the projects undertaken by the Widow's Might circle. If ever anyone needed help, it was Louisa and Cissy. But the group discussed, then voted on, their charitable endeavors. It wasn't up to Claire to commit without giving her friends the opportunity to approve it.

"Let me clean that cut before I leave."

Fifteen minutes later, she walked out the front door and stood peering into the hole in the porch floor. Seeing a small rocking chair nearby, she slid it over the hole and walked away determined to present her request at the next Widow's Might meeting.

MARK ADJUSTED THE WICK on the lamp he'd brought to the dining room table. More light helped his tired eyes focus on the lines he'd drawn, erased, and redrawn...over and over.

Two hours ago, he'd abandoned the coat and tie and rolled up his sleeves to settle into an evening of work at home. Several possibilities regarding the Dover house lay scattered across the table. One appealed to him more than the others, but he'd settled on nothing yet.

His thoughts tossed to tomorrow when Claire would return to his office expecting a normal working relationship. How could he continue to see her—to work with her—and not want more?

It was his fault. He had offered her employment knowing this temptation might grow stronger each time they met.

He scrubbed a hand down his face as if that would scrub away all thoughts of one Claire Kingsley. The action was akin to wiping a smudge of ink from his shirt, expecting not to leave a stain.

No matter what she said or did to deter his interest in her, no matter the harshness of his inner lectures, nothing worked. Even the office held her scent, as if it were a bottle containing an enticing perfume. Fine. When it came to the lovely widow's perfume, perhaps he tended to let his imagined sense of smell run too freely.

A month ago, he would have called another man irrational for having such strong feelings about a woman so soon in their acquaintance. Obviously, he was irrational. Too bad he was as stubborn as his mother, or he would forget any idea of something personal developing with Claire.

"Marek." His mother walked through the doorway that linked the kitchen and dining room. Cookie followed on her heels, no doubt looking for some scrap of food. The dog and her appetite had grown larger each day.

Mama held a cup of coffee. "Here. From what I see on your face, you can use this."

He nearly scalded his tongue on the hot liquid but felt an almost instant sense of revival. "That's good."

"You should go to bed."

"Not yet. I can't afford to let time escape without progress on this house design."

He had received a partial fee from Dover but wouldn't receive any more until the preliminary design was approved. What he really needed to make the loan payment was a partial fee from someone like Harris Lefler. Over two weeks had passed since he had sent the letter off. So far, no response.

"I thought you were working with Mrs. Kingsley." His mother's lips pinched before she asked, "Why does she not do her part to help you?"

After his conversation with Claire, Mark told his mother of their collaboration on Mr. Dover's project and Claire's clerical position in his office. Mama had said little at the time, which revealed as much about her unhappiness as any outburst.

"She is doing her part."

"It isn't right for an unattached man and a widow to be alone for hours. Who knows what people are saying."

"No one is saying anything. Even if they were, she's an employee, not a lover." At his mother's gasp, he sipped the coffee, ashamed of letting his annoyance control his tongue.

Many women might have misgivings about working alone in an office with a man. Nonetheless, for any woman who aspired to work in that man's world, she must trust him. At the same time, Mark understood that some men betrayed that trust. He would not be one of them and would guard Claire's reputation as diligently as possible—starting now.

He set the cup in the saucer. "That was an improper comment that neither you nor Mrs. Kingsley deserved from me."

His mother twisted her hands. "Then you are not pursuing a personal relationship with her?"

"She's made it clear it wouldn't be welcomed."

His mother's body relaxed, and she stopped squeezing her hands as though they were sodden dishrags. A broad smile took years off her appearance. "In that case, you will not mind that I invited guests to visit us."

"Aunt Gizela?" As soon as the question left his mouth, he dropped the pencil he'd picked up seconds ago. "You said guests, as in more than one, so it can't be your sister."

"No. But I would like to see her again. Perhaps I will write—"

"Who did you invite?"

She moved behind him, placed her hands on his shoulders, and kneaded them like they were made of bread dough. "You have been working hard and could use time to relax and have fun."

Rather than relaxing them, Mark's muscles tightened under the gentle manipulation. His mother had mastered the technique of evading questions she didn't want to answer. "Mama, tell me who you invited."

She released him and started for the kitchen. "Nadia Kowalski."

"Mrs. Kowalski and..." Where the mother went, the—

"Paulina."

—daughter was at her side.

Mark groaned. Mama and Mrs. Kowalski had planned the marriage between him and Paulina since they were infants. Not that Paulina hadn't grown into a fine woman. About eight years ago, he gave in to the curiosity over his mother's confidence that they were a match and escorted her to a neighborhood dance. He returned Paulina home early that evening having felt no spark. He'd tried to convince her they were better suited as friends.

"Nadia is my *przyjaciółka*."

His mother's best friend. The reminder of the closeness between the women tugged a reluctant smile from him. He didn't trust the intentions of either mother, especially his own. Nonetheless, he would never refuse her a visit with an old friend. "I know she is, Mama. As long as you harbor no illusions as to my future with her daughter, I'll welcome both and do my best to be a proper host."

Her wide grin declared triumph. "I knew you would, my dear boy."

"When will they arrive?"

"A week from tomorrow."

"That's"—he counted the dates off in his head—"Friday the eleventh? When did you issue this invitation?"

"Three weeks ago."

Of course. Not long after he met Claire at the store. "Keep in mind, I'll be busy and unable to spend as much time with them as will make you happy."

"I understand." She clasped her hands together. "I have much to do."

Regardless of his exasperation, he chuckled when she bustled off as if she planned to clean the house from top to bottom at eight o'clock at night. Cookie remained in the dining room, lying next to Mark's feet.

He picked up the pencil with the intention of resuming his work, but he couldn't stop the irony from blaring like a trumpet in his head. At one time, Paulina made it clear she would welcome a deeper relationship, but he hadn't been interested. With Claire, he wanted more, but she'd expressed her disinterest in flawless terms.

Maybe he wasn't meant to find that freedom in love he'd spoken of to his mother. Maybe she knew best.

Before he returned to work, Mark needed more coffee. As he rose from his chair, one of the drawings slipped off the table and floated to the floor. He'd get it later, after refilling his cup in the kitchen.

On his return to the dining room, Cookie peered up at him, a small slip of paper hanging from her mouth and her tail tucked. The rest of the paper that had fallen to the floor surrounded the dog in a multitude of pieces he'd have to put together like a jigsaw puzzle.

"You either found my sketch palatable, or you're telling me you hate it."

From what Mark saw of the lines and shading on each, it was the design he'd most considered developing for Mr. Dover. He could hear his mother's voice saying Cookie gave him a sign that the idea was a mistake. Normally, he'd pay no attention to her notion about "signs."

This time, maybe she was right.

# Chapter Twelve

M ark stood beside Claire's desk and shuffled through the envelopes the postal clerk had handed him. He pulled out the thick one. The envelope bore a crown in the top left corner and a Chicago return address.

Pulse pounding in his ears, he slid a finger under the flap, too eager to reach for the letter opener that came with the desk. He withdrew three sheets of paper, the first with a short, typed message.

*Dear Sir,*

*I received with interest your communication regarding the Riverport property of Mr. Harris Lefler.*

*It is my pleasure to inform you that Mark Gregory Architecture has been selected to join nine other firms in submitting the first round of a design...*

His neighbors no doubt heard Mark's shout. The elation dwindled at the next words.

*...by 30 June 1897.*

June thirtieth? He consulted the calendar tacked to the wall. The deadline gave him less than a month to come up with the perfect concept and deliver it to...

He skimmed to the bottom of the letter.

*Queries and submissions are to be made to the consulting architect, Mr. Joseph Arbuckle at the above address.*

*Yours respectfully,*

*Joseph Arbuckle*

These competitions required hours of work that resulted in labor and supply costs with no guarantee of a commission. Still, he was one of ten architects chosen. How had that happened when he'd built no name for himself yet?

Perhaps he had. His position as a draftsman in Burnham's office had earned him a good, albeit limited, reputation.

Why question it? He had won the right to prove his talent to someone with power and connections. No matter the reason for his choice, his design would be in Mr. Arbuckle's hands well before June 30...without fail.

He read the requirements, line by line and word for word. A rendering of the elevations for all four sides was due in—he double-checked the calendar on the wall—twenty-five days with three finalists from the first round chosen by the second week of July. Those finalists received a substantial stipend to help with expenses—a reward that would relieve the stress over his loan payment.

Lefler would have his design by June 28 and no later. Mark would hand-deliver it to Arbuckle. Under no circumstances would he entrust such an important task to the postal service.

Claire had warned him about her husband's former partner, George...Something. He wasn't afraid of the competition, but it was one more ghost from her past to stand between them.

CLAIRE OPENED THE DOOR to Mark's office. Bringing the

sketchbook he'd given her was probably a mistake. If he asked to see drawings for the Dover house, she would have to tell him there were none.

More than once in the past week, she'd opened the book and picked up a pencil, placing the graphite against the paper. Each time she attempted to draw something, her fingers froze.

She sniffed the air and crinkled her nose.

Mark met her at the door. "Forgive the smell of cigar smoke. Addison and I celebrated yesterday."

Claire removed her hat and gloves and set them on the desk. "I thought you looked cheerful."

"For good reason." Mark brandished a letter through the air.

She eyed the paper and chuckled. "Let me guess. You've been named a standard bearer waving a paper flag for king and country."

"For your information, Mrs. Smart Aleck, this paper happens to be an invitation." His grin stretched from ear to ear.

"Come now, Mr. Gregory. Spit it out. An invitation from whom and for what?"

"How would you like to work for the man commissioned to design an office building for one Harris Lefler?"

"You got it? The invitation to compete?" How had she not guessed his news? She snatched the letter from Mark's hand. As she read, her heart galloped. He had done it! Mark Gregory Architecture had received the invitation.

She had prayed for this result—for both Richard and Mark. *Thank you, Lord!*

"Mark, this is wonderful news. Congratulations!"

He handed her the other papers. His smile had unfurled like a frost-covered leaf warmed by the sun. Now, it flattened. "I have work to do. This competition has more than one round. Did you notice the deadline for the first judging?"

Claire had rushed through the sheets included with the letter, the ones outlining the requirements. Her groan confirmed that she'd missed it. "I hope you already have ideas."

"I haven't been idle since sending my request for an invitation, but the real work starts now. Based on your meeting with George...George..."

"Brant. George Brant."

"Based on your meeting with him, I'm behind the other architects."

"Being located in Riverport is an advantage. You know the property and the conditions better than the other competitors."

Mark pulled out the desk chair for her. "Sit. Please."

Claire set the sketchbook on the desk and covered it with her hat. She'd dreaded telling Mark she still had no drawings to show him. However, with his excitement over the Lefler invitation, perhaps the subject would never come up today.

Mark propped a hip on the edge of the desk. "Tell me about George Brant."

Despite the June warmth inside the office, a sudden chill swirled around Claire. "I've told you. He's a competent architect."

"And someone I shouldn't underestimate. But that doesn't tell me what it was like to work with him. It doesn't tell me why you felt the need to leave Indianapolis rather than remain a part of your husband's company." When she didn't reply right away, he asked, "Is it that painful, Claire?"

His soft voice dissolved her reluctance. What would it hurt to tell him a little of her past? "A week after Richard's funeral, I went into the office. I hadn't removed my hat before George told me to go home."

Mark frowned. "A week isn't long to grieve. Maybe he thought you weren't ready to return to work."

She ducked her chin and shook her head. "His agreement with Richard stipulated the surviving partner buy out the heir of the deceased—whether the heir requested it or not. I no longer had a role in the business my husband founded."

It left her a grieving widow with a satisfactory bank account balance, no purpose, and no desire to live alone.

"I knew of the agreement and should have expected George's reaction. Once my husband died, there was no one to argue for my presence." Not for the first time, a question wiggled its way into her consciousness. Would Richard have permitted her to help him with his work much longer? She shook off the doubt. "With nothing left to keep me in Indianapolis, I moved home."

"I'd call Brant a shortsighted fool for not seeing your ability. You do have talent, Claire. *I've* seen it."

The sincerity in his voice fostered a yearning to become the pioneer Mr. Dover encouraged. But it was a moot point if she couldn't even draw a simple sketch of an interior detail.

"Why did you ask about George?"

"He's the only competitor I'm aware of, and it never hurts to learn something about the competition. I can see it's a painful topic for you, so let's forget it for now."

She would reveal anything she knew about George if it helped Mark to win the Lefler commission over the man who had so easily removed Richard Kingsley's name from his own business.

"Let's also postpone work on Mr. Dover's project for today."

She'd received a reprieve but wasn't sure whether to be happy or concerned. Even though Mr. Dover indicated he was in no hurry, they should show him a design soon. "Is there something I can do to help you?"

"Wish me the best." He grinned. "Not that failure is in my vocabulary. I'm capable of providing a winning design, so whatever happens from here is up to me."

No doubt he believed his boast, which alarmed her. "I admire your confidence, Mark, but don't fall into the trap of thinking you alone control your future success."

"If not me, who else?"

"God."

Mark's features tightened. "I learned long ago that God isn't interested in my business, Claire."

"God is interested in everything you do. Everything."

He shook his head. "A man wanting to make a name for himself in this world must work hard and strike fast. He can't depend on having ample years to accomplish his goals before his life ends."

Her husband hadn't had those ample years to make the kind of name for himself that Mark seemed to want, but personal renown wasn't something Richard had dwelled on.

"So far, my confidence has worked well for me, Claire, and I haven't the time to wait for God to decide how I should proceed." He held his hand out for the letter from Mr. Arbuckle. "The rest of the mail is on the desk. I'll be busy in the drafting room."

Too busy to talk about the reason for his animosity toward God?

If anyone had a right to question God's loving care, it would be her. Even in the moments of dark despair, her pain brought her closer to Him.

"All right. I won't disturb you."

CLAIRE THREW OFF THE sheet, climbed out of bed, and lit the lamp on the bedside table. Although the hands of the alarm clock read twelve-thirty, she hadn't slept for the past hour. She thumped the bell on top of the clock, creating a hollow, tinny sound in the quiet room. She rarely needed the alarm to wake her, but Richard had set it every night. It was a ritual she'd continued.

The sketchbook sat on the table next to the clock. Things couldn't go on this way, not if she hoped to continue working with Mark. Surprisingly, she wanted to do so, more than she'd imagined.

Mr. Dover deserved an impressive design, and she was certain her ideas fit his vision—if she could only get them onto paper.

*"God is interested in everything you do. Everything." That applies to you too, Claire.*

With Mark's news today, Claire realized she had wasted too much time on her fear. Her best opportunity to help him was to ensure he had something to present to Dover when requested.

After staring at the sketchbook for what seemed another hour, she snatched it up and carried it and a drawing pencil downstairs to the kitchen table. She could do this.

"God, not in my power but Yours."

Her hand shook, but she flipped open the cover to a pristine page.

And she sat there.

Every previous idea for the interior of the house had scattered, hiding behind all the other thoughts in her mind.

She whispered another soft prayer, then closed her eyes and breathed—in, out—until her fingers relaxed and a familiar image came to mind. Oak columns rose on the sides of a fireplace mantel like guards stationed at the entrance to a castle. Each piece was carved to resemble a miniature willow tree. Glazed aqua tiles representing water surrounded the fireplace opening and flowed onto the floor. The oak-carved rays of a rising sun hung over the top portion of the mantel.

With the image as clear as a painting, her pencil slid across the paper, first in an outline, then in intricate detail. The instant she finished, her heart raced with excitement and thankfulness. She had drawn a new design.

By the time the rising sun spied on Claire through the kitchen window like a Peeping Tom, she had several rough sketches. It was a start, and something to show Mark when she saw him again.

She placed a hand to her stomach. Was this flutter a result of satisfaction over her night's work, or the anticipation of seeing Mark again?

# Chapter Thirteen

Mark was conscious of Claire peering over his shoulder. If he'd ever doubted her level of comfort in working alone with him, it vanished once her heat warmed the back of his neck.

For the past half an hour, he'd gone out of his way to avoid looking her in the eye. How could she insist on indifference from him? How was he to ignore the sweet scent that set off thoughts of an evening's walk through a fragrant garden with her at his side?

While he preferred her perfume to cigar smoke—he didn't even like cigars—there was only so much nearness he could take. His only salvation was to throw himself into his work.

She walked to the triple windows and looked out. "Do you think Mr. and Mrs. Dover will like the interior ideas?"

He hadn't expected her until tomorrow, but she'd arrived after her shift at the store, her step bouncing with excitement over her ideas for the Dover house. Good ideas. She truly had a mind for creative detail.

"I can't see why not. That was good work, Claire." Better than he'd done yet, despite his boast about his abilities and control over his future.

She looked over her shoulder and grinned, then glanced at the octagonal wall clock he'd purchased second hand, its walnut case and fusée movement in excellent condition. Hurrying to the table, she shut the sketchbook and pushed in her chair. "I have to leave."

Mark stopped in the middle of adding an idea for a bas-relief over the entrance door of the Lefler design. "You have a social engagement?"

"Yes." She smiled. "It's with my Widow's Might friends."

He exhaled. She had mentioned the group of widows who gathered once a week. "I thought you met with them on Sundays."

"This is a special meeting."

He walked with her to the front office. "Something important happening?"

"Do you remember Louisa Gruhn?"

"She's the woman whose daughter you saved?"

Claire rolled her eyes. Mark enjoyed reminding her of her bravery, probably because he found her reluctance to take any credit endearing.

"Louisa's home is in dire straits and needing repairs she can't afford. The ladies and I are meeting at her house Saturday morning to do what we can."

"That's generous of you."

"Verbenia always stresses that faith without works is dead. Part of our circle's reason for existing is service, to put our faith into action."

The mention of faith reminded him again of their last conversation. Frankly, it was one he'd thought of often in the hours that followed. He believed every word he said, but he'd sounded vain. Vain and smug. What must she think of him?

"You recommended helping Mrs. Gruhn?"

"We all make recommendations when we see a need."

Both humble and admirable. "What kind of repairs?"

Claire pinned her hat on her head. "For one thing, we'll replace the porch floorboards. Many of them have rotted."

Carpentry. Did the women know the best way in which to go about such work? Did they have the proper tools? "I'm sure your decision to help stems from a desire to see Mrs. Gruhn and her daughter come to no additional harm, but replacing a porch is a big job. Are there gentlemen who help you with your projects?"

"Not normally." She laughed. "Our usual activities include things such as knitting scarves for the boys and girls at the orphanage or preparing meals for the elderly and sick."

He couldn't help but tease her. "Women's work?"

She scowled, but the humorous glint in her eyes lessened its impact.

"I didn't realize Riverport had an orphanage."

"Yes, it's south of town."

"It's hard enough to live without one parent. I can't imagine the burden on children who live without both parents."

She stopped in the middle of pulling on a glove. "Do you...do you look forward to having children?"

"Very much. I'd like enough children that they will keep one another company. I know what it is to be an only child."

The color left her face, and it occurred to Mark that, unlike his widowed mother, she had no children to raise alone, but the prospect of indiscretion kept him from asking why.

He nudged the conversation back to the work at Louisa Gruhn's. "You said men don't normally help you."

The color slowly returned to Claire's face, and she resumed pulling on her gloves. "The Third has agreed to work with us since it involves carpentry. He's a proficient woodworker."

"The Third?"

"My employer at the store. We refer to the youngest generation of Spencer Newlands as The Third to keep them straight. He's courting Phoebe Crain, one of our members."

"I see." Courtship gave the store owner the right to join the ladies. Mark had no such right.

He really hadn't the time to help, anyway. The Kowalskis would arrive tomorrow, and he didn't know how their visit would affect his ability to finish the Lefler design in time.

But rotted porch boards. What if Cissy broke through one and was hurt? If Mrs. Gruhn's house was as bad as Claire indicated, they could use his assistance.

When allowed, he would not stand by and see a shoddy job being done by those who hadn't the experience to do better. What if one of the ladies injured herself on a saw or other tool? What if it was Claire?

"Could you use another set of male hands?"

Her eyes grew large. During several quiet moments, he decided he'd overstepped his bounds. Finally, she asked, "You want to help us?"

"My father was a construction worker and taught me a number of skills of the trade. I swing an accurate hammer."

She clutched the handle of her purse in a tight fist. "I-I don't know."

"If the ladies would be uncomfortable, say so and I won't bring it up again." What he really meant was that if *she* would be uncomfortable, she should tell him.

A slow smile graced Claire's face, one that prompted a near swoon at the dimples that popped out with it. Not that men did such a thing as swoon. But if they did...

"No, I don't think they would mind, but are you sure you want to place yourself in a position of being among a gaggle of unwed women?"

The question gave him pause. She had a point. He knew nothing about her friends other than they were all widows. Would his offer place him in a position of fending off desperate-for-remarriage females, or were they more like Claire and uninterested in matrimony? He was already on guard against the arrival of Paulina and her mother. Then again, helping Mrs. Gruhn meant less time for the two mothers' matchmaking.

"It's for a good cause. However, I'll defer to you and whatever you think is best."

Her expression softened, as though she were pleased by the fact that he wasn't pushing his way into her affairs. "In that case, we would welcome the help." She wrote down the time and address.

He opened the outer office door for her. "I'll see you there on Saturday morning."

Mark watched her hurry down the hall. He was an idiot for torturing himself through unnecessary contact with her.

He was a bigger idiot for volunteering for a day's project when the clock was ticking on the Lefler competition.

MARK ENTERED THE HOUSE, immediately drawn to the noise coming from the parlor. He recognized his mother's laughter, but not that of the stranger she entertained—a man. In all her years as a widow, Mark had never known her to show an interest in another man.

Intrigued, he tossed his hat on the foyer table and approached the room.

When Mama saw him standing in the doorway, her laughter drifted off like an untethered balloon. Pinched lips and a look of concern replaced the good cheer he'd heard from her. "I did not expect you home so soon, Marek."

Just what had he interrupted?

He glanced at the smiling man on the sofa and back to his mother. "I thought I'd work from here the remainder of the afternoon. It seems I've arrived in time to meet our visitor. Mark Gregory, sir."

The man stood. His smile stretched thin lips to near invisibility. Appearing to be around Mark's mother's age, a streak of gray ran jagged, like a lightning strike, over the top of his head. "Good afternoon. I'm Alec Olesky."

Polish? What else should he have expected? His accent was as American as Mark's.

Olesky's dark stare never wavered from Mark's face. A challenge existed in that look. If this was a social call, wariness of a son's response could be the source. Olesky couldn't know that Mark would never block his mother's happiness, unless he found the suitor unworthy of her.

Mark gestured for the man to take his seat again. "How long have you and my mother known one another, Mr. Olesky?"

The man glanced at Mama. "Well, we—"

"Not long, Marek." She sighed. "He is our new boarder."

New boarder? As in someone living in their house?

A series of emotions washed through Mark. Confusion led the way with disbelief following on its heels.

Anger shot past them both. She had done it. She had defied him and made good on her threat. His jaw worked back and forth as he formed a retort that never slipped past his lips. Instead, he gestured toward the foyer. "Mama, I'd like to speak with you in private."

She stood and squared her shoulders. "Excuse us, Mr. Olesky. We will return shortly." She led the way out of the parlor, through the dining room, and into the kitchen.

Mark paced in front of the stove. "He needs to go."

"You are overreacting."

"Are you determined to get all of us thrown out of this house? I told you we cannot sublet a room in a house we are renting."

Her chin rose. "There is no such provision in the lease, and I spoke with the landlord. He approved of it."

She'd already spoken with him? Their landlord had been an accommodating old codger in other ways, but in this one, he'd been Mark's best hope. Now what? "Do you even know anything about Mr. Olesky?"

Her face lit. "He is a widower with grown children who have moved away. He misses them terribly and does not like living alone."

Fear bolted through him. It was one thing to imagine Olesky as a possible suitor. It was something far different to imagine him as a live-in suitor—a *lonely*, live-in suitor with an opportunity to take advantage of his mother. "You let him move in here with you home alone all day? What were you thinking?"

"It is not as you suspect, *mój słodki chłopcze*. He is a working man and will not be here during the day."

"And what about non-working hours when I'm not here?"

"If you are so worried, perhaps you should adjust your schedule to be home more often."

"Olesky needs to go."

"I have already promised him the empty bedroom upstairs. I cannot ask him to leave when he has arranged to move his things in." She patted his arm. "Take a little time to get to know him. I think you will like one another. Having him here will give me purpose, Marek."

"What about the Kowalskis? Where will we put our guests with the third bedroom occupied?"

"I have already discussed it with Mr. Olesky."

Of course, she had.

"He will not move in until they leave."

The man poked his head into the room. "I'm sorry to interrupt, but I hope my presence isn't a source of trouble."

Mama eyed Mark, her expression pleading.

Wasn't a sense of purpose what he wanted for her? Would allowing Mr. Olesky to stay help her to adjust more quickly to living in Riverport?

Mark could imagine Addison's glee when he announced that they now had a boarder...until he could think of a way to get rid of the man.

MARK HAD DECIDED TO take Cookie for a walk—a long walk, while he pondered the best way to be a good host to the Kowalskis without giving his mother or either of their visitors any hope when it came to marriage. He'd use the deadline for the Lefler building as a shield to hide behind—a time-intensive project. After all, it was real, the truth, and he'd already warned his mother.

As they strolled up his street, Cookie's bark drew his attention to the porch. Paulina waved to him from the rail with the enthusiasm of a passenger greeting welcoming friends from the deck of a ship. He braced himself for what was to come and waved back.

Mark suppressed the sigh that longed to escape, climbed the steps, and positioned the dog between himself and his guest. He would kiss Paulina's cheek, but there was no sense in giving her the wrong idea. "I hope you had a pleasant train ride. When did you arrive?"

"About thirty minutes ago." His childhood friend crouched and rubbed Cookie's head. "She's a sweet thing."

"She has us at her beck and call." He bent and rubbed the wiry hairs on Cookie's back. "Mama feeds her too much."

"She's eating for a litter." Paulina's voice crackled with humor.

"An imminent one. In the almost three weeks we've had Cookie, she's grown quite large. Mama gave her an old blanket, and she's spent the last few days creating and recreating a nest with it." With puppies, the Kowalskis, and then Mr. Olesky, his house would soon be overrun.

"I hope they're born while I'm here."

How long did she and her mother plan to stay? He gestured for her sit in one of the wicker chairs on the porch. He'd find out sooner or later without sounding inhospitable.

"From what I've seen so far, Mark, I like the town you've chosen for your home."

"So do I."

She tilted her head. "How is your business progressing?"

"It's beginning to bear fruit." Was her curiosity due to hope for her future? "In fact, I have deadlines for a couple of projects. I'm afraid they'll take me away from my host duties more often than you might appreciate."

"I understand."

"Also, I promised a friend I would help her with repairs to a house tomorrow morning. I hope you don't mind."

Humor and curiosity danced through the vibrant blue of her eyes—darker than Claire's, but as striking. "This friend is a woman."

"She works for me."

"An older woman?"

It was a shame his heart didn't beat for Paulina. She had grown into a lovely woman—inside and out. Instead, each day, his heart pounded harder for Claire. "We're close to the same age."

Her sudden laughter jolted him. "Smooth those worry lines, my friend. I didn't come here to drag you before a priest."

Once his brain registered her words, the heaviness in his chest lightened. She was different than he remembered. "Can you blame me?"

"Unfortunately, no. I used to follow along wherever Mama led." Her countenance brightened. "That was before I met someone during my classes at the Society."

"Society?"

"The Chicago Evangelization Society."

"You're a follower of Mr. Moody?" Dwight Moody was well known for the institute he'd established in Chicago and for spreading the teachings of the Gospel. "He isn't Catholic."

"I'm a follower of Jesus Christ, not Mr. Moody or Pope Leo."

How had he not realized she was a woman of faith, like Claire? It was a faith he shared...within reason.

*"God isn't interested in my business."*

*"God is interested in everything you do. Everything."*

*"So far, my confidence has worked well for me, and I haven't the time to wait for God to decide how I should proceed."*

It had worked well, much better than his prayers, even if he regretted the conversation with Claire. Not only had he sounded like a man full of conceit, but at the time, he'd failed to recall that her husband died young and, most likely, before accomplishing all he'd hoped to do.

*"Don't fall into the trap of thinking you alone control your future success."*

Behind her words, Mark had sensed Claire spoke from experience. There was so much about her he didn't know and she hadn't shared. Yet.

"Who is this man?"

"His name is Frederick."

"I'm happy for you."

"Don't be too happy. My parents don't know yet, and I can't guarantee our mothers would find either of our attitudes acceptable."

"Ah, yes. The mothers. Where are they?"

"In the kitchen with their heads together. They wouldn't let me in."

"That doesn't bode well for us."

He started to get up from his chair, and she grasped his sleeve. "I came with Mama to seek your help."

"What kind of help?"

"I want you to convince our mothers that we have no future together."

He laughed. "While I'm at it, would you like me to wrap the moon for you as a wedding gift?"

She slapped his arm, but a smile curved her lips. "I'm serious. The only way Mama will accept Frederick is to know there is no chance of a marriage between me and the son of her old friend. When you mentioned your employee, I had hoped... Is she married?"

"Mrs. Kingsley is a widow." Not that it did him much good. "Do you anticipate matchmaking while you're here?"

"Do you need it?"

In all honesty, he'd welcome the help. However, he'd never admit it. "You assumed she'd be an answer to your problem."

She patted the arm she'd slapped earlier. "Our problem."

Mark didn't even attempt to suppress a sigh this time. He rose and opened the door. "Let's tell our mothers the good news, before mine contacts the priest and yours unpacks a trousseau."

The weight of worry over his relationship with Paulina had turned into nothing but a feather pillow. If only he could say the same about his relationship with Claire.

*Frankly, God, if You're so interested in my future, let's start with Claire. She's no closer to seeing me as anything other than an employer, possibly a friend.*

He waited to hear or sense a response. Nothing. Just as he'd received no response when he'd prayed for his father's recovery all those years ago.

As with everything, succeeding in winning Claire's affection would be up to him.

# Chapter Fourteen

As Claire pulled on her father's work gloves, her attention slid to the street and westward. No sign of Mark.

It was almost eight-fifteen. People stirred and, somewhere in the distance, an unpunctual rooster crowed—as late this morning as a certain architect.

Spence—as he had insisted that everyone call him—had arrived early and repaired the sagging windowsill on one of the front windows.

Before they began work, he demonstrated the proper way to hit a nail head without bruising a thumb. Verbenia and Mavis remained inside the house to care for Cissy and prepare the noon meal.

A few minutes later, Claire, Louisa, and Edythe began to pry up the old porch boards, preparing to replace them with new, solid wood—the most important of their tasks today.

Still no Mark.

After a while, Claire's fingers ached from wielding the crowbar. She could imagine the torment Edythe must be experiencing. The woman lived with a housekeeper and cook to accomplish the everyday domestic chores and was unaccustomed to strenuous activity.

On second thought, Edythe's fingers *were* accustomed to it. She embroidered everything in sight, from handkerchiefs to tablecloths to pillowcases. Plus, from what Claire had heard, those children of hers kept her running. But did Edythe's ears handle the screech of old nails wrenched from wood any better than Claire's?

Perhaps it didn't matter. When Edythe slid the clawed end of the iron piece under a board and yanked it up, her face glowed with more than a sign of exertion. It shone with a sense of accomplishment.

Verbenia walked around a corner of the house with a basket of apple muffins and handed them out. When she got to Claire, she asked, "Was Mr. Gregory unable to be here?"

Claire's jaw clenched at the quiet question, unsure why his absence disappointed her so. He had promised. If he couldn't make it, the least he could have done was to send word of his regrets. "I'm sure he'll be here shortly."

Louisa groaned with the effort of loosening her board, and Spence's handsaw rasped against new wood. Phoebe and Ruby ran their planes across the already-sawn pieces, smoothing the surface of the wood to be used for the porch floor. Everyone had arrived on time and worked hard.

Everyone but Mark.

Verbenia offered Claire a muffin. "No, thank you."

"How do you like working with him?"

"Fine."

Truthfully, she and Mark had spent little time on the Dover house. She had found a number of discarded drawings for the Lefler building wadded and thrown on the floor. Some were slashed through with a large X. No one would call Mark Gregory a tidy worker.

"Has this experience stirred a renewed interest in practicing the trade in the future?"

No matter how hard she'd fought the draw toward resuming her architectural work, it remained. With it remained the misgivings. "Some dreams aren't healthy, Verbenia."

"In what way?"

Claire pointed to the basket in Verbenia's hand. "They're like eating an overabundance of muffins. They're delicious until they give you a stomachache that causes you to retch on someone else. Then that person pays the price for your gluttony."

Verbenia's probing gaze left her uncomfortable. "Who paid the price of your gluttony, Claire?"

The woman's soft voice might have soothed had Claire not regretted saying too much and in a vulgar manner. She blamed her loose tongue on her irritation with Mark.

Verbenia turned toward the house, then back again. "You're right to proceed with caution. Paul himself said, 'All things are lawful for me, but I will not be brought under the power of any.' Even if you once filled up on something pleasurable to the point of overindulging, it doesn't suggest that God won't allow you an occasional muffin if He wants you to have it." With that pronouncement, Verbenia walked away.

Could she indulge in the occasional project without harming someone else? Without letting others' rejection cause bitterness?

The next board wouldn't budge. Claire shoved the crowbar farther under the plank and put all her weight into prying it up. The board snapped, sending Claire backwards to land on her posterior with a grunt. She winced at the throbbing ache the fall spawned.

Before she could order her legs to stand, a male hand reached down. "Thank you, Spence." She gripped his hand and rose to her feet.

"You're welcome, Mrs. Kingsley."

The cheerful voice left Claire lightheaded. She controlled the smile on her face and looked up. Mark stood at her side wearing a pair of workingman's denim trousers held up by suspenders and a blue-and-white-striped shirt with a bare collar, the sleeves rolled to his elbows. A grin completed the image of a solemn businessman replaced by a day laborer—a heart-stalling sight.

The others stopped their work to see to her soundness. She reassured everyone she was fine, though inside, she bemoaned the fact that anyone, especially Mark, had witnessed her clumsiness.

Louisa dusted off her gloves. "Thank you for coming, Mr. Gregory."

"I'm sorry I'm late, Mrs. Gruhn. We have visitors from Chicago. Mrs. Kowalski, my mother's friend, insisted her daughter walk to the butcher's shop for some sausage this morning. I was tasked with escorting her since she was unfamiliar with the town."

"You have visitors? Why didn't you tell me?" If Claire had known, she'd never have agreed to his coming. It wasn't fair to expect him to leave his guests.

"They understood my previous commitment."

With the frown between his eyes, Claire doubted his assurance.

How old was the daughter, anyway? She scowled. What business was it of hers?

Everyone introduced themselves to Mark—introductions Claire should have provided—and returned to work.

Mark turned to her. "Where would you like me to start?"

"As you can see, we've taken out half the boards. The new ones are stacked in the yard. If you'd like, you can begin nailing them to the frame."

Rather than go for one of the prepared boards, a hammer, and the can of nails, as Claire had expected, Mark walked to the edge, where they had removed the old planks. He jumped down into the empty space and ran his hands over the wood of the frame, studying it from every angle. He crouched and peered under the section the women hadn't finished removing.

Claire shivered with the remembrance of the spiders that had scurried along their disturbed webs as the women removed the floorboards.

Mark knocked on the wood under their feet. Shortly after, he climbed out and sauntered over to Spence, carrying on a conversation Claire couldn't hear from the porch. Spence bobbed his head and handed Mark the folding ruler he'd used to measure each board before cutting it.

Edythe asked, "What are they doing?"

"My guess is that Mark found rot in a few of the joists and needs to measure them before Spence can cut new ones. We can't install the top planks until that's done." Claire stretched, her back aching with the morning's exercise. "We should continue prying up these boards. He won't know for sure how many replacements he needs until he sees what's under our feet."

The women worked to the sound of sawing, screeching, and nails pounded into wood. In time, all the old boards were removed and most of the frame rebuilt to meet Mark's approval.

Verbenia, who had tended to Cissy while Mavis cooked the noon meal, opened one of the front windows and called out, "The stew is hot. Come around back."

The others left, but Mark continued to work. She tapped his shoulder. "We're stopping to eat."

He sat back on his haunches in the hole and wiped his brow on his shirtsleeve. He'd been replacing and adding additional boards in the frame at a feverish pace, saying the person who originally built the porch had used one-by-ten boards instead of two-by-tens, and it was a wonder the porch hadn't collapsed ages ago. "While you ladies eat, I'll finish up here. It's the least I can do to atone for my tardiness."

"Then I'll help you."

"Claire—"

"I'll eat later." She picked up the crowbar but paused at the sight of a woman trotting down the street toward them. "Someone is in a hurry."

Mark glanced in the direction of Claire's gaze. "That's Paulina, one of my visitors." He leapt from the hole onto what remained of the floorboards and leaned over the porch rail. He called out, "Is something wrong?"

Miss Kowalski drew up in front of him. She rested one hand on the porch railing and the other on her ample, heaving chest. "I think Cookie is ready to have her puppies. She didn't eat this morning. She's restless and keeps digging at the newspapers your mother put down."

The woman was about Claire's age, maybe a year or two older. She was beautiful with black hair, cobalt-blue eyes, a strong chin, and a corset trimmed waistline that Claire could only dream of possessing...if she didn't mind passing out for lack of oxygen.

Forced to escort her this morning, Mark probably cried all the way to the butcher shop.

"Isn't my mother home?"

"Yes, but she and Mama are a bit...flustered."

Claire stepped alongside Mark, "It does sound like Cookie is preparing to give birth."

"You have experience with such a thing?"

"I've seen several deliveries by dogs and helped my uncle on occasion." Strange how she could think of the birth of puppies with no ill effects, but when it came to children...

Mark rubbed the creases along his forehead.

"Don't worry," Claire said. "Cookie knows what to do."

"She might know how give birth, but I doubt she knows how to fend off 'flustered' women." He glanced between Claire and Miss Kowalski, appearing torn between staying and going.

She pulled off the work gloves and took the decision from him. "Go ahead. I'll come too."

The rigidity in his shoulders eased. He leapt over the railing, then grasped her waist and lifted her, setting her feet on the ground. "Let's go."

After informing the others why they were leaving, both Claire and Miss Kowalski trotted to keep up with Mark's long strides. Noting the woman's flushed face and labored breaths, Claire said to Mark, "Go without us. We'll be there shortly."

He slowed to let them catch up. "I didn't think. I'm sorry, ladies."

His houseguest stopped and inhaled a lungful of air. Despite her breathlessness, her voice was like melted chocolate, smooth and sweet. "No. Go. I'll be fine."

He glanced in the direction of his house and back at them. "Are you sure?"

Both women shouted, "Yes!"

Once he'd put distance between them, Claire said, "I've never seen a man quite so nervous over the birth of puppies."

"So nervous he forgot to introduce us. I'm Paulina." The woman pronounced her name as if it were spelled Pow-lena. "I assume you're Mrs. Kingsley."

"Please call me Claire."

"Mark is a good man, don't you think so?"

Claire had witnessed Mark's goodness multiple times. Rescuing the dog from her tormentors. Helping with the repairs at Louisa's house. Caring for his mother. Saving Claire from injury. "He is a good man."

At Paulina's speculative gleam, Claire attempted to explain. "From what I know of him, though I don't know him well. We met a little more than month ago." She shut her mouth to stop the awkward rambling.

With their energy revived, they continued walking.

As Mark's house came into view, Claire's steps faltered, her path to the door blocked by an invisible wall of her own construction. Why had she volunteered to come here? Would his mother even let Claire inside, much less near Cookie? There was no telling what the woman would say—first in accented English, then in Polish to drive home her point.

"What's wrong?"

"I'm rethinking my visit. Mark's mother..." How much should she say in front of a friend of the family?

Paulina slipped her arm through Claire's. "Come on. We'll focus on Cookie's welfare, then we'll work to help you win over Mark's mother."

"I don't need to win her over, Paulina. I only need to be able to stand in the same room with her without a white flag waving between us."

"No. It's for everyone's good that you win her over—yours, Mark's, and mine."

Why Paulina's?

"Please, Claire."

Mark hadn't shown a romantic interest in Claire since he'd walked her home one day—since she told him she would never marry.

Now Paulina was in town, and Mark had the admiration of the beautiful woman next to her. Surely, that meant she had no need to worry over Mrs. Grzegorczyk's opinion of her. Surely, she needn't worry about Mark's pursuit of her. In fact, wouldn't it be best for him if she encouraged his interest in Paulina?

The two women entered the house, and Paulina led her into the kitchen. Mark stood with his back propped against the counter. The steaming cup of coffee in his hand mirrored the pinched expression that said his temper ran as hot as the liquid. "They won't let me near the 'event' as they're calling it."

"Birth is not for a man to witness." Mrs. Grzegorczyk's voice came from the other side of the partially closed door to a mud room.

"Then how do you explain the presence of a male doctor when it's time for a woman to deliver her child?"

"Do not be impertinent, Marek." His mother slipped around the door and into the kitchen. The twisting of her hands drew an odd desire from Claire to caress her shoulder in comfort. A split second later, the woman got a glimpse of Claire and the concern reverted to the stiffness she was growing accustomed to seeing from Mark's mother. "Mrs. Kingsley."

Since Mrs. Grzegorczyk showed no surprise at her presence, Claire suspected Mark had told his mother she was coming. Still, she expected Mark's mother to insist she leave. "Good afternoon. How is Cookie?"

"She is fine."

"Mama..." With Mark's set jaw, the growled word sounded less like encouragement to be hospitable and more like a threat.

His mother huffed. "See for yourself."

Mark gave Claire an encouraging nod, so she entered the mudroom. Pressed in a corner, between a broom and a washtub for laundry, stood an older woman, presumably Mrs. Kowalski. She wore an expression no more friendly than Mark's mother's. Claire flashed a half-hearted smile and turned her attention to Cookie. Each time the dog moved, she crinkled the newspapers spread across the floor.

Kneeling, Claire ran the flat of her hand along the dog's abdomen and felt the strong contractions of the muscles, strong enough to prove birth loomed soon.

With five people in the room or crowded around the doorway, Cookie became even more restless. Claire got up. "She's nervous with everyone standing around."

Mrs. Grzegorczyk said, "I will stay."

"I will keep her company." Mrs. Kowalski remained in her corner.

Mark started to protest, but Claire stopped him with a touch to his shirtsleeve and a low voice. "As long as they let her do what's natural, it shouldn't hurt anything."

"All right." He escorted Claire and Paulina into the dining room and saw them seated. "I'll bring you ladies coffee."

Claire thought of telling him that she could get it, but the repeated glances over his shoulder toward the kitchen told her he wanted another look to reassure himself of Cookie's welfare—or reassure his mother and Mrs. Kowalski.

He was a good man.

"Don't take Mrs. G's animosity personally. She's a nice woman when she's content to leave Mark's life to him." The comment drew Claire's attention across the table to Paulina, who shook her head. "Don't misunderstand. Unless he has no strong feelings one way or another about something, Mark runs his own life."

No question about it, but... "He cares about his mother's happiness, and she doesn't like me. I don't want to make things difficult for him."

"Any difficulty is the sole responsibility of Anastazja Grzegorczyk. Will you bow to her hostility and deny Mark his right to choose his own friends?"

Could she and Mark be friends without anything deeper coming between them? He wanted children—more than one. He'd made it clear when talking the other day about the orphanage.

Yes, if his interest shifted from her to the woman across the table, they could be friends.

# Chapter Fifteen

Paulina's comment about his mother stopped Mark near the door between the kitchen and dining room, a tray in his hands.

"I'll admit that Mark's mother and I have something in common. It's been difficult to put the past behind me and accept something new." Claire's words were like an electric light flashing on and off, calling attention to themselves and her plight.

Mark had recognized her difficulty in moving forward from her marriage. He understood and accepted her wish to remember what she'd had with Richard Kingsley and expected it of a loving spouse.

That didn't alleviate the nagging feeling he'd never measure up to the memory of her late husband. Every time she said the man's name in a tone of near awe, he couldn't imagine her speaking of anyone else in the same way.

"Since we were children, our mothers have schemed to bring Mark and me together in marriage." Paulina held up both hands and pressed her index fingers side-by-side. As if they were one. Married. For life.

He should make his presence known, but if the women chose to look his way, they would see him. He stood in plain view. Almost.

Claire frowned. "You're saying you came here to—"

"To enlist Mark's help in convincing them that it will not happen."

"Then you two aren't..." Claire pressed two fingers together.

"No. We aren't."

"But you said yourself that he's a good man."

Before he moved a step, Paulina shrugged. "Mark let it be known years ago he didn't want me."

He winced, hoping he hadn't put it in such blunt terms. Listening in had gone too far and become embarrassing. Sooner or later, he was bound to hear something unpleasant. Besides, he was tired of holding the tray and the steam from the coffee was dissipating. If he didn't get the coffee to them soon, he'd deliver it cold.

"To be honest, Mrs. Grzegorczyk's invitation to visit was an answer to my prayers. I came to Riverport because I have met someone, and we want to marry."

Claire's frown grew deeper, before she forced it into a smile and enclosed Paulina's hands with hers. "I wish you much happiness. Does your mother know?"

"Mark and I had a long talk with both our mothers last night. Based on their attitudes toward you this morning, I'm afraid it did little good."

Claire arched a brow. "That brings us back to Mrs. Grzegorczyk and her attitude toward me, doesn't it? She wants you to marry Mark and—"

Mark cleared his throat. Time to silence this discussion. He walked into the room and set the tray down. A firm look bounced between the women. An unspoken agreement to pretend they hadn't discussed him?

After handing each lady a cup of coffee, Mark took his normal place at the head of the table and tried to wipe any sign from his features, any guilt over having been privy to their discussion. He suspected he was no more capable of pretense than the women.

MARK'S STIFF POSTURE and the way he paid special attention

to the flowered design on his coffee cup told Claire he'd probably overheard their discussion. But how much of it?

After seeing Paulina's beauty and appraising her sweet spirit, Claire had contemplated the prospect of doing a little matchmaking on Paulina's behalf. The old friends would make a nice-looking couple, and it would assure Mark's interest in someone other than her. But she hadn't considered the possibility that Paulina loved someone else.

Claire stirred cream into her coffee and felt the side of her cup. Barely warm. Mark must have eavesdropped on most of their talk. "How is Cookie?"

He set his cup on the saucer, and his features tightened. "I don't know. They shut the door on me...again."

"They should let Cookie get on with her business and stay out of it." A somewhat bitter laugh rang out from Paulina. "What am I saying? They don't know how to stay out of anyone's business, not even that of a dog's."

"What do you ladies think Cookie's offspring will look like?"

Mark's rushed question added more fuel to Claire's belief in his eavesdropping, but addressing it would discomfit them all. "With no idea of the father's breed, it's hard to guess."

Paulina clasped her hands. "I only know the puppies will be precious, and I can't wait to hold one."

Weren't all babies precious? Claire brushed away the thought. For some reason, she'd become too preoccupied with children lately.

With a break in the conversation, she listened for noise from the mudroom. "How long has it been since we left the kitchen?"

Mark pulled out his watch. "At least twenty minutes. Why?"

"When I checked Cookie earlier, the contractions were strong. I'd expected your mother to announce a birth by now."

"Is that a bad thing?"

"Not necessarily, but I'm concerned about the time it's taking.

Too long could be a sign of trouble. Will you check again?"

Mark put his watch back in his pocket and pushed out of his chair. "Come with me and ease your mind."

The three of them entered the kitchen. Paulina remained inside the doorway while Claire waited in the middle of the room.

Mark opened the mudroom door and asked, "Any progress?"

His mother jerked around. "Nothing. She gets up. She lies down. Gets up. Lies down. The whole time, she whines."

When added to the delay in birth, the dog's whining and fidgeting wasn't a good sign.

Claire moved closer. "Would you mind if I looked?"

His mother shrugged. "You will do better at watching over her than Nadia and me?"

Claire glanced at Mark. His jaw hardened into steel. "For Cookie's sake, let her see, Mama."

Remembering Paulina's comment about winning over the woman, Claire said, "No one will do better than the person who loves her most, Mrs. Grzegorczyk, but if I can help, I'm happy to do so. My uncle raised hounds and I've helped him with his puppies many times. Sometimes, there were difficulties. I'm concerned that the first birth is taking so long."

His mother's eyes widened slightly. She backed away and made room for Claire to examine the dog.

Claire felt the dog's middle all the way to her hips. "Will someone get me a basin of water and soap, please?" Mark brought her the items she'd asked for, including a towel. She washed her hands, then rolled up her sleeve. "This might look rather shocking to you." A quick examination revealed the problem.

Behind her, one of the women whispered, "Did you see where she put her fingers?"

Crouched at the dog's head, Mark scowled, quelling further exclamations of disgust.

Claire washed her hands a second time, knowing it wouldn't be the last. Her pulse pounded like a toy drum in her ears. "There is a puppy, but I believe it's stuck."

Mark rubbed Cookie's head. The dog pushed into him as though she needed reassurance that everything would be well. "What happens if it remains that way?"

Not wishing to cause the others more anxiety, she kept her voice optimistic. "The puppy needs a little help is all."

Mark paused. His penetrating stare told her she hadn't fooled him into thinking there was no danger. "Paulina, why don't you take Mama and Mrs. Kowalski to the parlor."

"Cookie is a part of our family, Marek. Why does Mrs. Kingsley stay? What if my poor *kochanie*...?"

"Your *sweetheart* will be fine, Mama."

Claire's heart went out to Mark's mother, but this time, she was more concerned about the welfare of Cookie and her pups than winning over the woman. She stepped out of the mudroom. "Don't worry, Mrs. Grzegorczyk. I'm leaving."

"Claire."

With a plan of her own, she raised a hand to stop Mark's protest. "You can encourage the birth as well as I can, ma'am."

Mark's mother's eyes bulged. "Me?"

"Yes. I'd only be in the way."

"I-I've never..."

"It isn't hard. You do as I did a moment ago. You place your—"

Mrs. Kowalski gasped, and Mrs. Grzegorczyk's face lost all its color.

"Fine, you may help Cookie, and Paulina will help you."

"Me?" Paulina shook her head with exaggerated violence. "No, ma'am. I know nothing about... Well, I know nothing about it and plan to keep my ignorance." She bolted from the room, leaving no time for either mother to protest.

Mark stood with his feet apart and arms crossed. "I'll stay here."

Cookie whined, and his mother sighed—long and loud, then stomped away with her friend. Evidently, he did assert himself when his wishes opposed those of his mother.

Once they were gone, Mark relaxed and grinned. "A clever maneuver, Mrs. Kingsley."

"I should feel guilty, shouldn't I?" She didn't. In fact, it felt good to stand up for herself against his mother. "If I thought she would be willing to do what was necessary, I wouldn't have interfered or been vulgar about it."

"She'll get over it. I appreciate your help with Cookie."

The soft expression in his steady gaze warmed Claire from head to toe.

When Mark crouched beside Cookie once more, the dog whined and fidgeted again. He caressed her head with calming strokes. "What do you need from me?"

Time wasn't on the puppy's side, and they had already used too much. "Clean rags."

"They're upstairs."

When Mark left the mud room, she said to Cookie, "Let's get your baby moving."

A few minutes later, Mark returned to the mud room with a pile of rags. "It took me longer to find them than I'd expected."

Claire glanced up at him, her brows drawn with the concern that encumbered her. "It's close, but still hasn't emerged, and Cookie is tired."

"You can do this, Claire."

She threw up her hands. "I have an idea, but what if it doesn't work?" What if she caused more harm than good?

He crouched beside her and laid a hand on her shoulder. "Do what you can. Do what you know."

The warmth of his palm and communication of trust in his gaze gave her the confidence to try. She tugged with firm but gentle movements, waiting in between for the pup to be born naturally. "I've never tried this, but I saw my uncle do it."

The dog whined.

"I'm being careful, Cookie." Another tiny tug downward and the baby dropped to the newspaper where its mother took over, licking and pushing the inert pup around with her nose.

Claire breathed easier until she observed the puppy. "Something is wrong."

"What is it?"

All she could see were two tiny, human bodies...still and lifeless. She shut her eyes, but it did no good. Her stomach twisted and curled into waves of nausea.

"Claire?"

Mark's voice vanquished the most horrific of images. A sob broke loose from her, and she picked up the tiny, gray pup. Her trembling lips imprisoned the answer to his question.

"Claire, what's wrong?"

*Lord, I can't do this. I can't be the reason for another death.*

Under Mark's stare, she forced out the words. "It isn't breathing."

MARK'S STOMACH LURCHED at seeing both the motionless puppy and Claire's distress.

"I must have done something wrong."

"No, Claire. Surely you realize that, if not for you, Cookie might have died." Feeling helpless, he observed the small body in her hands. "What now?"

"I don't... Wait." She reached out for a rag. "Hurry. Let me have one." She swaddled the pup in the rag and swiped the cloth over its mouth and snout, as if it were a child with a dripping nose. With gentle but brisk strokes, she rubbed its body. "My uncle showed me how this can encourage a puppy's breathing."

When her hands halted, he asked, "Did it work?"

Claire's eyes filled with an ocean of blue waves. She shook her head and tears splashed onto her cheeks. "I don't know what else to do."

He lifted her chin, whipped a handkerchief from his pocket, and wiped away the dampness on her face. "You and the puppy have come this far, Claire. Keep at it."

While she continued to rub, she closed her eyes once more. "Father, you made this sweet little being and care for him as you do for all your creation." Her words were as soft as her touch. "We ask that you provide him strength and the breath of life."

Mark watched for the slightest sign of that life, expecting nothing to come from Claire's prayer and feeling no satisfaction when the poor thing continued to lay limp and lifeless in her palm. He dreaded seeing her disappointment when—

"He moved his head!" Mark laughed. "He's alive."

It was the barest of movements, but another followed. In no time, the puppy squirmed.

Cradling the dog in the crook of her arm like a swaddled baby, Claire jumped up and squealed. "He is alive."

"Your rubbing worked. It urged him to breathe."

"It wasn't me. I'm not the one who gives a body life."

She referred to God? Could it be? But why would He pay any heed to whether a tiny animal lived or died? Regardless of a spark of a past hope that flickered inside him, Mark wasn't ready to acknowledge God's role in saving the puppy. What was a dog's life in comparison to a man's?

"Thank you, anyway." Carried away with appreciation, he leaned forward and kissed Claire's cheek. A friendly kiss. Chaste. Given in gratitude.

*Wholly unsatisfactory.*

Like a youth after sipping his first taste of sherry, he craved to drink in something more potent. Something sweet and warm. Something that implied a future and family. Something only Claire could provide.

From her soft expression and parted lips, he wasn't the only one feeling that craving.

He stepped closer and reached out, prepared to encircle her waist and —

"Marek! What is happening in there?"

Claire backed away from him, still clutching the puppy.

*Nothing is happening. Nor would it now.*

"I'll be out in a minute." Mark's struggle to control his longing, to taste those sweet lips, surfaced with the sharpness of his voice. It was as though his mother had known what she would interrupt.

Still holding the puppy, Claire wrapped it in one of the clean rags and carefully passed it to him. "I-I need to check Cookie. Take him to show her, but don't stay long. He needs his mother."

The pup's eyes were sealed shut and mouth open to release squeaks and cries. Cookie's intense stare said she would hold him responsible should anything happen to her new baby.

Claire sat on the floor near the door leading outside. She passed a hand over the dog's belly. "You're such a good mother."

Evidently, they were to ignore whatever transpired between them. He could do that. But he wouldn't. Not when the flush that tinted her face and the quick rise and fall of her shoulders confirmed that their moment of closeness had affected her every bit as much as it had him.

"Claire."

Her chin inched up. He expected her to look anywhere but at him. Instead, her gaze met his with boldness and confidence, rather than the anticipated alarm and regret.

It encouraged him to finish what he had planned to say. "I want you to know my arms are open. Whenever you're ready to walk into them for all time, they'll be open." It was a bold statement, but he meant each word.

She hesitated, then her head bobbed once—a minor movement, a reassuring movement, no more perceptible than he'd initially noticed from the pup. Even so, it gave him hope that one day soon she would remove the ring that bound her to the past.

That one day soon this woman would be his.

# Chapter Sixteen

On Sunday, Claire arrived at Verbenia's house at the same time as Phoebe. They paused on the walkway before approaching the door.

Claire smiled at her friend. "I haven't seen you in the store lately."

"I've taken on a number of new piano students and been invited to perform a concert at the theater on Independence Day."

"A concert? How wonderful!"

Phoebe would return to the stage where she belonged, once more realizing her potential. Claire was happy for her friend. But she also wanted to ask why. Why was the exercise of Phoebe's gift acceptable to society and Claire's discouraged?

"It's a tremendous opportunity and a lot of preparation in a short time. Fortunately, Spence has allowed me to use his grand piano to practice." Phoebe laughed. "If he had his way, he'd move it to my house. Can you imagine a piano of that size in my small sitting room? I wouldn't be able to use the room for anything else."

"There's not much sense in moving it when you'll soon be moving your things into his house." When Phoebe's face grew pink, Claire added, "Don't be coy. It won't be long before he proposes."

Phoebe's head dipped. "Wishful thinking on your part."

Claire laughed. "Not nearly as wishful as you claim, and we both know it."

Phoebe's grin gave her away.

"I'll plan to attend your concert."

"And I'll spend more time practicing. I wouldn't want to disappoint you."

"I've heard you play, remember? Your talent brought many customers into the store during the Christmas season. You are incapable of disappointing anyone in the audience."

From what Claire had heard, there was a time when Phoebe filled concert halls all over the Midwest. She was billed as "The Darling of the Ivories." That came before her unfortunate experience with her daughter's father.

The front door opened and Verbenia said, "Come in, you two. We're ready to start."

After they took their seats in the parlor, their time together began with prayer, followed by the reading of scripture. Each Sunday, they took turns leading a short scripture lesson. Today, Mavis addressed them and, as usual, she ran longer than normal. Sweet Mavis did enjoy talking.

During much of the time, Claire fought to focus on what was being said. Her mind continually drifted to yesterday and Mark's desire to kiss her—a real kiss, not merely one on the cheek. As had happened then, her stomach dropped with the surprise, the anticipation, and the failure of her previous efforts to keep him at arm's length.

Relief over the puppy's welfare had elevated their emotions and prompted her reaction to him. A simple explanation for her response. Too simple, perhaps.

For once, she'd appreciated Mrs. Grzegorczyk's intervention.

Afterward, she had retreated, but Mark's hazel gaze bore into hers, the amber flecks shining like polished gold.

*"My arms are open. Whenever you're ready to walk into them for all time, they'll be open."*

Those words had amazed, invigorated, and alarmed Claire all in one suspension of time. They exhorted her to do something she hadn't thought possible—to imagine a life with someone who wasn't Richard Kingsley.

She could imagine it all she wanted. It didn't change her circumstances. It didn't lessen the joy she found in working as an architect, and it didn't change her inability to bear children.

When Mavis finished her lesson, they spent over half an hour socializing before Verbenia took control. "Ladies, I'm proud of you. You provided a much-needed service to Mrs. Gruhn yesterday. You worked hard and did a marvelous job. After the rest of you left, Louisa cried in my arms with gratitude."

Claire stood up. "I want to add my appreciation. Now, Louisa won't need to worry about falling through a rotted floorboard. I do feel terrible that Mr. Gregory and I ran off without finishing the job."

"You missed the moment Spence hit his thumb with the hammer." Phoebe grinned. "In his pain, he forgot he was among a group of ladies."

"You should have seen his eyes when he realized it, Claire." Ruby Kelly did a fine impression of someone with saucer eyes and brows raised to the hairline.

"I wish I'd seen that." Claire told them of the births of Cookie's puppies and the trouble the first one caused. After two more puppies arrived without difficulty, squiggling and crying, Claire had walked away from Mark's house with a lighter step than had carried her there, as well as a prayer of gratitude for being granted the opportunity to save a newborn's life. For once.

"If anyone would like one of the pups, I'm sure Mr. Gregory would be pleased to let you take them off his hands when they're ready."

The women laughed and shook their heads, rejecting the offer with enthusiasm.

Edythe was the only one not laughing. "Please do not mention them to my Sarah Jane. We're already overrun with animals."

"I won't breathe a word to her." Claire changed the subject. "Lumber is expensive. I'm sure I speak for everyone when I thank you for buying the boards for the porch." Claire often felt guilty relying on Edythe's money. Although they all worked hard to help others, most of the ladies couldn't afford to purchase the supplies needed for their volunteer projects. Edythe's father wasn't known as the most openhanded of men unless the charity benefited him in some way. How did he feel about his daughter's generosity?

Edythe's lips tipped upward in a self-deprecating smile. "It was the least I could do."

"We'll try not to take advantage of your generosity in such an expensive manner in the future. However, Louisa can use additional help. Even more, she needs the support and company of good friends." Verbenia's glance bounced off each woman. "How do you feel about extending her an invitation to join Widow's Might?"

A multitude of "Yes" responses and nodding heads filled Claire with gratitude toward these women whose empathy with Louisa caused them to eagerly accept her into their midst.

"Well, that settles it." Verbenia gestured to the hall. "Ladies, Lucy's delicious-looking cake awaits us in the dining room. Lemon chiffon, I think."

Claire followed the others making a beeline for the refreshments. Her mind returned to Saturday's events and the grudging appreciation she'd earned from Mrs. Grzegorczyk. For now, she was satisfied with their tentative truce—a truce easily broken if Mark's mother knew what had transpired in that mudroom.

ABSENTLY, CLAIRE FOLDED a petticoat and placed it on a store display table. Not for the first time in the past two days, she touched the spot on her cheek where Mark had kissed it. Why couldn't she get that moment off her mind? She didn't want to dwell on it. She didn't want to encourage anything similar in the future.

A customer passed behind Claire, her tongue issuing a *tsk*, a chastisement of her for being idle. She nodded to the finely dressed woman, who dipped her head in acknowledgment but continued to scowl at Claire until she disappeared behind a display of shirtwaists.

*Bother!* Embarrassed over being caught in a daydream and with a finger stroking her cheek, Claire snatched the shabbily folded petticoat from the table. If she didn't pay more attention to her job, she would be looking for another one.

Over all the other noises in the store, Wallace's laughter rose to greet her from the first floor. She ambled to the wrought iron railing, petticoat in hand, and peered down. Her brother came into view and stopped next to Spence Newland's seventeen-year-old sister, Laurie. Both laughed at something Wallace said. Laurie reached out and patted his upper arm.

The two had become thick over the past several months. Normally, Claire would relish the notion that her brother was sweet on a girl, but he and Laurie were from different backgrounds, different financial circumstances. Claire didn't want to see him crushed when Laurie grew up and realized he couldn't provide for her in the way in which she'd been raised. She didn't want to see the same look on his face that she had placed on Mark's the day he walked her home from his office.

She smelled a strong mixed scent of perfumes before Roslyn slid up next to her and leaned over with her arms crossed on the top railing. "I think they make a nice-looking couple, don't you?"

"But they're not compatible, are they?"

"What does it take to be compatible? I thought Gil and I were well-matched." Roslyn hung her head. "I lied that day we had lunch on the roof. Sometimes, I do feel sorry for myself. Sometimes, I wish I could join you in your widow's circle."

Claire's heart iced over. As much as she loved her friends in the Widow's Might group, she would give anything to never have qualified as a member.

Roslyn stared at her with a stricken expression. "I'm sorry. I didn't mean it the way it sounded. It's just that, he's left me in a terrible position, unable to move ahead with my life. If I could find him, I would seek a divorce. That I do mean. This is not how I saw my future three years ago."

"Would you marry again?" The question burst from Claire's mouth.

Her friend stared off in the distance. "Even if I said yes, I ruined my best opportunity years ago." She shook off whatever memory disheartened her. "How is your work coming with the architect?"

"How did you know about that?"

"Everyone knows."

Not her parents. At least, she still hadn't told them.

How could she? More than once lately, they had commented on her job at the store and how well it suited a widow. They believed she'd found something she was good at, but it wasn't something so consuming—something like architecture—that it couldn't be dismissed for marriage.

Sometimes, she wondered if they knew already about her work with Mark. Surely, with his job here at Newlands, Wallace had discovered the reason for her occasional absence. However, her brother had said nothing to her. Had he told their parents?

"My goodness, are you that touchy about it?"

Claire had voiced her question in a harsh manner. "No, of course not. Sorry."

"Well then?"

"It's fine."

"I'm glad to see you returning to where you belong. Speaking of belonging..." Roslyn backed away from the rail, preparing to leave.

"Don't go yet."

What was she doing? Yes, she wanted her independence, but was it the right time? Was she ready? And Roslyn lived down the street from Mark. After Saturday, he might believe her intention was to pursue him. Of course, that was as easily done while working with him.

Claire's fingernails tapped a slow rhythm on the rail. She had lived like a coward, hadn't she? Afraid to draw, afraid to move out on her own, afraid to pursue what pleased her most, afraid of a friendship growing between herself and Mark...afraid of pregnancy.

Fear had become a habit and one to be broken...if she found the courage to do so.

*Courage.* The word, like a mist in her mind, provoked her into spurning any lingering reservations. "Are you still interested in having me move in with you?"

A wide smile graced her friend's face. "Of course, but are you sure?"

"I'm sure." With that declaration, Claire sensed true independence for the first time in almost two years. Roslyn's house wasn't as large and fancy as her parents' house, but it was nicer than Louisa's or Phoebe's. Could she afford it without relying on the money she'd received from George? "There is one thing we haven't discussed."

"The rent."

"Yes."

Roslyn named a figure.

"That's awfully low."

"It's no secret that I can use the money, but I'm more interested in the company."

Claire's parents would call the move a waste when she already had a room in their house, but this would grant her some of the freedom she missed. "Is Saturday afternoon too soon for me to move in?"

"It's perfect." Roslyn's sigh indicated her happiness. "Now, if I don't return to my station, I'll be let go and will need to raise your rent. Don't worry about Wallace. He's a good man who will choose wisely, and Laurie is no snob."

After Roslyn descended the stairs to resume her position at the perfume counter, Claire remained at the railing. In the past few weeks, her life had taken many turns.

How would she tell her parents about this one?

# Chapter Seventeen

"**A**re you ready?" Paulina leaned over the sales counter in the women's department. Her smile brightened Claire's hectic day.

"I'll get my things and be back in a few minutes." Claire returned from the fourth floor with her hat and purse.

The women's first stop was the soda fountain in Hendry's Drug Store for a glass of Coca-Cola. They sat on small stools at the counter. Claire took her first swallow and licked her lips. "I plan to enjoy this treat. There won't be many more in my future."

"Why not?"

"After I move Saturday, this will be a luxury."

"You're moving out of your parents' house?"

"I'll be living with a friend. Actually, Roslyn lives down the street from Mark."

"You'll be neighbors." Paulina watched her finger run down the side of her glass. "That means you'll see more of him. I mean, more than during working hours."

"Possibly." Had she committed herself to seeing Mark every day? To spending additional time around him? More opportunity for him to wear down her resistance?

Claire thought Paulina supported Mark's interest in her, so the idea of her spending time with Mark should please the woman. Instead, she appeared preoccupied and gloomy. "Is that a problem?"

Paulina shook her head, her smile strained. "No. Not at all."

Claire sipped her drink, not persuaded that her new friend told the truth. She changed the subject. "I haven't seen the puppies lately. How are they?"

"Sweet, but active. They bounce around the house as though they haven't a care in the world. I've staked my claim on the female and will be back to pick up Bella as soon as she's ready to leave her mother."

"Bella?"

"Frederick says it means beautiful." Red crept up from under the collar of Paulina's dress to spread across her face.

Claire nudged her with an elbow. "I'm sure Frederick misses you."

"I miss him."

They were the right words but said with a distinct lack of enthusiasm. Was Paulina having second thoughts about her relationship with Frederick, doubts of her love for him? Perhaps, during these past days of becoming reacquainted with Mark, she'd come to the realization that she didn't fancy the man waiting for her in Chicago after all.

Claire should be happy to know someone was willing to take Mark's attention from her, but like Paulina, she couldn't summon much enthusiasm. "What time does your train leave on Friday?"

"Twelve o'clock."

"I wish you could stay longer." Staying longer gave Paulina more time with Mark, more time to turn his head in her direction. More time for Claire to convince him to do so. Again, she sensed an unwelcome pang of regret at the idea.

"My father hasn't been feeling well lately, and Mama doesn't want to leave him alone much longer."

Claire frowned. "Is it serious?"

"Indigestion." She laughed. "He insists that sodium of bicarbonate is a wonder drug."

161

"The miracles of modern science."

Finished with their Coca-Colas, they left the drugstore and stopped outside the building. Claire asked, "Where would you like to go?

"I haven't seen the park. Mark says it's nice. Would you mind if we walked there?"

True to its name, Riverside Park meandered alongside the river. Claire opened her mouth to suggest somewhere else to walk, then remembered her recent determination to show more courage in life. "It's not far."

Inside the park, the splashes and laughter of children playing in the water added to the sudden melancholy that hit her as soon as she'd stepped past the rock pillars at the entrance. How innocent the children were. How fancy-free and merry.

Claire pointed to a small path running parallel alongside a wall of trees that blocked much of the river. It seemed her courage still only went so far. "Would you mind if we walked this path?"

"Yes, that's best." As they passed a sycamore tree, Paulina pulled a leaf from a low-hanging limb and proceeded to fold it into various sizes and shapes. Her shoulders sank. "I wanted to walk someplace private, so we could talk."

"About what?"

"When you married your husband, how did you know he was the right man for you?"

Claire's earlier suspicion wasn't unfounded. "You're having doubts about Frederick?"

"I don't know. Perhaps." Paulina groaned. "I thought I was sure about him until..."

"Until you saw Mark again?"

Paulina grimaced. "I think he truly likes you, Claire, but you're not interested in him, are you?"

That was a question packed with emotional nitroglycerin. "I'm not interested in remarriage at this point, so whether or not I'm interested in any man has nothing to do with how another person feels."

"Why won't you remarry?"

"There are reasons." Reasons she chose not to get into with someone she'd known for such a short time. "The real question is, what are your plans?"

"I don't know. I was so sure I was meant to be Frederick's wife." She released a quiet huff. "Maybe I'm letting my mother control my thoughts. She still can't accept that I'm not married to Mark." She tossed the leaf away. "I can't believe we're discussing this. Forget I said anything."

Claire pursued an answer to the question that had been on her mind since last Saturday. "What did you mean when you said I should win over Mrs. Grzegorczyk for yours, mine, and Mark's sakes?"

Paulina stopped and let a young couple pass by before she answered. "My family and Mark's arrived here from Poland thirty years ago. They sought to escape oppression in a country divided by Germany, Austria, and Russia.

"Our mothers became friends on the ship. Sometimes, I believe their bond developed because neither of them adjusted well to the idea of coming here. Like many who find themselves in a strange land, they missed family and their way of life."

She clasped her hands behind her back as they walked. "Mark and I were born here. We don't have the memories of another homeland. And memories tend to become glorified over time, don't they? People see things, not as they are, but as they want to remember them. When that happens, it's possible to reject the present as not good enough when it comes to memories of the past. People become afraid to embrace what is before them."

Paulina's explanation substantiated Claire's conversation with

Mark three weeks ago. "I understand that they're afraid to adjust to America because, deep down, they fear they'll like it. What does that have to do with their attitudes toward me?"

"Mrs. G considers any non-Polish woman a threat to Mark's appreciation of his ancestry. My mother is the same where I'm concerned. Neither Mark nor I have ever seen Poland except on a map, yet our mothers think we should treat it as our homeland."

The answer to her question fell into place, and she regretted her ignorance in not fitting the pieces together before now. "Frederick isn't Polish?"

"No. That's why they've worked harder to bring Mark and me together during this trip—relentlessly harder. Don't you think that, like countries, everyone should be judged on his or her own merits? Our mothers can't continue to let the past control them."

"That's true." The United States didn't measure up to the women's memories of Poland, just as...

Claire's shirtwaist stuck to her back, but the warmth she felt wasn't from the sun.

She stared at a pileated woodpecker perched on the trunk of a nearby tree. As it dug a hole in the side of an elm tree, the *tap*, *tap*, *tap* of its beak was as persistent as the little voice inside her that struck at her sense of right and wrong.

*Stop. Stop. Stop.*

Measuring up applied to people, as well as countries. Mrs. G, as Paulina called her, might never come to like her, but Claire was every bit as guilty of failing to give Mark the credit due him. Though she knew his skill, in her thoughts, she'd often judged his professional ability by Richard's standards. Her husband had been a gifted architect, but she'd let her bias coax her into believing Mark wouldn't measure up to her husband as an architect...and, conceivably, as a man.

Or was she afraid Mark would measure up too well?

She couldn't deny his quick wit, intelligence, and manners. Yes, he was handsome, but many men's looks faded over time as their hairlines receded and their bellies expanded, so that didn't sway her. Somehow, though, she couldn't see far enough into the future to imagine those changes in Mark.

What she could see was his disappointment in her inability to have children.

Mrs. Grzegorczyk was right in one respect. Her son was better off with someone else.

MARK LEFT THE HOUSE at seven in the morning, seeking the peace and quiet of his office to concentrate on his work. Entertaining visitors had put him behind and triggered a hunger for a couple of hours of privacy without the constant feminine prattle rattling his ears, the odor of cooking cabbage, and coos over endearing but lively puppies.

It did little good. In the stillness of the drafting room, daydreams muddled his mind. Restless, he crossed to the open windows, careful to look over the rooftops and not down at the street.

He regretted not ignoring his mother's voice on Saturday in order to finish that kiss. Claire was willing. He'd seen it in that wistful stare. He'd heard it in the slightest sigh that escaped her lips. She was willing until she turned away from him.

He wouldn't rush her. He meant what he'd said about waiting with open arms.

In the meantime, Paulina was acting strangely, studying him as though he were an extraordinary butterfly specimen. Then there was Claire and her "Paulina this" and "Paulina that." One would think she was trying to influence his feelings for an old friend.

Mark returned to his desk and picked up a three-inch protractor. He laid the brass tool on the paper in front of him. The only thing he should let influence him this morning was his work.

Two new projects came to him late last week, small jobs, but one of them had required his immediate attention. Mr. Dover still awaited his preliminary sketches and Claire's interior details. The Lefler design must be finished soon if he was to meet the deadline.

Mark studied the elevation in front of him. According to his research, Harris Lefler's recent office buildings incorporated the current Palazzo style with its symmetrical shape and uniform windows.

Essentially, it was a box with decorative cornices at the top of the building. Nice, but too comparable to the drawing in front of him and, most likely, too similar to many of the other nine designs Lefler would receive for the Riverport building.

The end of Mark's pencil tapped a disjointed beat on the paper as he stared at the wall. He wanted something bold, something different. But what? How did he draw the man's attention to something unique without the design being rejected for being too different?

Addison walked across the room and cleared his throat. "Good morning."

Mark stood. "You're here far too early. The baseball game doesn't start until five o'clock."

"I'm afraid I won't be able to go with you. I received a telegram last night."

"What's wrong?"

Addison crushed a paper in his hand that Mark assumed to be the telegram. "My parents were visiting a cousin in Louisville, and my father had an incident."

"What kind of incident?"

"The doctor believes it's heart disease. He's alive, but my mother needs me."

"I understand."

"I never really thought about what it would be like to lose a parent."

Until it happened to him, Mark had not considered it, either. Was there a difference between losing a parent as a child and as an adult?

For him, it had meant growing up sooner than normal. It meant scrounging odd jobs as a twelve-year-old to help his mother make ends meet rather than playing baseball with friends after school. It meant spending his non-sleeping hours keeping up his schoolwork, determined to improve his life. It meant missing the love and laughter of the man who gave his life to protect him.

"Your father will recover."

"Sure." Addison cracked a slight smile that suggested he wanted to believe Mark but couldn't quite manage it.

"Will Lizzie and the girls go with you?"

"No. It's an expense we can't afford. Plus, with Lizzie expecting, she isn't in a condition to travel."

"Then I'll look in on them while you're gone. Tell Lizzie to let me know if she needs anything."

Addison visibly relaxed. "I would appreciate it."

"When do you leave?"

"Two hours. I have a ticket for the ten-thirty train." Still, he stood as though unsure what to do next.

"O'Keefe?"

"Yes?"

"Go."

His friend froze, his face a picture of indecision and dread, then his head bobbed.

"Addison, best wishes for your father's health."

Claire and Paulina would mention praying for Addison's father. Did his friend expect to hear something similar from Mark? How empty were encouraging words of God's love and care when he didn't believe in them. How hypocritical to pretend otherwise.

Addison settled the slouch hat on his head. "I'll see you when I get back."

The outer office door shut, leaving Mark alone once more in a room that was suddenly too quiet.

He grabbed a sheet of paper from a stack on the table and skimmed the short list of client changes for the guesthouse. It shouldn't take long to make them, but what if he trusted Claire to do it? She was familiar with the project, and it would allow him to concentrate on the Lefler design.

Would she take on the task, though?

When it came to architecture, Claire was a conundrum. She showed enthusiasm over a design and never shied away from giving an honest opinion when asked. He liked that about her. He liked that she approached an idea from various angles, seeking the right one. With admitted reluctance, he credited her husband for teaching her well.

On the other hand, there was indecisiveness in her. Something held her in check. Something kept her from showing the true passion he believed roiled under the surface—as if she were afraid to give it free rein.

He compared her reluctance to throwing a stick for Cookie to fetch. The dog jumped up and down in anticipation, but when Mark finally tossed the stick, she simply stared up at him as though waiting for permission to run after it.

Did Claire feel she needed permission to indulge that passion? Permission from whom?

# Chapter Eighteen

No sooner had Claire removed her gloves and hat than Mark rushed into the front room of the office. "I have a job for you."

She prepared for another errand to town hall, or to pick up the mail, or any one of the miniscule tasks he assigned her, and she saw as busy work. Mark didn't need her here, not really. While she enjoyed being privy to the world of architecture again, was she costing him needless expense? She had seen the ledger. He was making strides, but not as quickly as his self-confidence had foreseen.

"What is it?"

He slapped a sheet of paper on her desk that contained a typed list. "I'd like you to make these changes to the guesthouse."

"Me?" *No, no, no.* A second project had not been part of their agreement. She never hesitated to give her opinion on his work and had finally convinced herself to sketch a few interior designs for the one project she'd agreed to. This was different. This was more like the duty of a draftsman, not a secretary or bookkeeper. "Why me?"

"Because I believe you're able to do them. They're simple, Claire, and I want to work on the Lefler design."

Lately, most of his time had been devoted to the competition. They had spent little of it on Mr. Dover's plan. If she did this small thing he asked of her, not only could they return to the house project sooner, it afforded him the chance to present Lefler with the best possible office building submission...one that showed George he wasn't the only competent architect in the state of Indiana. She wanted Mark to succeed, as much for the previous reason as for their friendship.

She glanced at the list. "I'll do my best."

Claire worked on the guesthouse, making sure her work was meticulous and that it met Mark's standards and proved her skill.

She stood and stretched her back before taking the plan and change list to Mark. "What do you think?"

He studied the floor plan for several minutes, comparing it with the list of items on the sheet of paper. "Perfect."

"You were right. They were easy."

He pulled out his watch. "I think I've reached my creative limit today. It's getting late, and the game starts soon."

"The game?"

"Pilots versus the Gobs."

Yes, the baseball game. She had attended a couple of the at-home games with Wallace, but he had to work tonight, and a woman didn't attend those types of events unescorted by a gentleman. But how she would like to attend another game.

"Gobs." His lips twitched. "Odd name for a baseball team."

"With Indiana's glass industry, it makes sense. A gob is a drop of glass that goes into a feeder, which sends it into a mold to form bottles and such."

"Beauty and intelligence." Mark slipped into his coat. "I'd planned to go with Addison, but his father is ill. He's left for Kentucky to be with him."

"I'm sorry about Mr. O'Keefe's father."

It should be a good game. Temptation flooded her. But, no, it wasn't wise.

Mark grabbed his hat. "I'd better go."

"You'll go alone?" Her rash question smacked of seeking an invitation. Would he interpret it as such? Hadn't she intended him to do so?

"I have no choice. Unless..." He cocked his head. "Does your brother enjoy baseball?"

He wished to ask Wallace? He knew about her interest in the sport and intended to ask her brother instead of her? "I'm sure Wallace would be delighted to go with you, but I happen to know he can't tonight."

"That's a shame." Mark started for the front office.

She toggled the switch on her way out, dousing the electric lighting in the room. "You're going to do it, aren't you?"

He glanced over his shoulder, his wide-eyed gaze as innocent as an impish toddler's. "Do what?"

"You're wrong if you think I'm going to invite myself." Claire smiled and brushed past him. She gathered her things, stalling to give him time to rethink his teasing.

He stood near the desk. She didn't look his way but felt his gaze on her. After several wordless and nerve-wracking moments, he leaned around her. "Would you like to attend the baseball game with me, Mrs. Kingsley?"

She tugged on a glove and slipped by him to stand at the door, pleased with the victory. "Why, yes, Mr. Gregory, I believe I would."

He opened the door for her, letting her pass into the building's hallway. "Claire."

"Yes?"

"I wouldn't have left here without asking you to accompany me."

With his superior grin, she realized she'd stepped into a trap of her own making, but she would have the last say. "We can't leave Paulina out. Let's ask her to join us."

Just like that, he lost the grin, and she found hers.

AT THE TICKET BOOTH, Mark paid for their entrance to the baseball game over Claire's objection that she should buy her own ticket. He said, "I invited you, remember?"

"What I remember is that I bullied you into it."

"No one bullies me into doing anything, Claire." The statement came out gruffer than he'd intended, so he smiled. "I heard it as you begging me."

"Begging you? If that's what you heard, I recommend you clean your ears." She flashed a saucy grin and preceded him into the park.

Mark laughed, anticipating quite an invigorating life with that lady one day.

The thought of expecting a lifetime with her should surprise him, but he'd grown accustomed to the idea over the past few weeks. Now, he simply needed to convince her that they belonged together.

Regardless of his words to Claire the day the pups were born, must his arms grow weary before she afforded him so much as a morsel of hope?

They found seats on the second row of the wooden bleachers overlooking a fenced-in field appropriate for the size of Riverport. It was a simple baseball park with the typical neatly trimmed lawn and diamond-shaped path.

"It is a shame Paulina couldn't join us."

"Isn't it." Frankly, Mark had been pleased when Paulina had declined with the excuse that she must wash a few things before they left for Chicago in a couple of days. Frankly, he'd be glad to end the strain of the mothers' constant matrimonial hints.

Mark gestured toward the players for the Pilots as they stretched and practiced their swings at the edge of the field. "Are they better than the competition?"

"Our Riverport team has a good record this year, but the Gobs are four wins ahead."

"We'll have to cheer the home team on louder then." He pressed his tongue against the back of his teeth and freed a loud whistle. "Smash that glass, Pilots!"

Several of the men surrounding them replicated his whistle and shouted their own encouragement as the first batter approached the mound. Claire covered her eyes with her hand, but he caught the smile that told him she only acted embarrassed over his behavior. He wouldn't put it past her to wish to add her own whistle. Out of the question, because she was every bit a lady.

Each time a player for the local team came to bat, she angled closer to provide information she believed Mark should know. Some of it wasn't new to him. Other statistics were appreciated. Mostly, he enjoyed the way her shoulder pressed into his and her flowery perfume scented the air. To keep it happening, he kept his mouth shut and listened.

Mark bought them each a bag of peanuts, and they settled in to pay attention to the game. When the Riverport team scored a home run, the man seated beside Mark jumped to his feet, jostling Mark's arm. His peanuts flew into the air, showering Claire on the way down. Even during the man's profuse apology, neither Mark nor Claire stopped laughing.

During the seventh inning, when the Pilots were ahead by two runs, the amateur teams imitated the recent practice of their professional counterparts and announced a time for those on the benches to pause and stretch.

"Would you like to walk, Claire?"

"That would be nice." She stood and winced. "Perhaps one day they'll pad these benches."

They slipped from their row and ambled away from the crowd.

As they strolled the grounds, Claire asked about the health of the pups.

"Plump and fit, even the runt. I'm still becoming used to the idea of a house full of frolicking animals, though."

"It will help to prepare you for the day you have a houseful of frolicking children." The last couple of words faded, as though she regretted having made the comparison.

"That reminds me. Addison informed me the other day that they'll be blessed by a child near Thanksgiving, if all goes well."

"If all goes well?"

"They've lost three infants in the past, but they're happy for another chance to add to their family."

Claire's jaw sagged. "I wish them well."

Mark barely heard Claire's soft answer over the jocular noises from the park and the call to resume the game. They strolled farther from the field and stood on the other side of a hedge of bushes. It was an audacious gamble to ask, but he felt audacious at the moment. "I've already told you that, one of these days, I'd like a number of children. What about you?"

Without a wasted second, Claire pivoted. "What I would like is to see the rest of the baseball game."

It wasn't the answer he'd expected. It wasn't an answer at all. He had assumed she would turn coquettish and tell him it wasn't a subject for the two of them to discuss so early in their...whatever one would call their association. He should know by now that she wasn't the coquettish type.

As Claire took a step away, Mark said, "Wait." He pulled a partial peanut shell from a strand of hair above her ear and held it out. "A fashion statement, Mrs. Kingsley?"

A slight smile crept across her face to cast aside the gloom left over from their previous conversation. "The latest, Mr. Gregory."

He tossed the shell and reached out, intending to remove a second, smaller piece. Instead, his fingers bypassed it to skim the soft skin of the valley beneath her cheekbone. They drifted downward with ease and purpose, like a hawk homing in on its prey, and combed through the hair at the back of her head.

He leaned closer. Ever closer to her mouth. Ever closer to the prize.

She tipped her head at an angle to welcome his kiss, and Mark's pulse quick-stepped. His mouth hovered over hers, ready to seize the treasure he'd imagined for weeks. Still, he warned himself to stop there and not dare a touch without giving her a moment to choose. It must be her choice.

Her eyes slipped shut and she breached the space between them to touch her lips to his. Soft. Tentative. Salty. Hungry.

The splendidness of the moment snatched every bit of reserved air from his lungs, but he'd never complain. She had opened her arms to him, and it was well worth his labored breaths.

At the roar of the crowd, Claire backed away. Her voice trembled as she said, "It seems as if someone succeeded in scoring a home run."

Indeed. And it wasn't on the baseball field.

WITH THE NIGHT AIR coming from the open window, Claire woke to a temperature more bearable than when she'd gone to bed. But her nightclothes clung to her body, and remnants of a dream stuck in her mind.

In that dream, a scruffy dog chased her as she ran through Mr. Dover's lot. A man watched from among the trees, his shadowy features indistinct. Nonetheless, Claire recognized him. He was the reason she ran.

Her fingertips covered her mouth. Shouldn't she regret kissing Mark? Somehow, she hadn't dredged up any remorse over it in the moment, not when she had begun that kiss...not when she had welcomed his lips on hers. He had promised open arms, and hours ago, she had stepped right into them.

In this present hour? Regret? No. Only a soothing warmth in the pit of her stomach.

Even so, the dream left her head spinning with confusion. In it, she ran from Mark, yet she could no longer deny that her feelings for him were far from that of a colleague or friend.

Claire climbed out of bed and lit a lamp before padding across the floor in her bare feet. The chirp of a cricket outside her window told her she didn't prowl the night alone.

Stopping at the bureau across the room, she opened the bottom drawer and pulled out a large roll of paper she had saved from her husband's effects. Shoving aside the covers, she laid it on the bed and unrolled it, using her mattress as a table. The faint smell of lingering chemicals and dust tickled her nose. Paper turned blue through the process of cyanotype exposed the white lines of the drawing on the page—a design she and Richard began mere months after their marriage. His creativity drafted the outside and hers the inside.

The house was unlike anything she had ever seen and nothing like the tired repetition of the classical but typical European styles. Instead, it represented a freedom and natural beauty found in the environment of the Midwest's plains. Richard was convinced that given time the novelty of the design would gather a universal appeal and become a standard in home construction.

As she studied the lines and angles, the walls and rooms, the air in her bedroom swirled with the ghost of her husband's laughter. Her skin warmed with the remembrance of his breath on her neck and his arm draped across her shoulder as he pointed out the staircase that led to the second floor—a sample of her work. Thick, bare treads seemed to float on air. They were supported not by risers but decorative cast iron rods running from floor to ceiling.

She and Richard had foreseen building this house one day...together.

*"This will be our home, Claire. What do you think?"*

*"I think I can't wait until we build it."*

In the end, they left their old house, not together or in a way she had anticipated. And the home of their dreams was rolled away and shoved in a bureau drawer.

Although she had begged George Brant to present the project to a client, he had declined to use it after Richard's death. He had declined to use her.

The house deserved to be built by someone. It deserved to be filled with the children she and Richard hadn't brought into the world.

Hearing the O'Keefes had lost *three* children had almost crushed her. How had they borne it? What convinced them to look at this next possible loss as a blessing?

She rolled up the plan, returned it to the drawer, and crawled into bed. Someone should live in that beautiful home, but it wouldn't be her. She would never live in a place that represented so many unanswered dreams.

Claire pulled the sheet up to her neck. She tried and failed to recall a memory from the one time she and Richard attended a baseball game. Funny, but all she heard was Mark's laughter when his peanuts flew up in the air and rained down on them. All she saw was the longing in his eyes when he waited for her to accept his kiss. All she felt was the way her lips tingled afterward and the hope it stirred in her.

In the next instant, her sense of awe succumbed to the single, horrible realization of why she ran from him in her dream. Like Richard, Mark wanted children one day.

If things continued on this course and their relationship grew into love, she was bound to disappoint him, and that would break her heart all over again.

# Chapter Nineteen

M ark had lost all ability to control his smile. His foot tapped the floor below the drafting easel as he stared at the endless blue of sky outside the bowed windows. The expanse offered a canvas to display the images that repeated in his mind—mainly, the look of acceptance on Claire's face in the instant before they kissed.

They had advanced a step toward something grander than friendship. Although he'd erred in kissing her in public, as hard as he tried, he couldn't summon even a smidgen of guilt over it. It was the only time he'd touched her last night. He hadn't even taken her arm as he accompanied her home. He surmised from her refusal to let him see her as far as the house that she still hadn't told her parents about her connection with him.

That begged the question, where did they go from here? How did they move forward? He didn't want to rush her, but neither could they return to their former relationship.

An hour later, as Mark attempted to add the finishing touches to a scrolled design above the street-side door of the Lefler project, Claire arrived for their meeting with Mr. Dover.

Yesterday, she had made the changes to the guesthouse, and he'd approved them. Now, with his lack of busywork for her to do, she stood behind him, peering over his shoulder. How was he supposed to focus when her every movement drew his attention like a shooting star?

Mark couldn't work this way. Did she realize how he tortured himself with the need to kiss her again?

He'd had a lot to lose with the move to Riverport. Meeting Claire doubled the stakes. If he lost his business and his reputation, and was forced to return to Chicago, most assuredly, he would lose her, too. What woman wanted to associate with a failure?

*Act like a man and steel yourself to the circumstances with a stiff upper lip.*

Because she'd changed the subject when he tried to bring up what happened at the baseball field, he might as well settle for that stiff upper lip. Her softer ones were once more unattainable.

Claire moved to his side. "He'll be here soon."

"I know."

"What will you show him?"

Mark laid a hand on the stack of sketches for Charles Dover. He'd stayed up into the wee hours finalizing his ideas, pleased with a specific elevation. It answered the problem plaguing him for weeks. This plan took advantage of the beautiful surroundings of the Dover lot. His eyes had blurred to the point of barely seeing the paper, much less completing an interior layout.

"I'm ready. However, I'm not sure I can concentrate on presenting it properly when such a lovely assistant attracts my attention with her every move."

Claire glared at him—a counterfeit glare, he hoped. She shrugged a shoulder with a show of indifference and sat in the extra chair he'd purchased a week ago.

Even though she'd raised a wall between them, and it was his challenge to erode it little by little, he was grateful that he no longer stared up at her.

Deliberately withholding his favorite, Mark seized four other sketches and handed them to her. "Tell me what you think of these."

She flipped through them, barely taking them in, then she started over, this time giving each sketch a proper amount of attention. As she worked through each, her mouth pursed more and more. Was that good? Bad? He couldn't tell.

Mark drummed his fingers on the surface of the table to match the beat of the pulse that drummed in his ears. This was worse than the day he'd turned in the draft of his first sketch at D. H. Burnham and waited for the verdict.

She went back to the third sheet. "I would begin with this one."

"Why?"

"I like it best."

That was it? "I hoped for more input. What's wrong with the others? You don't think he'll like them?" Why shoot questions at her like an insecure novice?

"There's nothing wrong with them."

"But?" She forced him to add that tiny word to draw out the truth.

She released a frustrated sigh. "They are all good elevations, Mark, but I'm not convinced any of them will work for Mr. Dover. They don't satisfy his primary request to save as many trees as possible."

Mark spread the papers on the table and studied them for the hundredth time. He rubbed his tired eyes with the heels of his hands. She was right, of course. He reached for the one he'd held back.

"I agree. But they are possibilities in the event he doesn't like this one." He handed her the sketch.

Claire laid it on the table in front of her. She bent to study it, and those pastel eyes grew larger with every second she scrutinized the drawing.

Her silence heightened his skittish heartbeat. "Without all the gables and fancy detail, the simplicity of the elevation allows it to blend in with the scene in which it's set and not the other way around. I believe it will also lend itself to some of your ideas for the interior. We can—"

"I don't need convincing." She turned to him and smiled. "This is striking and distinctive. There is a definite feel for nature in the outline of the roof and the house in general. What about the floor plan?"

"It's rough at the moment." He grabbed a pencil. "I see the main rooms of the house in the front. The rear is angled to give the structure a triangular shape to accommodate the wooded area. Like this." He drew linear and angular lines that formed an irregular triangle with the depth on the southeast side of the house. The more he drew, the harder his heart beat with the excitement of finalizing the plan. "There's a slight break in the trees here"—he pointed to the northwest side—"so we'll include ample windows to overlook the yard to the creek."

Claire straightened and laid a hand on his shoulder. "Mark, I think you've—"

The outer office door closed with a discernable click.

"That must be Mr. Dover." Her hand leapt from his shoulder as though the sound lit a fire that scorched her palm. For him, the fire still smoldered.

Mark dropped the pencil and pulled his suit coat from the back of his chair. A coat rack was on his list of items to purchase soon. He entered the front office followed by Claire.

Dover's secretary stood at the desk. "Good afternoon, Mr. Gregory, Mrs. Kingsley. Mr. Dover sent me with his regrets. He's had to leave town unexpectedly and will be unable to meet with you today. He apologizes but won't return for almost three weeks. He asks if the sixth of July will fit into your schedule."

Three weeks? He checked the calendar. That was after the Lefler design was due and before learning whether he'd advance to the next round of the competition. "That would be fine with me. I assume he'll still want Mrs. Kingsley in the meeting. Will that work for you, Claire?"

"I believe so."

The man pulled a small book from his pocket and wrote the appointment in it. "He wanted me to assure you that he is eager to see and discuss your ideas."

After the secretary left, Mark gathered his sketches. "I have a good idea of the interior layout, but until we meet with him, we can't proceed too far. The good news is that I can now finalize the Lefler design."

Truthfully, the Lefler project took priority over his other work. It was the project with the potential to bring him the success he desperately desired...or ruin him.

"How is it coming?"

"Good. It's taking shape."

He had come a long way in drafting a design for the businessman but had much work to do before personally delivering it to Mr. Arbuckle in Chicago next Wednesday. Time was running out on both the deadline for the design and the deadline to meet his loan. However, his confidence in his current plan had begun to deteriorate.

"While I work on it, you can take that sketch we talked about before Dover's secretary arrived and draft some ideas for the interior details."

She hesitated, the same as she had done whenever he'd asked her to work on a project. "Mark, I have a plan at home I'd like to show you. Richard and I designed a house for our personal use but never..." She drew in a breath. "We never built it. I think many of the interior elements will work with the Dover house. Would you like to see it?"

Mark's enthusiasm fell. "I'm sorry, Claire. I won't consider implementing a plan from another architect."

"The design is mine. There are no issues in using it."

He turned back to the drawing table. "Dover is paying for my work, not someone else's."

"Mr. Dover is paying for something from both of us."

"Exactly. You and I." Not her husband's. His sigh broke the prolonged quiet in the room. "Please, just come up with some interior samples to go along with this idea."

"Whatever you say."

That tiny pout tempted him to wrap her in his arms and kiss it away.

Oh yes, working under these conditions tested the strength of his patience and integrity. Now, the question was where was his breaking point?

CLAIRE STROLLED WITH her parents along the sidewalk toward the restaurant down the street. Her mother paused outside the grocer's and examined the broccoli stacked in a bin between rhubarb on one side and asparagus on the other. It wasn't unusual for her to suddenly stop at such displays.

Claire and her father had no choice but to wait—right across the street from the building housing Mark's office. She contended with the temptation to glance in that direction. It wouldn't do to draw her parents' attention since she still hadn't told them about working with Mark. Nor had she said anything about attending the baseball game with him or her upcoming move.

Ma picked up a broccoli spear and the top slumped. She dropped it back in the box and dusted her gloves, a sign she'd dusted the poor vegetable from consideration.

A steady clip-clop and children's laughter announced the approach of a vehicle—Judge Danby's open barouche. Claire waved to Edythe, who sat in the seat beside her father and across from her three restless children. "Edythe!"

The judge's daughter searched for the person calling her name. When she spotted Claire, she returned the wave in a friendly manner, yet as restrained as the woman herself. Edythe's father said something to her, and she turned to speak to the children.

Claire worried about her. The judge was known as a respected man of the court, though gossip said he was an unpleasant man in the home. Claire suspected him to be one of the reasons for Edythe's keen participation in the Widow's Might group. Their meetings were an escape from his control. They were also an escape from the antics of her high-spirited children.

Claire's gaze shifted and her smile froze.

Crossing the street, Mark dodged two carriages and stopped on the sidewalk next to her. "Good evening, Mrs. Kingsley."

Dread rose in Claire. She'd hesitated in letting him walk her to the door after the baseball game. Didn't that show him she still hadn't told her parents about them? Yet, he'd purposely crossed the street to greet her. "Good evening."

She glanced toward the second floor of his building. His mother watched from the window, aiming a hostile glower at Claire. Apparently, the truce between them had expired.

Next to her, Claire's father's gaze dissected Mark in the way most fathers mentally tore apart male strangers who talked to their daughters on the street. She sought a way to get past this meeting without figurative bloodshed—hers—once her parents realized Mark's identity.

Pa held out his hand, his brow now twisted with curiosity. "I'm John Pittman, Claire's father."

"Mark Gregory." The two of them shook hands. "It's nice to meet you, sir."

"Gregory?"

Claire held her breath, waiting to see if he recalled where he'd heard the name, or if Mark would help him remember.

"Yes, sir."

"How do you know our daughter, Mr. Gregory?" Leave it to her mother to come right out and ask.

"My mother and I are new in town. We met Mrs. Kingsley at Newland's when she assisted my mother in her search for a new hat."

The air left Claire's lungs in relief.

"Regrettably, Mama found nothing to suit her that day. However, I was impressed by your daughter's thoughtfulness and good humor. As her brother told me, she's quite a saleswoman. I'm sure, in time, she and my mother will find common ground"—he paused a tick—"in hats."

Claire's unrestrained soft snort of disbelief brought her parents' attention to center on her. Time to dispel any thoughts they might entertain as to she and Mark being anything more than customer and sales clerk. "Isn't Miss Kowalski with you?"

Mark's eyes narrowed. "She's waiting in my office."

"In that case, we wouldn't want to keep you from her company. It was nice to see you again, Mr. Gregory."

A muscle jumped in his jaw. Mark wasn't happy with her. Not at all. "Good night, sir. Mrs. Pittman." Without a second glance at Claire, he crossed the street again.

Not only was he a good man, but one who had used discretion. And right now, he was a very angry man.

Her father's mouth flattened as he aimed a pointed look in Claire's direction. "He's the new architect, isn't he? I recall the newspaper article."

Her deceptive efforts had proven useless. There would be no keeping the news from them now. "Yes, he is the new architect."

That announcement drew a frown from her mother.

No further word was said on the street, and Claire followed her parents into The Moonglow Restaurant. She prepared to be sliced thin by the upcoming interrogation, like the roast beef her father always ordered.

# Chapter Twenty

M ark climbed the stairs to the second floor. No, he stomped.
He should have minded his own business. Claire's
parents were ignorant of his acquaintance with her. He'd known
that. Why try to force the acknowledgement and place everyone in
an awkward position?

Even during the short and stressful introduction, Mark had
noticed that she took after her father in looks and her mother in a
forthright nature. Well, somewhat forthright.

But why continue to keep their relationship a secret from the
people closest to her?

The Pittmans' late son-in-law was an architect. Had they not
gotten along? Did she think they would frown upon Mark for that
reason—guilt by association?

Worse, even after kissing him as she had last night, Claire
continued to push him toward Paulina. It made no sense.

Long strides carried him down the second-floor hallway. The
pungent odor of pipe smoke hung in the air, coming from the open
door of the office on his right. The smell reminded him of his father
and evenings spent adding and tamping tobacco in the bowl of his
father's pipe.

Inside his office, he expected to find his mother chatting with the
Kowalskis and showing them every nook and cranny. He opened the
door. His mother sat at the front desk with her mouth drawn into a
scowl. Mrs. Kowalski and Paulina were nowhere to be seen.

"How was your conversation with Mrs. Kingsley, Marek?"

Now he understood the source of the scowl. "It was brief. I saw her on the street and walked over to meet her family."

His mother pushed up from the chair. "Walked? It looked as though you *ran* to meet them."

Mark forced himself to remember that he respected his mother. He wouldn't chide her in front of friends.

She pressed a palm against her forehead. "Forgive me, Marek, but my head hurts. I believe I will go home and rest."

Paulina and her mother must have waited in the drafting room. At his mother's announcement, they entered the small office. Paulina's sympathetic gaze washed over him. She pressed his arm in wordless encouragement as she and her mother walked out the door.

Before she stepped into the hall, his mother turned. "You will be home soon?"

"In a couple of hours or so. Don't wait supper on me." As she lumbered through the doorway, Mark caught her up in a hug, his irritation waning. "Feel better."

She pushed away and nodded.

After the women left him alone in the office, he sank into the chair his mother had occupied. Attending the game with Claire had convinced him even more that she was the woman he wanted to court. If she would let him.

What was he to do about his mother's aversion to her?

Claire's help with the puppies had earned Mama's regard—for a few days. Now, she'd slipped back into an attitude of resentment toward the loveliest, funniest, most intelligent woman he had ever met.

His droll chuckle split the silence. In some ways, Claire was the most frustrating.

The sooner he convinced her to see him as a possible suitor, the sooner he'd dissuade his mother from the ludicrous idea that he belonged with Paulina or any woman simply because she was of Polish descent.

And Paulina...

In the past few days, whenever possible, she had stuck to him like wallpaper paste. He understood a desire to keep company with someone her own age, but her constant reminders of their friendship led him to believe there was more to it. What happened to Frederick?

In the drafting room, he removed his suit coat, hung it over the back of his chair, and pulled the plan for the Lefler building from the pile of papers on the table. He sat back in his chair and stared at the drawing, not really seeing it. What he saw instead was a detailed rendering of a large, three-story office building. Perfect in every detail.

Mark tossed the previous design aside in favor of a blank sheet of paper. He couldn't transfer the images in his head to the paper fast enough. Bold, modern, and the right submission for Harris Lefler's competition.

CONFESSION AND CANDOR were long overdue.

After ordering their meal, the Pittman family sat silent in the restaurant, which intensified the sounds around them—sounds of clattering dishes, laughter, chairs screeching along the floor, even a loud belch from somewhere in the busy room and the tittering it produced.

How was Claire to start the conversation?

She was saved added struggle when her mother said, "Mr. Gregory seems like a nice man."

A flutter in Claire's stomach betrayed her effort to remain dispassionate. "Yes."

"And when did you determine that, before or after you visited his office?"

"How did you know I've been there?"

Her mother huffed. "Really, Claire. You knew exactly which window to look at, second floor in the corner."

The glance had been a spontaneous reaction, not meant to be noted by others. "Yes, I have been to the office...numerous times."

"Why?" Up to now, her father had been content to let her mother speak.

Claire hated causing her parents concern. "Ma, do you remember the invitation I received last month to meet with Mr. Dover?"

"I remember. I also remember advising you against going."

"I went anyway."

"I assumed as much."

Nonetheless, she had never asked, so Claire hadn't mentioned it again. "As I told you, I met the gentleman when we both stopped to observe the building being constructed on Henning. While we talked, it came out that I'd had some architectural experience."

Her mother jerked upright. "You rarely talk about that anymore."

Claire added the words "with us" to the statement.

The waitress brought their food to the table. Her father blessed the supper. Before the "Amen" drifted from one of Claire's ears to the other, he said, "Continue, Claire."

He hadn't called her by his nickname for her, Clairie, which stressed his disappointment.

"When I reached Mr. Dover's office, I discovered Mr. Gregory had also received an invitation to the meeting." Claire sliced into the pork chop on her plate and inhaled the delicious smell of the meat and spices. Too bad their conversation would ruin the taste. "He was asked to design a house for Mr. Dover, who had one request."

"What was that?"

"That I assist in the design."

Her mother set down her fork and looked to the ceiling as if begging God to tell her that what she'd heard wasn't true. "Is it what you really want?"

Claire laughed to break the tension. "Are you talking to me or to God?"

Ma scowled at her. "You know perfectly well to whom I'm speaking."

Claire grew solemn. It was her life and the decisions she made were her choice. "Yes, Ma. This is what I want to do. It's only for one design. Although..."

"Although what, Claire?"

"Mr. Gregory and I reached an agreement that I would clerk for him two afternoons per week. My work on Mr. Dover's plan is secondary." Before they could argue, she told them about the project, including her meeting with George and the announcement that had driven her to accept Mark's offer.

"But you have a job at the store."

"I'm still there, Ma."

"Surely, your brother knows of this. Why didn't he tell us?"

Perhaps because he wasn't a snitch.

"That wasn't his place, Ida." Her father speared a green bean. "Why didn't you tell us, Claire?"

"For the past month, you and Ma have articulated your feelings on the subject over and over. I didn't want to disappoint you."

"You've disappointed us more by not being frank with us. Neither was Mr. Gregory. He had a chance to say something and didn't."

"I'm sorry." She sipped her tea, her throat parched from nervousness and the humiliation of being talked to like she was a six-year-old. Confession might be good for the soul, but not the body. "Please don't blame Mark for any of this. He told the truth when he said we met at the store...originally."

Her father pinned her with a stare. "Yet he also withheld more important information."

"Because of me. He realized I hadn't told you about our...situation and chose to be a gentleman about it."

"Ha! A gentleman doesn't lie to a woman's parents."

Claire's teeth clenched. Why couldn't her mother understand? "And a grown woman's parents don't try to control everything she does."

"Ida, she's right. She's an adult. As much as we don't want to see her hurt again by the opinions of others, we can't stop her from doing what she finds fulfilling."

"Fine, but so you both know, I don't go along with this. That scoundrel George Brant broke your heart when he dismissed you so blithely, Claire. Others have criticized you. Are you going to let another architect do the same?"

"George is a bully and a backward thinking man who can't be compared to Mark."

"You sound as though you know him well."

"I know him well enough to have attended a Pilot's game with him last night." Feeling emboldened, she added, "While we're having this discussion, there's something else I haven't told you."

Her mother groaned. "I'm not sure I want to hear."

"I hope, like me, you think of it as good news." She prayed that was the way they would see her leaving. "First, I must tell you how much I appreciate your letting me stay with you while I struggled to get over Richard's death. You gave me a place to go when I had nowhere else."

"It's your home. That's true for both my children. We're a family."

"Thank you, Ma." Claire swallowed past the mountain of emotion stuck in her throat. Clearly, her mother wouldn't make this easy. "Your love and care have meant more to me than I can properly express. You allowed me time to grieve and heal until I could face the day without tears. With fewer and fewer of them, anyway. Now, you must allow me the opportunity to stand on my own again."

"John!" Claire's mother gripped the forearm of Claire's father in what must be a bruising hold. "She plans to marry Mr. Gregory."

Claire blinked at the panic in her mother's voice. "What? No."

She might be attracted to Mark more than she wished, but under the circumstances, that was as far as it went. It was why she persisted to insinuate that he belonged with Paulina.

On the other hand, if things were different, why wouldn't he be welcomed as a son-in-law? Just because he was an architect, it didn't make him the wrong man for her. In fact...

She froze amid salting the rather bland potatoes on her plate. She mustn't continue down that line of thinking.

"Then, what is this about?" asked her father. "What is your plan?"

"As I said, for some time now, I've desired to live on my own, so I'm moving out of the house on Saturday."

"Saturday? So soon? Where will you go?"

Claire picked up a piece of toasted bread. "I've agreed to move in with Roslyn Malone."

Her announcement suspended all movement at the table. Her mother's mouth dropped open. "Mrs. Malone? From the store? The wife of the embezzler?"

"She's a friend who had nothing to do with what happened. She was as much a victim as the Newlands."

"Is this really what you want, Clairie?"

Her father's use of the nickname warmed her. "It is."

His tentative smile gave her a smidgen of hope that he supported her plan. "If you're bent on leaving, we'll miss you. Our place will always be home for you when you need it, a place of sanctuary, but I'm happy that you've found your feet again."

"Thank you, Pa."

"But, John, it's a waste of money. She has a perfectly good room in our house."

"That's just it, Ma. It's your house, not mine."

"You'll be a woman alone. How will you care for yourself?"

*For heaven's sake.* "Ma—"

"Ida, we've already established that our daughter is a grown woman. She's been married and lived away from us before. She has a job, a brain, a lovely face, and an endearing personality. Now that she's ready to resume her life, I'll wager she won't be alone much longer. Wallace and I will help her move her things to her new home Saturday afternoon."

Buoyant relief swept through Claire. She hadn't expected her father's easy agreement and wasn't sure if she should kiss his cheek in gratitude or discourage his obvious hope for an impending marriage with...whomever...as long as it wasn't with a reviled architect.

"ARE YOU SURE YOU WANT to leave so soon?" Mark asked the question as a matter of courtesy, while he removed Paulina's bag from the boot of the carriage and carried it toward the depot.

Their guests' stay of one week had seemed like two. Claire, Paulina, and both mothers had joined forces in an assault on his life, and he was ready for the end of the battle, or at the least, a ceasefire.

It would be nice to have the house back in order again, to enjoy evenings without feeling he must entertain guests. Unfortunately, that left Mr. Olesky free to move in.

Paulina grinned. "You're asking us to stay longer, Mark?"

How did he extricate himself from this pickle barrel?

People passed, coming from or going to the station, some with wide smiles, others with the sad faces of those who've said goodbye to friends and loved ones. Paulina's laughter shattered the awkwardness of the quiet moment between them. "Don't worry. I'm as eager to return to Chicago as you are to have your peaceful home returned to you."

"Frederick?"

"I wish he were free to meet us when we arrive."

"There's something special about having someone you care about waiting for you, someone who will welcome you home and tell you how much he missed you. You'll get that greeting soon enough."

Thoughts of his trip to Chicago next week intervened with an image of Claire meeting him upon his return. Possibility? Or fantasy? With Paulina's departure, what material would Claire use on that wall she'd built to keep them apart?

"You will take his breath away when he sees you in that beautiful new hat." Mark flicked a feather and laughed when it bounced.

"I will, won't I? Your mother's gift." Paulina pulled on his sleeve and took a step backward, dragging him with her. She lowered her voice. "I have a confession to make."

"A confession?"

"I spent much of last night praying for direction. I'm afraid I gave in to our mothers' persuasion. I started to believe you and I had a future together."

Their mothers Mark could understand. Claire's encouragement was another matter. "You recognize the truth now?" *Please.*

"I do. Like them, I let fear of the unknown lead me to question my relationship with Frederick. Memories of our friendship and their hounding caused me to doubt the present as well as the future."

"Paulina, I do value our friendship, but I must ask. You're sure about Frederick?"

"Surer than I've ever been. As sure as you are about Claire." She picked up a small valise. "Take care of my little Bella."

Unlike the day Paulina arrived, he didn't hesitate to embrace her. "She'll be fine until you return."

Paulina grabbed hold and whispered in his ear. "By then, I expect to see you and Claire as more than an employer and employee."

While Mark had similar hopes for the two of them, they grew fainter with the passing of time. A moment in his arms, and she had jumped out.

"Remember what I said about helping Claire tomorrow." Paulina released him, a satisfied smirk on her face. "Time to go, Mama."

The two women walked across the platform and waved from the steps of the train car. They disappeared inside, and the train chugged away from the station.

"I'll escort you home, Mama." He wrapped an arm around her shoulder. "How would you like to make *Piernik* for when I return from work?" It was a spur-of-the-moment thought intended to take her mind off the departure of her friend, but at the mention of the gingerbread, Mark's mouth watered, already tasting the various spices.

She shook her head, her mouth as straight as a ruler. "The young have no interest in their heritage."

His mother was wrong. There were many things he appreciated about being Polish, such as *Piernik*. "Does that comment have to do with me not pursuing Paulina?"

Her chin jutted. "Had you paid more attention to her, she would not have chosen someone else."

"Mama, how do you not understand that she is in love...and not with me?"

"How do you not understand that she would be if your Mrs. Kingsley had not bewitched you? I saw how Paulina looked at you this week. Now, you have spurned her and missed your chance."

"No one has bewitched me." How he said that with a straight face, he wasn't sure. "Paulina does not love me and never has. We do not love each other. Period. There are no missed chances. You and Mrs. Kowalski must accept it."

"What choice do we have?" Mama pulled a handkerchief from

inside her sleeve and dabbed it at her eyes. "We are broken in our hearts."

For the first time since meeting her, Mark wondered if pursuing Claire was a wise decision—for her sake. Should he succeed in marrying her, would she and his mother forever be at odds?

# Chapter Twenty-one

With her shift at the store behind her, Claire returned to her parents' house Saturday evening to find her father and Wallace moving her grandmother's trunk to a wagon borrowed from a friend, the owner of the feed store.

The trunk joined the few boxes she had packed, her two suitcases, and the already-loaded bedroom furniture. Everything might arrive at Roslyn's smelling like oat dust, corn, and horse liniment, but it was getting late and the wagon would save them transport time. The rest of her belongings—a few keepsakes and more furniture pieces—would remain in the attic.

After a short trip, her father reined in the horse in front of the quaint yellow house with white trim—her new home. He stared at the porch. "You invited him?"

Sitting on the street side of the wagon seat, Claire peered around her father. It was Mark. What was he doing here? "I mentioned moving in with Roslyn on Thursday."

Mark skipped down the porch steps, his brisk stride bringing him to the wagon before her father's feet hit the ground. Like the day they worked on Louisa's house, he had relinquished the suit for the striped shirt and denim pants of a carefree young man. "Good afternoon, Mr. Pittman."

"Mr. Gregory."

Claire winced at the chill in her father's voice. Surely, he didn't still blame Mark for her mistake in not telling him of the Dover project.

Mark's frown disappeared...mostly. "Since I just live down the street—"

"You live on the same street?" Claire winced at her father's strident voice. He turned to her. "What else haven't you told us, Claire?"

"I..."

Wallace jumped from the back of the wagon, and the opportunity for a response passed. Her brother smiled at Mark. "I haven't seen you at the store lately. I trust your mother is well. Is she enjoying the hat she bought?"

Mark and Claire exchanged a glance, then he said, "I'm afraid she didn't find anything that day."

"What a shame. Send her back to Newland's. Claire will suggest something new she won't pass up. Won't you, Claire?"

Her father grabbed the leather handle on one end of her trunk. It scraped along the wood of the wagon box as he pulled it toward the edge. "Wallace, take the other end."

"I'll help you, sir."

"We'll manage, Mr. Gregory." Pa took a step, then in a more conciliatory tone, he said, "Thank you, though."

Wallace's confused glance brushed Claire before he did as he'd been told. Together, *family* carried the trunk to the porch.

Mark reached over the side of the wagon and lifted a box—the one with her rolled house plan standing up in a corner. "I assume I made a poor impression on your father the other day."

"He's upset with both of us." Claire tugged at the leather suitcase holding her undergarments and lugged it up the front walk. "I do appreciate your discretion that night. I also appreciate your help today, but you have the Lefler building to finish."

"I've worked all day and can use the distraction. I'll finish tonight."

The screen door screeched when Roslyn opened it. She moved aside to let everyone enter, then shut the door. "I haven't had such a crowd in my home in months."

"I hope you don't mind."

"Not at all, Claire. I enjoy meeting new people." After introductions, Roslyn leaned closer and whispered, "You didn't tell me my neighbor was so attractive."

A grunt from her father reminded Claire that he and Wallace still carried the trunk. "Would you mind if they took my things upstairs? The trunk is heavy."

"You know the way."

Mark laid the box down in the small entry and turned back to the front door. "While they do that, I'll bring in what I can."

A good man, a competent architect, and sensitive to her father's wish to protect her.

Then again, his reluctance to go upstairs probably boiled down to self-preservation over her father's reaction to him entering her bedroom.

Upstairs, she set the suitcase down and opened the door off the hallway that led to the room Roslyn had shown her at the beginning of the week. She stood aside to let the men by.

Once they placed the trunk against the wall, Wallace spun in a circle, taking in a space slightly smaller than her room at home...at her parents' home. He whistled. "Nice."

"It is, isn't it?"

Feminine wallpaper with tiny rosebuds and interlocking vines filled the bedroom from corner to corner. A painting of women strolling through a restful garden engendered a sense of serenity, and sheer and ruffled white curtains let sunlight in to brighten the room.

Wallace strode toward the door. "I'll bring up the rest of your things."

He left and Claire faced her father. "I'll enjoy it here."

"I believe you will, Clairie." Her father crossed his arms. "I can't say I'm comfortable with your Mr. Gregory living close by and coming around."

"He's not my Mr. Gregory, Pa, and he won't be 'coming around' as you say." Probably not. Maybe not. And if he did? "Why are you uncomfortable with Mark?"

She would add that he was nothing more than a friend, but honestly, she didn't know how to describe him anymore. Did a friend volunteer his labor for a woman and child he didn't know solely for Claire's sake? Would a friend declare his arms open anytime she felt the urge to feel them around her? Would a friend kiss her as he had at the baseball park?

He tweaked her chin. "Because I'm your father. No matter your age, it's natural for me to distrust any man who would give of his time to help you move from our house to a place of your own." The side of his mouth cocked up, letting her know he teased her...a little. "Are you sure you can trust him, Clairie?"

"He's a gentleman, Pa."

"Then it's settled." He turned and left the room.

She exhaled a pent-up breath and descended the stairs. Halfway to the first floor, she overheard Wallace say, "It is uncommon. I suppose it's something that might grow on a person."

Claire stepped into the entry hall. Wallace and Mark stood with their heads bent over a large sheet of blue paper her brother had unrolled—a sheet of blue paper that belonged to her.

Mark glanced over his shoulder at her, guilt written on his face and in the awkward step he took away from her brother. Or did he step away from her?

She had given him an opportunity to view the plan and supply his opinion. Why should she let him peek now? Why should she let him critique something she cherished and he rejected?

Claire held out her hand. "That is mine, Wallace."

He grinned. "You've never shown me this plan. It's different."

"So you said." She focused on Mark. "I just assured my father you were trustworthy."

Wallace glanced from her to Mark and back again. "He is trustworthy, Claire. I'm the one who took your plan from the box and asked him to look at it. If you want to blame someone, blame me."

She snatched the plan from her brother and rolled it up. Anger burned inside her. Both men had invaded her privacy and her...her past...without permission. "Next time, please ask me first."

"Sorry, sis." Wallace moved to the door. "There's more in the wagon to be brought inside."

When he'd gone, leaving her alone with Mark, her strained smile was little more than a tick in her cheek. She gripped the plan tighter. The two of them eyed one another. She looked away first.

"You were hard on him."

Claire had been hard on them both. She had overreacted to the curiosity of her brother with a temper tantrum. She knew it. All three of them knew it. "This plan means a lot to me."

"Is that why you're holding on to it as if it were a rare antiquity?" His voice softened. "Are you afraid to let go of your life with Richard?"

A lump the size of a baseball clogged her throat. She loosened her grip on the roll and jammed it back into the box. "I'll take these things to my room and get them out of Roslyn's way."

In her new bedroom, she set the box on the floor and pulled the plan out, ready to drop it in the bottom drawer of her bureau. Until she realized the bureau hadn't been brought upstairs yet.

MARK RAN HIS HANDS through his hair, tugging on it, pain searing his scalp. If fury had a name, no doubt it would be Claire

Kingsley. If he hadn't listened to Paulina and, instead, stayed home where he belonged...

So far, he'd been quite the little helper today.

Mr. Pittman treated him with a cold shoulder, and Claire accused him of being untrustworthy.

Why did Claire consider the plan so private that anyone who laid eyes on it earned her wrath? From his short perusal of the design, he'd found it remarkable and had to admit—though grudgingly—to the skill of Richard Kingsley.

With the urge to escape the house, he marched outside and down the front path to the street where Mr. Pittman pushed and pulled a bureau over the bed of the wagon.

"Let me help you, sir." Mark didn't wait to be told that his assistance wasn't necessary. He grabbed one end and lifted the piece of furniture.

Claire's father jumped to the street. With a quick glance at Mark, he bobbed his head and lifted the other end. Together, they carried the heavy bureau to the porch.

Mark turned to climb the three stairs backward, allowing Mr. Pittman to walk forward. The man said, "I'll do it. You just keep your end up, Mr. Gregory."

Though it was against his better judgment to let Claire's father take the less safe lead, Mark yielded rather than initiate more ill will. As her father reached the top, Mark's foot hit the second step. The noisy hinges of the screen door shrieked.

"Clairie, watch where—" Her father hadn't finished his warning before he lurched toward Mark.

The bureau slammed into Mark's chest, knocking him off balance. His breath whooshed out and his feet peddled backward off the second step, skimmed the first, and flew out from beneath him. By instinct, he pushed the bureau sideways and hit the ground on his back. His head smacked the dirt path. Pain shot through his back, and he fought for air.

The bureau lay at his right, covering his fingers.

"Lord, please, no." Claire's prayer penetrated the fog of Mark's pain and disbelief. Footsteps pounded down the wood of the porch steps. She fell to her knees beside him. "I'm so sorry, Mark. I wasn't watching where I was going and didn't realize you and my father were there."

"Clairie! You can explain later." Her father shifted the bureau and bent over Mark, furrows between his eyes. "Are you all right? Can you move, Mr. Gregory?"

Could he move? He drew in a shallow breath, and gingerly wiggled the toes on one foot. Fine. He wiggled the toes on the other one. A twinge of discomfort but so far, so good. He was grateful for having had the sense to shove away the heavy piece of furniture before it crushed his chest.

He raised his aching head, then his shoulders. The world spun, and his lunch threatened to reappear. Moisture beaded on his forehead and above his upper lip. "I..."

When his stomach settled, he tried to rise to his elbows. The fingers of his left hand dug into the dirt that worked its way under his nails. His right hand was useless.

"Ahh..." Pain roared through his lower back.

With progress fit for a race with a snail, he eased down once more, until he reached a prone position on the ground, panting as though he'd run a mile.

As he lay sprawled on the ground, the three Pittmans gathered around, staring as if they waited for him to either get up and dance or shut his eyes in death. The young Mrs. Malone hugged the porch post.

"I'll go for the doctor." Wallace straightened, then sprinted away.

"Stay still, Mark." Claire laid a gentle hand on his shoulder.

He focused on her face and blinked, clearing his vision. She'd lost all color. Her trembling fingers smoothed the hair from his eyes, and she whispered, "I am so sorry."

While he basked in the lightness of her touch, he wanted to reassure her. "It will be all right."

Mr. Pittman's expression had softened toward him. "Where does it hurt, son?"

*Son.* In his vulnerable state, Mark fought against the emotion that rose from the memory of the last man who referred to him in that way. "It's mostly in my back, sir. If I remain still, it isn't bad."

"But when you move..."

"When I move, my muscles spasm."

At least, he could move. People suffered paralyzing accidents every day. The idea of it struck Mark with a terror he hadn't known since he was eleven years old and fell over that balcony to land on his father. Out of habit, his damaged fingers reached out for the arm that had broken with the fall that day.

Mark's father hadn't been paralyzed in the accident, but he'd suffered with his back and other ailments the rest of his short life. Would Mark suffer incapacitating pain from now on? Would his life be cut short?

Wallace returned a few minutes later, accompanied by a doctor. After introducing himself as Dr. Jamison, he knelt beside Mark and began his examination, right there in Mrs. Malone's front yard, in full view of the neighbors. Right there, where Claire could witness his childish moans and groans. The word "mortified" didn't do him justice.

The middle-aged physician leaned back on his heels. "You've broken a couple of fingers, young man. Otherwise, I'm confident you only strained the muscles in your lower back. You'll be in pain for a time, I'm afraid. But with a few days of bed rest the inflammation will disappear, and you'll eventually recover fully. Consider yourself fortunate."

Fortunate? How nice to know he wasn't doomed to a lifetime of confinement to his bed. "A few days?"

"A week at a minimum." Dr. Jamison smiled down at Mark as though he hadn't just pronounced a death sentence on his patient's career.

A week. Seven days. He couldn't stay in bed that long. He had too much work to do. His chest froze. *Lefler's design.*

Yesterday, he had received a letter that the deadline had been moved up to Monday, the twenty-eighth—two days before the original deadline. The change was minimal, but under these circumstances, that was two days Mark needed to heal.

His entry was almost complete, but not quite. How could he complete it with broken fingers? Even if he managed it, with his back in agony, how was he to travel to Chicago next week to deliver it? He'd already bought his ticket for the Wednesday train.

"I must be up and on my feet in four days. It's important." He tried to rise but the fist of pain knocked him down a second time.

If the ache didn't keep him still, Claire made sure he didn't move. "Mark, you need time to heal."

"You don't understand. At this point, everything hinges on the competition." His business future. His ability to make the payment on the bank loan. Even his relationship with the woman pinning his shoulders to the ground. It all hinged on winning the right to move to the next round of the competition and, eventually, designing Lefler's building.

If he had known an hour ago that he would soon lie on his back in a neighbor's yard, sentenced to a week of bed rest, he would never have ventured from his house.

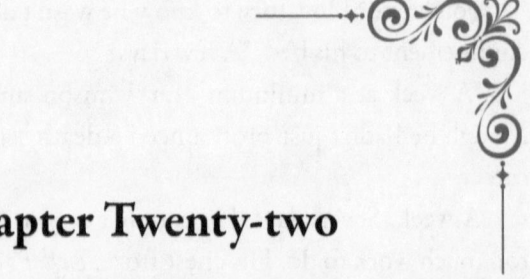

# Chapter Twenty-two

Claire knocked on Mark's front door and braced herself for Mrs. Grzegorczyk's reaction. The woman had burst into tears upon seeing her son carted home in such agony yesterday. Claire had fought hard against joining her but saved her weeping for the privacy of her bedroom.

Weeping over the pain she'd caused Mark. Weeping over the future she'd cost Richard. Weeping over her failure to enrich the lives of those she loved, rather than damage them.

Weeping. Weeping. Weeping.

When the door opened, Mark's mother stood on the other side. Dark circles shaded her eyes. The gloom added to Claire's guilt.

"Good evening, Mrs. Grzegorczyk. How is Mark today?"

"He is in the bed where he belongs."

Where Claire put him.

"He asked to speak with you should you pay a call on him, Mrs. Kingsley." She moved aside, stopping short of outright asking Claire into the house.

Claire stepped into the front hall. Cookie trotted into the area to greet her, nails clicking on the floor. Three balls of fur bounced along behind their mother, their high-pitched puppy yips adding a bright note to the somber visit. "They've grown."

"They fill my heart with joy as much as they test my patience."

The statement reminded Claire of why she couldn't dislike this woman who disliked her.

Mrs. Grzegorczyk led the way upstairs, leaving the dogs to wander back toward the kitchen. She knocked on the second door down the hall. "Marek, Mrs. Kingsley is here."

There was a pause, then he called out, "Send her in."

His mother aimed a firm stare at Claire. "Do not stay long. He must rest."

"No, ma'am. I won't."

Mrs. Grzegorczyk opened the door, allowed Claire to pass, then swung the door wide until it tapped the inside wall of the bedroom. She moved a chair brought up from the dining room, setting it several feet away from the side of the bed.

Propped up and supported by pillows, Mark eased the covers almost to his neck, exposing little more than his nightshirt-clad arms and beard-shadowed face dotted with perspiration. Claire wanted to tell him his modesty was not mandatory when the temperature outside neared ninety, and the air in the room was stifling. Not wishing to rile his mother, she said nothing.

She scanned the bedroom with its walnut furniture and dark drapes. Sparse. Masculine. In the corner on the other side of the room stood a drawing board. Next to it various tools of the architect's trade were scattered on the top of a small table.

"Have a seat, Claire." Mark had tamed his hair on one side, as though he'd run the fingers of his good hand through that side and left the other one wild. His shadowed eyes matched his mother's, a testament to his discomfort and inability to sleep well.

Once Claire was seated at a proper distance from her son, Mrs. Grzegorczyk retreated from the room, leaving the door open. Claire half-expected the woman to stand in the hall, acting as a moral guardian.

"How do you feel?"

"As long as I remain still, I'm fine."

And if he didn't, the pain was excruciating? "I can't tell you how sorry—"

"Claire, it was an accident." He cocked his head. "It *was* an accident, wasn't it?"

"I'd never..." At that teasing glint in his eyes, she frowned. "I'm happy to see your sense of humor suffered no permanent harm when you tripped over those big feet of yours."

His laughter boomed in the small room, quaking his shoulders and back, causing him to wince. Claire grimaced with the weight of his pain. "I'm so sor—"

"Don't say it." Mark raised his hand, exposing the bandage wrapped around the index and middle fingers he'd broken. Splints extended past each fingertip.

"Where is the sling the doctor prescribed?"

"It's only two fingers, not a wrist, and the sling is uncomfortable. In a few days, I'll be moving around as normal."

His stubbornness reminded Claire of his declaration that he controlled his own life, his own fate. "Your mother said you wanted to see me."

"I was worried about you."

"Me? I'm not the one in pain."

Concern branded his steady gaze. "Don't blame yourself for what happened."

How could she not? If she'd attended to her surroundings instead of focusing on her anger, Mark would not be lying in his bed, trying to make her feel better.

Richard wouldn't be lying in a grave next to their babies.

"Is there anything I can do for you?"

His wry laughter echoed through her. "Not unless you want to deliver the Lefler design to his agent in Chicago on Wednesday."

"The design isn't due for another ten days. You should be well enough by then to deliver it yourself."

"I wish that were the case, but I received notification that Lefler will be leaving the country at the end of July, so the deadline for the first round has been moved up by two days."

It was crucial to get the design into the hands of Mr. Arbuckle on time, but deliver his entry to Chicago herself?

Since she was responsible for the setback that faced Mark, she owed him. "I'll be happy to deliver it for you."

His eyes enlarged, then dipped into a glower aimed at her. "No. I was teasing you. I didn't mean—"

"I'm capable of finding my way around the city."

The lines between Mark's eyes deepened. "It isn't finding your way around that I worry about, Claire, and you know it. You can't go alone."

"Why not?" She grinned to hide her unease. "I'll carry a baseball bat. I'm quite good at hitting what comes at me, you know."

His shoulders shook. "Don't make me laugh at that mental image, or I'll be in this bed for a month."

"Mark—"

"Suggesting you deliver the plan to Lefler wasn't a serious statement, Claire."

"Let me do this for you. If I were a man, you wouldn't think twice about asking me."

His lips twitched. "If you were a man, I'd be very disappointed."

She ignored the way the statement sent a series of pleasant goosebumps skittering up her arms. "You have no choice, Mark. Even if your back could stand hours in a train car, you can't hobble into Mr. Arbuckle's office and let him see you as anything but healthy and ready to work."

Silence met her common sense, but in his expression, she saw a brief spark of hope, a flash of possibility before it flickered and vanished.

"I can't do it. I can't ask it of you."

"You're not asking. I'm insisting."

"Claire, you're an intelligent and informed designer who would have the answers to any questions asked."

Giddiness bubbled up. He trusted her skill. "Then what is the problem?"

"I won't allow you to walk Chicago's streets alone for my sake. If something happened to you, I'd never forgive myself."

"I'll ask Wallace to go with me." She groaned. "No, he can't. Mr. Newland will be out of town the first few days of this week, meeting with his partner in the new five-and-dime stores. He's requested that Wallace see him when he returns to the store." She smiled. "I believe he's going to promote my brother to a position as a department manager."

"That's great news for him."

But not so wonderful when it came to the problem at hand—finding a chaperone for Claire's trip to Chicago.

"Don't you give up. We'll work it out."

"That's not the only problem." He touched the bandage on his hand. "I'm right-handed."

"I know."

He stared at the chenille-covered bed. "The design is complete but not the rendering for presentation."

Claire eyed his broken fingers and realized what he meant. She almost choked on the solution.

First, it was the Dover design, then the guesthouse. Mark had no idea what he was asking of her this time. Placing another important design in her hands was little different than offering opium to an addict.

*A single project. I accepted one project to defend Richard's memory. Why are you tempting me with more, Lord?*

Mark waited for her response, that searing gaze once more trained on her. Could he not see her desperation?

"YOU WANT ME TO PREPARE the rendering."

Mark hated hearing that anxiety in Claire's voice. He didn't understand its cause, especially after witnessing her talent over the past weeks. "I'll guide you."

She crushed one hand with the other. Maybe she thought that, if she broke her fingers as well, he wouldn't ask this of her and would be forced to find someone else.

It hadn't been in his mind to turn the project and its delivery over to Claire, but there was no one else, was there? Not in Riverport.

Even while Mark despised the idea of sending any woman, much less Claire, off to a city teeming with people—some of whom slithered through the streets like snakes—she had raised his optimism with her offer to take the design to Chicago.

He had said he didn't blame her for the accident, and he didn't. But she had the ability to change the course of his future. He couldn't let whatever drove her fear drive his downfall. The plan made sense...if he found a chaperone for the trip.

"You can do this, Claire. Just as I knew you could deliver Cookie's puppy, I know you have the skill to create a rendering."

"It's been over two years since I've done one." Her voice trembled. "What if I make a mistake that costs you the commission?"

"There will be no commission without your help. And you will be paid for your work, like any other draftsman."

She drew back as if he'd slapped her. "I am not concerned about payment."

"I am. This project is more important than I can express. I would do it myself but..." He raised the arm with the broken fingers.

"That is unfair of you."

Her rebuke didn't faze him. What concerned him more was the reason for her reluctance. "I won't push you any further, but our previous discussion of delivering the entry to Chicago was pointless.

You can't deliver what doesn't exist."

She shut her eyes for a nail-biting minute. "I'll do it."

Had remorse convinced her? He hoped not. He preferred to think she recognized his desperation.

TWO DAYS LATER, MARK fidgeted in his bed. He coveted escape, even if he had to crawl on his hands and knees toward freedom, defying the medical advice and dodging the matron downstairs.

Two days spent in this prison of a bedroom. Its stagnant air and gloom had grown in proportion to the sounds of a cheerful life carried on outside the walls and windows.

If the doctor was right, there were more days of confinement to come. Every minute he stayed in this room, in this bed, was another minute closer to the day the first loan payment was due, another minute of time wasted in acquiring new clients to salvage his business, and another minute that ticked by toward the loss of his good name.

Why had he ever agreed to such stringent loan terms? A growl vibrated in his chest. He'd agreed, because calamities like his mother's illness and this injury had never occurred to him. He never doubted losing control over his success.

Complete escape might be unrealistic today, but the quicker Claire saw him even halfway back to normal, the quicker she would move past her unnecessary guilt over his injury—something she continued to apologize for.

He tested the consequence of leaning forward to sit straighter in the bed. The insignificance of the spasm in his lower back—nothing like he had experienced yesterday or Saturday—encouraged him to maneuver a leg over the edge. He waited for a sharp pain. When it didn't stab him unmercifully, he slipped the other leg over until both feet touched the floor.

No matter the throbbing, Claire would find him sitting in the chair next to the drawing board when she visited in another half hour, not lolling about in bed.

Mark paused a moment. This next part would test his mettle. He grabbed the bedstead with his good hand and pulled himself up. The muscles in his throat constricted to lock away a spontaneous groan.

"What are you doing?"

He twisted. Bad move, but he congratulated himself on not screaming like a hysterical woman. "You're early." And he stood before her clad only in his nightshirt.

Claire's lips pinched, and her eyes narrowed. It was a wonder she could see him. She crossed the floor. With the pouch containing sketches of the Lefler design trapped under her arm, she yanked off her gloves one at a time. "By the scene before me, I'd say I'm late."

"Don't mother me. I have had far more of that than I can take these past two days."

She clutched his arm. "My goodness, we are testy."

"Just hand me my dressing robe and help me to that chair." Too late, he remembered his manners. "Please."

She cast a glance around the area near the bed, her brow furrowed, before she turned her attention to the doorway. "Your mother will have my head on a pike."

"Claire."

A frustrated puff of air whooshed from between her lips. "Fine."

She helped him into his robe, then stood in front of him and smoothed the lapels, patting them for good measure afterward and resting her hands on them.

This was too much to endure.

He placed his good hand over hers, savoring the warmth of skin like velvet, the fingers gentle and delicate, yet with the underlying power to save a dog's life and pull a child from danger.

She lifted her gaze, a slow rise of long lashes to reveal soft blue depths in which to swim forever. Mark dipped his head and leaned in, defying his back to protest, positive he wouldn't feel it if it did. Not at this moment. Not when she tilted her chin to meet—

Shuffling noises, a scrape, and a cough came from the other side of Mark's bedroom wall. Claire bolted from his hold. He sighed, trying to bear in mind that it was for the best, given their surroundings.

"Is your mother moving furniture?" Her voice wavered.

"If only that were the case." His wasn't any better. "You're hearing the arrival of our boarder, Mr. Olesky."

"You brought in a boarder?"

"Not my idea." To lighten the sharp response, he asked, "Will you help me to the chair?"

It took them what seemed like a week, but Mark maneuvered onto the seat of the chair. He'd never imagined the necessity of relying on anyone else to help him in this way. He detested it. He detested giving up the control he always held to so tightly. The control Mark loathed losing for fear of the consequences. Now look at him, unable to walk without help.

His previous conversation with Claire had haunted him during the endless hours confined to his bed. She had argued that disaster awaited those who thought they controlled their lives without relying on God. He hadn't consulted with God about anything in years. Now, he found *his* plans jeopardized by a misstep.

He had claimed success was up to him because he couldn't count on God taking an interest in his life. But was God really indifferent to him, or had Claire been right in saying his life and all things in it were important to God?

Contrary to her contention at the time, he'd attributed her prayer for the puppy that almost perished to coincidence, a result of her persistent efforts. What if he were wrong? What if God breathed life into that tiny body because she believed He cared? What if He'd honored her faith? What if He simply cared for the puppy?

As a child, Mark had wanted to believe God cared about his life, that He had a better plan. That belief changed with his father's death.

Then Mark's plan became a desire to establish a well-respected name before it was too late. But what did it matter if generations to come forgot that name? What had he really accomplished of lasting value?

When it came to trusting in God's love and care, was it as simple—yet hard—as remaining faithful through all circumstances whether good or bad?

He took a moment to calm his racing heart before he pointed to the pouch. "You had no trouble finding everything?"

"It was all on the table as you said." She reached into her pocket and pulled out the key to the office he had given her.

"You keep it. What will I do with it for the next few days?" Tired of his grumpy attitude, he mumbled an apology. "You can clear the washstand and lay out the sketches for us to go over."

She placed the pitcher and basin on the floor and spread the individual papers across the surface of the washstand, then unrolled the plan across his lap. "It's a wonderful elevation, Mark. I can't imagine Lefler not being attracted to it."

"I hope you're right." Her words of affirmation helped lighten his mood.

She fingered the tools on the washstand. "What would you like me to do first?"

"As you can see, all that was asked of us in this round was to create the exterior sections of the building with examples of the detail work, a list of building materials, and an estimated cost. Everything we need is in this room. We'll put it together in a draft before preparing the rendering for presentation."

She slid a smile his way, her humor sunnier than yesterday. "We, huh?"

"Look at it as another joint project. You can start by cutting a sheet of paper thirty inches by twenty-one from that roll in the corner. We'll save the Whatman paper for the final rendering." The fine paper was too expensive to waste on a draft.

In no time, she had the paper cut and tacked to the drawing board. Except for a small break for the supper his mother brought, they spent the next two hours going over the plan and putting the sketches together to suit Mark. Every fifteen minutes or so, his mother peeked into the room to remind them of the impropriety of the two of them being in his room—alone.

But they made good progress. For the first time since his accident, Mark held out true hope that his design would reach Chicago on time.

When he caught Claire yawning, his conscience pricked him. "That's enough for now. You're tired after working all day at the store."

"Actually, I'm surprised by how invigorated I feel."

"You've done a wonderful job, and I'm grateful. There's a train out on Wednesday before noon with a return the next morning. I'm afraid you'll have to stay overnight, but I've sent a telegram to the Kowalskis to expect you."

"The Kowalskis?"

Now was the time to tell her his news, as much as he dreaded it. "I found someone to accompany you to Chicago."

As she put away the materials, she asked, "Who?"

If Mark believed in the effectiveness of such prayers, he'd kneel and beseech his Creator for protection for himself, for Claire, and for... "My mother."

She halted while placing the drawing pencil in the kit on the table. Resuming the task, her voice was little more than a mumble as she asked, "Are you sure I can't take that baseball bat, instead?"

# Chapter Twenty-three

C laire folded her nightdress and packed it in the bag on the bed, along with everything else she needed for an overnight stay in Chicago. She looked forward to seeing Paulina again, but whenever she thought of spending twenty-four hours with Mrs. G and several hours with Mrs. Kowalski, her nerves tightened like the high wire in a circus act.

Almost as tight as the moment Mark nearly kissed her again, the moment she would have let him. Again.

She must end this attraction to him, but how? She could no longer use Paulina as a shield. Now, the only armor she held between her feelings for him and an unfortunate future was the reminder that he desired children.

Roslyn stood in the doorway to Claire's bedroom. "I admire your courage."

"My courage?" Since when had she shown courage?

"From what you've told me, Mrs. Grzegorczyk won't be the most pleasant of chaperones. You're willingly walking into a lion's den and taking that lion with you to Chicago."

During a late night, cozy conversation, Claire had confessed the trepidation she felt in the presence of Mark's mother, so she couldn't fault Roslyn for her opinion of a woman she hadn't met, especially when a similar judgment had just run through her mind. "I'll assume Mark has requested she be on her best behavior."

Roslyn laughed. "If you really want to tie the woman in knots remove your ring." She dipped her head in a gesture that pointed toward Claire's hand.

Claire twisted the piece of gold in circles around her finger. "I've worn it all this time. I see no reason to remove it now." Perhaps it was ludicrous, but she equated removing Richard's ring with betrayal—almost as bad as George wiping the Kingsley name from Richard's business.

"All right, so I'm speaking out of turn, but I watched you and Mr. Gregory on Saturday and have come to the conclusion that it won't be long before I'll be looking for another roommate." Wisdom beyond her years gleamed in Roslyn's eyes. "As much as you want to remain dedicated to your marriage, don't let loyalty to someone who is gone shackle you to a lifetime of being alone."

Without saying a word, Claire slipped the lacy gloves on, covering the symbol of her marriage and hinting at her wish to end the conversation about it. She closed her suitcase, fastened the straps, and lifted it from the bed.

Roslyn returned to the doorway. "I won't say any more, but you know I'm right."

With her bag in one hand and the wrapped design with its mounted watercolor wash in the other—awkward but not heavy—Claire pasted on an artificial smile. "I'll see you tomorrow afternoon."

Roslyn followed her from the room. "Who will watch over Mr. Gregory while you and his mother are gone?"

"Fortunately, Mr. O'Keefe's father is out of danger, so he's returning to town this evening and will see to Mark's needs during the day tomorrow. Mr. Olesky will be there during the night."

"Good. I'm not one for emptying chamber pots."

Claire couldn't help herself. She laughed all the way down the stairs and to the front door. She figured it was the last laugh she would have before seeing Paulina again.

CHICAGO IMPRESSED CLAIRE more than she had imagined, even as its size intimidated her.

She held on to her hat as she tilted her head back to scrutinize the giant structures of the city from the relative safety of the sidewalk.

The traffic. The pedestrians. The noise. The variety of smells from restaurants and people and animals. She'd lived in Indianapolis for four years, yet this... It thrilled and overwhelmed her at the same time.

Mark had walked these same streets when he lived and worked in the city. If he were here today, would he find them as exhilarating as she? Or, since he'd grown up here, would he yawn at the sights around him?

At the mere thought of seeing Mark again, her heart hopped with the momentum of a fleeing rabbit, and she scolded herself for its silliness. How could she be gone less than six hours and miss him?

On State Street, Claire paused outside a four-story, brick-and-limestone building. She checked the number in black and gold on the glass transom over the door. "This is it."

"May I help you, ladies?" A tall, well-dressed gentleman stopped alongside her, his stare discomfiting Claire. It was a bit too oily for her taste.

"You may not." If there was such a thing as an evil eye, Mrs. Grzegorczyk targeted the man with its malice. "In fact, you may leave us."

After he'd found the means to close his mouth, he backstepped, tapped the brim of his bowler, and trotted down the walkway.

Claire made a show of looking behind her to check the material of her skirt.

"What are you doing?"

"You lit such a fire under the poor man, I was afraid it singed my dress."

The woman grunted. "That is why my Marek was wise to insist I chaperone you. You are too pretty for your own good."

A compliment?

Mrs. Grzegorczyk elbowed past and opened the door. "Let us get this done."

She followed Mark's mother inside the lobby. In reality, she had followed her most of the day. The woman enjoyed being in control—not so different from her son.

Over and over on the train, Mark's mother had complained about the design being in her way. Yes, it took up room where they were seated, but Claire wasn't about to let it out of her sight. Not only because she had worked for hours the past two nights to complete the final rendering, but because Mark depended on her to see that Mr. Arbuckle received it in excellent condition.

They crossed the small and unimpressive lobby with its dark walls and poor lighting. When they reached the elevator, her companion asked, "Which floor?"

"Third."

The third floor was no more impressive than the lobby—narrow and smelling of tobacco and sweat. The exception was Mr. Arbuckle's office. They opened the door to sunlit rooms, pale walls, and the strong scent of a man's cologne.

Claire gave the male secretary her name and the purpose for her visit and was asked to wait. Mrs. Grzegorczyk found a wooden chair along the wall of the front office. "I will sit here until you are finished."

A few minutes later, Claire was ushered into Mr. Arbuckle's office. The wiry man, not much taller than her and with thinning gray hair, met her halfway across the room. His spectacles did nothing to soften the hard look in his eyes. "May I help you, Mrs. Kingsley?"

"Yes, sir. I'm here to deliver a design entry for Mr. Lefler's competition. It's from Mark Gregory." She held up the thin but bulky package and prayed her hands didn't tremble. Despite his slight size, the man was as intimidating as a heavyweight boxer.

"Gregory?"

"Yes, sir. From Riverport, Indiana?"

"I recall the name now. Last minute entrant chosen by Mr. Lefler himself. Frankly, being such a new firm, I would have expected Mr. Gregory to deliver it and introduce himself."

How much should she disclose? If she said too much, might it affect Mr. Lefler's decision to choose Mark as a finalist? "That was Mr. Gregory's plan, and he sends his regrets, but it wasn't possible for him to make the trip today. Eager to have it in your hands early, he asked that I bring you the design."

Mr. Arbuckle perched against the front edge of his desk and crossed his arms. "And who are you?"

He already knew her name, so what was he really asking? "I beg your pardon?"

His nostrils flared. "I want to know your connection to Mr. Gregory, madam."

Claire risked renewing the man's ire with Mark for sending the mere help to deliver the rendering, but what was she to do? Lie? Clearly, the man was a natural sourpuss. "I'm his office clerk, sir."

His body relaxed at her answer. "Well then, let's see what you have for us."

Claire unwrapped the design and held it up for him to examine. She heard him move but couldn't see him from behind the board.

"Nice. Very nice."

Inside, she smiled. Outside, she remained impassive.

"A traditional palazzo style but softer. Good detail." He poked his head above the board, and Claire flinched with the sudden appearance of his face inches from hers. "This C. E. Kingsley listed as the renderer...a relation to you?"

Some architectural competitions were anonymous, with the submission being unmarked and the designer a mystery. This one was not, and Mark had asked that she ink her name in the lower left corner of the rendering opposite his. She argued, but he insisted. After all, it was a common practice for those hired to prepare a rendering.

"I am C. E. Kingsley."

Mr. Arbuckle's frown drew the two tarnished silver eyebrows together as one. "Exactly how much work did you put into this design, Mrs. Kingsley?"

"The design is Mr. Gregory's. I only prepared the rendering...under his direction."

Claire's arm muscles grew rigid and her fingers pinched the sides of the board she held as Mr. Arbuckle stared off into a world where she didn't exist. By his expression, ogres occupied that world.

The silence grew ever more discouraging. "Where would you like me to place this?" When he didn't answer, she propped it on the shelf of the easel and shifted the legs, cocking the easel a couple of inches to the left to give him a full view of Mark's design.

"A few years ago, I met an architect by the name of Kingsley. Good man. Heard he passed away a while back." Arbuckle turned his sharp gaze on Claire. "Mr. Lefler once considered him for a building design in Indianapolis."

Lefler had wanted to work with her husband? "Why didn't he hire him?"

"He doesn't believe decent women belong with men in the professional world. When he learned a woman worked in Mr. Kingsley's office, he changed his mind and hired someone else."

Claire felt the swallow all the way to her toes. She glanced at the rendering, fully comprehending the moral behind Mr. Arbuckle's story. Because of her, Kingsley and Brant lost an important client.

Because of her, Mark hadn't a glimmer of a chance in winning the commission for the Riverport building.

In less than a week, she had cost Mark unnecessary physical pain and valuable time lost from work. Now, she may have cost him the biggest job of his short career.

With as much polite audacity as she could muster, she said, "This is a competition for the best design, Mr. Arbuckle, not an indictment on the prejudices of our society. Mr. Gregory's entry deserves a fair appraisal."

"I'm afraid that's not for me to decide."

"Then you're saying everything he has done to present Mr. Lefler with a stunning option for his building has been a complete waste of time?"

"Not complete. I would suggest you urge him to find a more...suitable client."

"With all due respect, Mr. Arbuckle, I am his four-hour-per-week office clerk. Are you telling me that no firm submitting a design has a woman in any position in the company?"

"No firm but Mr. Gregory's. Are *you* telling *me* your only responsibility is as his clerk?" He gestured to the rendering.

Unable to deny the evidence, Claire searched for a deeper argument, but she'd long known that when a man's bias took over his way of thinking, there was little to be done about it. She carried the rendering with her to the door.

"If it helps, Mrs. Kingsley, I do believe your employer shows considerable talent."

Claire glanced over her shoulder. "I will be sure to tell Mr. Gregory you approve of his work, Mr. Arbuckle, before I add that Mr. Lefler won't even give him the courtesy of considering it. Thank you for your time."

His shoulders rose and fell. For a moment, she thought he might change his mind and ask her to return the design to the easel. "My next appointment is due. If you'll be so kind as to tell my secretary that I'm ready."

Claire chomped on her tongue to keep from saying he should tell the man himself. The architectural community was small. She wouldn't risk doing more damage to Mark than she'd already done. "Yes, sir."

"Thank you, Mrs. Kingsley."

In leaving Mr. Arbuckle's office, Claire concentrated on the swish of her skirt as she walked, the paintings on the hallway walls, something—anything—other than the tears gathered along the bottom rims of her eyes.

She had shattered one man's dreams. How was she to tell Mark she had also shattered his?

# Chapter Twenty-four

After hugging Paulina, Claire thanked Mrs. Kowalski for her hospitality, and climbed into the streetcar that would take Mrs. Grzegorczyk and her to Union Depot for the return trip to Riverport. She still hadn't found the words for telling Mark about her conversation with Mr. Arbuckle.

Mark hadn't said as much, but she had access to his books, so with that knowledge and his near panic over getting the design in on time, she suspected he had counted on the money from the competition, even if it was only a stipend from having passed the initial round. While he had accumulated a modest amount of business for someone so new to the area, each project he lost had an impact on his account, not to mention the impact on his reputation and confidence.

They boarded a streetcar. Mark's mother slid across a seat to sit near the window. Claire sat next to her, the design that shouldn't be there propped against her legs.

Even with people standing in the aisle, she could see the city through the open sides as they snaked through the flood of traffic that never thinned—pedestrians, carriages, bicycles. It was no less hectic when the driver turned onto Canal Street.

The conveyance stopped in front of the central entrance of the three-story Union Depot. Opened over fifteen years ago, it was still a beautiful building.

On their arrival in the city yesterday, Claire had appreciated its exterior of cut stone and red brick. Looking at it now only reminded her that in hours her train would pull into Riverport's station and she'd be forced to confess to Mark how she had failed him.

She helped Mrs. Grzegorczyk with her bag and the two of them passed under the iron-roofed covering out front, walked through the entrance doors, and crossed the expansive floor to the grand staircase that would take them down to the tracks and their train.

They occupied a portion of a bench in the waiting room until called to board. Neither of them had said much from the moment they left the Kowalski family.

Claire had attempted to act normally when around Paulina and her family last night, and thankfully, no one appeared to notice anything wrong with her. In fact, the whole visit was a strain. Paulina, preoccupied, shot odd looks at her mother, father, and Mrs. Grzegorczyk. Then Paulina confessed to Claire that she suspected something strange was going on and worried that it involved her relationship with Frederick.

After that discouraging news, Claire couldn't bring herself to speak of her conversation with Mr. Arbuckle and seek her friend's advice. Instead, she painted a pretty picture of her day and worked to distract Paulina with news about her puppy, Bella, and life with Roslyn.

Claire's experience yesterday contributed to her reticence this morning. What was Mrs. Grzegorczyk's excuse? Paulina had been right to be suspicious. Mark's mother and Mrs. Kowalski had both been quieter than normal.

They found a seat in the center of the train car and settled in for the ride home. The wheels began a slow roll and the car jerked as they pulled away from the station. Looking out the left-side windows, Claire kept her gaze on Lake Michigan, so vast she was unable to spot a far shore. As vast as the chasm that would grow between her and Mark when she related to him the result of her trip.

Once they had reached open land, Claire said, "Thank you for accompanying me, Mrs. Grzegorczyk. I wasn't eager to travel alone."

"What will you tell Marek?"

After leaving Mr. Arbuckle's office yesterday, Claire had given Mark's mother a brief account of the meeting. Mrs. Grzegorczyk had said little. Now the astonishing compassion in her voice burst the dam that had held back a flood of Claire's words. "I don't know, but I would like to be the one to tell him that Mr. Lefler refuses to work with a firm that employs a woman." She shook her head. "I can't believe that Mark's design, this trip, turned into so much wasted time and expense, all because of me."

She waited for the condemnation she expected from Mark's mother. The silence lasted a full half minute with life going on as usual around them. The crinkle of a newspaper read by the man in the seat in front of them. Two children fighting over who received the biggest piece of cheese given out by their mother. The piercing laughter of a young woman that caused heads to turn toward the rear of the car.

"Did you know of the man's prejudice from the time you began working in my son's office?"

"If I had, I would never have agreed to it." Claire raised her chin. "I do know one thing I'll tell Mark. I'll tell him I'll no longer work for him. He can inform Mr. Arbuckle and perhaps save his chance at submitting the design for the competition."

"Now you talk nonsense."

"It isn't nonsense if it helps him gain an important commission. I don't know what I was thinking." Claire exhaled a sigh. She had learned two years ago that she wasn't meant to be an architect. What made her think that lesson no longer applied simply because a nice gentleman urged her to be a pioneer?

Mrs. Grzegorczyk's lips drew inward, as though she denied them the opportunity to answer. Then she said, "I received some disturbing news last night myself."

"I'm sorry." Claire waited for her to continue. When the woman turned toward the window and stared out at the passing landscape without saying anything further, Claire leaned against the seat back and watched the scenery out the window across the aisle. Farmhouses, barns, and other outbuildings sat on patches of land like islands surrounded by seas of corn and soybeans. After a while, it all looked the same.

The two of them rode for miles, each in her own world, while around them, people spoke quietly. Some laughed. A baby cried. Men read newspapers. Women did needlework.

"Nadia told me her husband is dying."

Claire jolted upright in the seat. The words were spoken with such a hush, she wondered if she'd dreamed them. "Did you say Mr. Kowalski is dying?"

"Yes. Cancer."

"Paulina never mentioned anything to me about it."

"They did not learn of it until yesterday morning before we arrived. Paulina believes it is nothing more than stomach trouble."

"They haven't told her?"

"They chose to wait until we left."

Poor Paulina. No wonder she'd felt tension between her parents. "Has the doctor given them any hope?"

"None."

Claire grasped the woman's hand and sent a silent intercession heavenward for the whole family, including Mark's mother. Mrs. Grzegorczyk either sensed the prayer or needed the comfort of another's touch. Whichever, she squeezed Claire's hand and didn't let go until they reached Riverport.

MARK GINGERLY SHIFTED his weight in the parlor armchair.

He had awakened this morning to discover he could move without the throbbing ache in his back, so he'd asked Mr. Olesky to help him downstairs. The man had obliged. In fact, he'd been quite obliging since moving into the empty bedroom on Monday.

What Mark didn't understand was hearing footsteps traipse down the stairs about ten o'clock last night, and then what he thought was the door off the mudroom closing. Since the man occupied a room in his home, not a cell in a prison, Mark hadn't questioned him about it this morning.

Frankly, his mind was on Claire's return today. And his mother's.

Although he had hoped to meet them at the station, Mark soon discovered he wasn't well enough for the trip. Most likely, he would be tomorrow, but they weren't arriving home tomorrow. He couldn't afford to reinjure himself with so much work to catch up on. His dry chuckle echoed his frustration. What work could he do until his fingers healed?

Mark tapped his unbroken fingers on the chair arm and gazed at the clock as if he could will the time to go faster until the ladies arrived.

Anytime now.

A few minutes later, the front door opened and shut again. Footsteps plodded across the floor.

"Mama?"

She stopped at the door to the parlor. "What are you doing out of bed, Marek?"

With tentative movements, he rose from the chair. "I'm much better, but forgive me for not meeting you at the station. Claire didn't come in with you?"

"I'm here."

She walked around his mother, a breath of fresh air to his senses. Nevertheless, something appeared to weigh on her shoulders, crushing any pleasure at being home. Had it been a mistake to send his mother with her? Had they argued?

Cookie trotted into the front hall, trailed by three frisky pups that grew larger each day. They yipped and bounced around the women.

Mama glanced at Claire, then him. Her countenance drooped with sadness. "I will take my things upstairs."

She ignored the dog begging for the stroke of her hand, a snub that set warning bells ringing in Mark's brain. Claire's concerned gaze followed his mother. He was wrong in thinking they hadn't gotten along on the trip.

"What's wrong with my mother?"

Claire set her bag on the floor. "She'll explain later."

Until he sent her back to Chicago—to her friends—Mama had shown signs of feeling a little more comfortable with life in Riverport. Had the return, even for twenty-four hours, wiped out the progress she had achieved in accepting her new home?

Mark ignored the slight ache in his back and crossed the room. "How is it possible that I missed you so much after only a day?" He peered over her shoulder to be sure they were alone.

"Mark—"

"May I kiss you?"

Distress poured from her like rainwater off a roof. His gaze dropped to her right hand and the wrapped package he'd failed to notice. It looked suspiciously like the one she'd carried to Chicago. His stomach sank, along with his good humor. "I see Mama's not the only one who has something to explain."

"Mark, I tried. Please believe me, I—"

"Calm down, Claire." He rested his good palm against the side of her face and rubbed his thumb across her cheekbone in an effort to soothe both of them. "Calm down and tell me what happened."

She closed her eyes a moment, then reopened them. "He wouldn't accept it."

His hand fell. "The rendering? Why not? I followed all the specifications, all the rules of the competition. You delivered it in plenty of time. What was Arbuckle's excuse in rejecting it?" The more he talked, the more his voice rose, so he stopped and took his own advice with a relaxing breath. "Come over to the sofa and tell me why you weren't able to leave our entry with him."

She stuck to his side, helping him to the chair. He didn't argue. The sooner they were seated, the sooner she could relay the story. After he'd eased into the armchair, she sat on the sofa across from him, the rendering propped against the back of the seat.

She shook her head. "That was the problem, Mark. Mr. Arbuckle saw it as *our* entry."

"And?"

Claire sprang from the sofa before the upholstery had a chance to warm. The brisk movement knocked over the design. She paced in front of the furniture with her hands folded into fists at her side. "Lefler may be a successful businessman, but he's also a narrow-minded nincompoop!"

A nincompoop? Had she met the man and he insulted her? Mark almost sprang from his seat but stopped himself in time. "What did he say to you?"

"Lefler? I didn't meet him."

"For heaven's sake, you called him a narrow-minded nincompoop. He must have insulted you somehow."

"His insult came through his representative." She shook her finger at him. "But I assure you, if I had met him, I would have given that man a piece of my mind."

This was getting them no closer to the reason for her anger. Another minute of not knowing why she returned with the design instead of leaving it in Chicago might drive him to say something he'd regret. "Claire, will you please just tell me what happened?"

She slapped a hand against her chest, her features twisted with misery. "Me. I happened." The anger seeped from her. "Mr. Arbuckle asked about the name associated with the rendering. I told him I'd done it but assured him it was your design. He informed me that my husband was once denied the opportunity to work with Mr. Lefler because the man would never consider working with a firm that hired women."

"What?" The cruelty of the man to be so blunt!

Mark pushed up from the chair, trying to control the wince that narrowed his eyes. "Did you tell him why you did the work?"

"Well, I..." Her countenance sagged. "No. I was afraid it would be another black mark against you. That it would give him the impression you weren't in a condition to follow through with the next phase of the design."

"Claire, I'll be healthy by the time the next stage of the competition begins."

"I don't think it would have mattered. He knew I did the rendering. He knew I worked with Richard. There wasn't much I could say."

It wasn't her fault. *It wasn't her fault.* "You did your best, and I'm grateful."

"Mr. Arbuckle did ask me to tell you he liked your design. I think his words were 'Very nice.' In fact, I think he liked it more than a little bit."

Encouraging, but that didn't help him right now.

"I'll stop by the office after my shift at the store tomorrow, gather whatever you need, along with any mail, and bring it to you. That will be my last task as an employee of Mark Gregory Architect."

Mark blinked several times as if his eyes were responsible for hearing her words. "You're quitting? Claire—"

"It's for the best."

"Don't be rash. Lefler isn't the only client in the world."

"It's not a rash decision. I've thought of little else since meeting with Mr. Arbuckle yesterday."

"Claire, I need you."

Her lower lip trembled. "I won't destroy another man. It's enough to live with having killed Richard."

# Chapter Twenty-five

Mark struggled to steady his breathing. What Claire admitted—blurting out that her husband died because of her—knocked the wind from him.

She resumed pacing back and forth in front of him, faster this time.

"Why would you say such a thing, Claire? You told me Richard drowned."

The pacing stopped and she stared at him, her eyes overflowing. "He did."

"Then tell me what happened. I need to understand."

"I've never told anyone but my family."

Mark handed her a handkerchief. There was an explanation and he must hear it. Now.

She wiped the tears away, then began to talk about an anniversary celebration with a picnic at the river. "We'd had a lovely time until"—she shrugged—"until I ruined everything."

Like prey paralyzed by a cobra, he couldn't look away, couldn't move, so he waited for her to gather herself and continue.

"Numerous times, I'd asked Richard why George wouldn't recognize my work in the office. Why he refused to increase my role or even admit it before colleagues and clients. I asked why he'd taught me so much only to refuse me the opportunity to show others what I'd learned.

"Richard wasn't one to lose his temper easily, but when I asked again that day, he shouted at me. We'd been over and over the situation, he said, and I should be grateful George tolerated me in the office at all. We carried on a lengthy argument that ended with him apologizing. Still angry, I couldn't find the words to respond in kind. A few minutes later, he said he was too warm, and a swim would cool him off. He invited me to join him, but I was hurt because he refused to stand up to George on my account.

"I pulled out my sketch pad and lost myself in drawing interior pieces for a new project. I wanted to try once more to impress both men with my work. Putting the images in my head down on paper calmed me, but eventually, I realized that Richard had never returned. I went to find him."

When Claire pressed her eyes shut and her lips trembled, Mark forced himself to keep from reaching for her.

Her fingers curled into a fist and her eyes closed. "Richard was nowhere to be found. I knew he wouldn't just leave me, so I dove into the water. By the time I located him, it was too late."

"Claire—"

"My selfishness and anger led me to pay more attention to my sketch than to my dying husband." Finally, she opened her eyes. Her voice shook. "I could have saved him, Mark. He wouldn't have died with no one to realize the trouble he was in. He wouldn't have died with my anger standing between us. If I'd been less concerned about myself, my husband would be alive today."

"We all lose our tempers at times. We all become distracted by our own interests. You did nothing wrong, Claire."

"Going against the constraints of society cost my husband his life and you an important client."

Mark stepped closer and cupped her cheek—warm and soft and wet on his palm. "I remember a day not long ago when you answered the request to meet with Mr. Dover. You suspected his purpose but went because that goal to be an architect still called to you. Do you remember what happened on the way to his office?"

She whispered, "I saw Cissy playing in the street."

"No. You pulled Cissy from the street. You kept her from harm when her mother had other things on her mind. Because you followed your heart—your dream—you were there at the right moment to save a child from injury...or worse."

She didn't answer, so he said, "If you blame yourself for Richard's death, then I must blame myself for my father's injury and eventual death."

She shuddered. "How are the two alike?"

His thoughts reverted to the day eleven-year-old Marek Grzegorczyk had finally had enough of being picked on for his size and his name. The memory of the day his father broke up a fight between Mark and an older boy.

"I was small growing up. Others used to tease me, one boy particularly. There came a day when I fought back with my fists. My father found us and intervened. The boy, who was older and larger than me, shoved my father as he grabbed me to pull me away. We broke through the weak rail of a low fence. He landed on his back in a ditch fifteen feet below, taking me with him. I broke my arm, but my father never fully recovered from his injuries."

Claire's eyes widened. "No."

"The point is, he never blamed me or the boy I fought. He blamed the builder's design for his injury. He said if the barrier had been built higher and of better materials, if the ground had been leveled, it wouldn't have happened. I'd already chosen architecture for my future, so before he died a year later, I promised him I would design buildings that he, as a construction worker, would be proud to build."

"I'm sorry about your father, but the situation is not the same."

Before he could think of an argument, she disappeared into the front hall. A moment later, the door opened and shut. Cookie sat in the middle of the floor with her pups gathered around her. The dog eyed the entrance to the house, then turned her brown-eyed gaze to him, her cocked head asking him for an explanation.

Mark lowered his body onto the seat of the chair. His insides were tangled in knots. Somehow, he must convince Claire she was not a liability to him—professionally or personally. At the same time, he must convince himself.

He slapped the arm of the chair, then suppressed a howl from the pain that ripped through his injured hand and tore a hole through the fabric of his own dreams.

AS PROMISED, CLAIRE picked up the mail at the post office, then stopped at Mark's office to gather the account book and anything she thought he might need while he continued to recuperate.

After a full day of letting her story sink in, surely, he would realize the wisdom in her leaving his employ. She'd hardly slept a wink last night while wondering what he thought of her. How relieved he must be that she no longer worked for him.

And she hadn't told him the rest—the true reason she and Richard argued that day by the river.

Though neither man would know, Mr. Arbuckle had done Mark a favor.

Claire put the key in the lock of the office door but found it already open. She stared at the knob. Had she forgotten to lock it before leaving on Wednesday?

With a slow twist of the knob, she pushed the door open and wary steps carried her inside. Light shone from inside the drafting room. "Hello?"

"I'm back here."

Her breath hissed with relief, and she followed Mark's voice to the large back room. How had he managed to walk to the office and up a flight of stairs? Stubborn man.

He stood near a stool at the drafting easel, a fresh sheet of the costly Whatman paper tacked to the board. The case with its blocks of watercolor paints she had used to finish the rendering sat on the nearby table, brushes alongside it.

"What are you doing here, Mark? You should be resting at home."

His excited grin covered the pinched eyebrows that told her, despite standing straight, he still felt the consequences of his injury. "I've been waiting for you. I have an idea."

She set her purse and the mail on the table, his tone tensing her muscles. "What kind of idea?"

"We'll do the rendering over, and I'll take it to Arbuckle myself. We have a couple of days. It should get there in time."

"What good will that do? I told you, he won't accept it."

"He wouldn't accept it with your name on it." Mark turned away from her. "This time, leave off your name."

Claire's breath stalled. He wanted her to redo the rendering without acknowledgment? The first time he'd been adamant that she put her name on it, even when she resisted. Now her name wasn't good enough? He wouldn't support her?

"Why would you think Mr. Arbuckle would accept a new rendering when he already knows you employ a woman?"

His mouth tightened. "You quit, remember? I don't employ a woman anymore."

"Yet you want me to do the work. What is the difference?" She gripped his arm, digging her fingers into the material of his suit coat. "I'm sorry you lost the opportunity for the commission, but there will be others. Leave your future in God's hands and carry on from here."

He gazed out the window. "I won't give Him the control."

"Because you're afraid of what God will or will not do with it? Then you'll never fully live the life He wants for you."

He whipped around to face her. "And what does He want for you, Claire? Where has He led you? To widowhood. To a department store when you should be using your talent designing buildings. Where did He lead Richard? To an early grave?"

Claire gasped. As the seconds passed, she worked to control the hurt over his words and the rise of the old resentment from her time at Kingsley and Brant.

Yet, according to Mr. Arbuckle, Richard had lost an important project because of her. He'd never told her. He'd been an honorable man. She wished to say the same for Mark but couldn't. He hadn't measured up to Richard after all, and certainly not in the matter of his faith.

Mark's body sagged. "I'm trying to save my business."

"I understand, but I can't do what you're asking of me."

"Why not?"

"For one thing, it's insulting. For another, it's dishonest." She grabbed her purse from the table and walked out of the drafting room.

"Claire, come back. I'm sorry for what I said. It was thoughtless."

On the sidewalk outside the building, she paused and leaned against the brick wall to collect herself. Peering up at the turret's second-floor windows provided a bittersweet moment.

She'd thought Mark an honorable man. Apparently, she didn't know him at all.

IT WAS TOO QUIET. CLAIRE might have occupied space in the office only a few hours a week, but knowing she wouldn't return gave the place the atmosphere of a graveyard.

Mark fidgeted in the chair at the table in the drafting room. Two hours and not a line drawn on the paper in front of him. He'd tried, but who could grip a pencil with two trussed up fingers? If only he'd broken the fingers of his left hand instead. How was he to complete any of his work this way?

All he'd accomplished this morning was to stare at Claire's handwriting in the ledger. It had summoned the memory of the last time he saw her on Friday, perhaps the last time he'd ever see her.

Regret corkscrewed in his chest. He hadn't meant to say those dreadful things. He hadn't meant to shock her by dragging her husband's death into their discussion. He hadn't meant to offend her with his plan to remove her name from the rendering.

Both actions were wrong. Both demeaning and cruel. And she was right. His idea was dishonest.

Mark considered himself an intelligent man, talented, and able to run his own future, but had he ever had a worse idea?

Possibly the day he signed that paper for the loan without allowing for unforeseen events.

Then again, his worst idea probably originated with his boast to Claire and others of his ability to accomplish everything on his own. How pompous that sounded. How tired he was of shouting his own efforts with the pride of a raucous peacock.

Being trapped by his own superiority was a new experience, as if he'd designed a structure around himself—one with no door, no window, no way out.

He'd lost control.

Mark crossed the room to look out on the town he had come to think of as his home and saw something he hadn't noticed before. He'd stood at this window numerous times, ignorant of the steeple that rose above the rooftops of the businesses along Commerce, a cross at its pinnacle. Likely, he'd never noticed because he hadn't cared to notice.

Now, it was all he could see. A cross at which he could lay his troubles, his failures, his self-centered attitude, and lack of faith.

A door with a way out.

He shut his eyes and sat motionless until the words—more a nonverbal yearning—took shape within him and blossomed like the petals of a lily into his first prayer in years. He didn't even know why he bothered. He only knew that, if he didn't pray, he'd burst into a thousand tiny, miserable pieces.

*I've tried it my way, God. Now, I'm willing to try yours. I'm not asking for success or an easy way out of the mess I've created. I'm asking for forgiveness in thinking I knew best. I still don't understand why good men and women die young. Maybe I never will, but I'm asking for guidance and the growth of my faith while I'm here on this earth.*

Mark opened his eyes. The threat of shattering had gone, replaced by a subtle sense of belonging and peace the swept over him with the depth of an incoming tide. He was prepared for the necessity to guard against slipping back into old habits, but for now, he felt accepted and loved once more by a father—the Father.

# Chapter Twenty-six

When he heard the outer door of his office open, Mark left the drafting room to meet his visitor. Inside the doorway of the front office stood a medium-sized man, broad in the shoulders and wearing an expensive-looking suit.

"Good morning."

Without batting an eye or acknowledging the greeting, the man said, "I understand Mrs. Kingsley works here."

Mark's interest shot sky high. He'd come to see Claire? "May I help you with something?"

"She does work here, doesn't she?"

Bits of that recent peace started to chip off with the smugness in the man's roaming assessment of the tiny front office. Until learning who this person was and why he sought Claire, Mark owed him no information. "Is there a reason you're asking?"

"You must be"—the stranger made a show checking the name on the door—"Mark Gregory." He turned that smug appraisal into a smug smile. "My name is George Brant. I'm a friend of Claire's from Indianapolis. I was in town and thought I'd say hello."

George Brant? "Ah." According to Claire, the man was far from a friend.

"I see she's brought up my name to you. I suppose she also told you I'm competing for the Lefler building."

Mark pulled out the desk chair with a sudden eagerness to get to know his guest better. "Please, have a seat."

Before placing his well-dressed rump on the seat of the chair, Brant checked it as though looking for cookie crumbs or spilled ink. Finally, he made himself at home and placed his hat on the desk. The two of them stared at one another until Brant broke the hush in the room. "Will Claire return shortly?"

Mark leaned a shoulder against the wall and crossed his arms, ignoring the contraction in his still-healing back. "You were her late husband's partner?"

"Richard. Yes. Fine man and a good friend." The somewhat somber timbre of Brant's voice almost convinced Mark that he had cared about Claire's husband.

Brant leaned back in the chair and crossed his arms. While Mark's stance was designed to be casual, his visitor's posture was haughty. "I'm afraid the last time we spoke, I upset Claire when I talked of taking on a new partner. I believe she saw it as an attempt to erase her husband's memory."

That wasn't all she thought he'd erased. Mark answered with a droll, "Life does go on."

"I'm glad you understand." Either the man didn't recognize sarcasm when he heard it, or he didn't care.

What did Brant really hope to gain through this visit, and how would Mark explain Claire's absence?

Brant drew in a deep breath. "I was surprised to hear she had found work as an architect again."

"Why? She's a talented designer." One he had sent away in his drive to succeed. One he would fight to get back if God so deemed it.

"I should warn you that some consider her a liability."

Mark's jaw tightened. "Because people like Lefler disapprove of women working in the profession of architecture?"

Brant lost a degree of his smugness. The furrows between his eyes deepened with a hint of regret. "Your attempt to submit a design for the Riverport building failed."

"I didn't realize it was common knowledge."

"It isn't, but I've past experience with the man."

"Is that why you dismissed Claire after her husband died? You wanted work from people like Lefler?"

Brant unfolded his arms and leaned over the desktop. "Look, I'm not here to dredge up the past or rub your nose in the situation."

"Then why bring it up? Lefler isn't the only client available. I do have other projects." Claire had been right to remind him of that fact.

"We both know that working for Harris Lefler is a promising feather in any architect's cap." The chair squeaked as George Brant rose. "*If* you see Claire, please tell her I stopped in to say hello."

Halfway out the door, he paused, his expression thoughtful. "You know, Mr. Gregory, those competition rules are explicit. They call out what is and is not permissible."

Mark stared at the door Brant shut behind him. An odd ending to the conversation. The longer he pondered it, the less he understood it.

He returned to the drafting room, irritated by the man's visit. Brant may not have come here to rub his nose in his failure, but it sure felt like it. Frankly, his nose was already so deep in failure, he couldn't breathe.

If panic hadn't pushed him into a corner last week, he'd never have suggested that Claire rework the rendering and leave off her name. He was no better than Brant.

Old habits—old sins—died hard, as did regret.

Wouldn't God want him to stop wallowing in his perceived failure and trust in His best for him—whatever that meant for his future?

Mark's life was no longer in his hands. For once, he would listen to Someone else rather than act in his own power.

He gathered the plan for Charles Dover. If he couldn't draw now, he could ponder what he would draw when able.

*"You know, those competition rules are explicit."*

Explicit.

Mark marched back to the front office and dug through files on the desk for the original letter he'd received from Mr. Arbuckle. He read every word twice, looking for whatever information Brant attempted to pass along in his cryptic manner.

"Lord, help me find the answer." His grip tightened on the letter. The plea had rolled off his tongue as though it were a common occurrence, instead of one he would have rejected an hour ago.

After the third read through, it jumped out at him, revealing what Brant tried to tell him without saying it.

He sank into the chair and laughed. "Thank you, Father."

Whether or not he achieved victory in the end, no one could convince Mark that God hadn't sent Brant to him for a purpose, even if it was simply to enhance his faith.

FOR ONCE, MARK HAD not acted on his own. He hadn't taken lightly his prayer to be led in the right direction. As the Indiana scenery rolled by outside the window of the train headed northwest, he clenched the rendering under his arm.

Today was the deadline for submitting the designs. He checked his watch. If nothing interfered, he should make it with a few minutes to spare.

This might be a fool's errand, a waste of time and money. If nothing came of it, he would face the bad news with grace and not bow to the pressure of a fair-weather devotion. This time, he would give God the benefit of the doubt. What else had he to lose?

Once Mark's train reached the Chicago station, he boarded a streetcar and rode it to within a block of Mr. Arbuckle's office.

Not even three months had passed since he'd left the city for a less hectic location. At first, he had thought he'd miss the excitement, the entertainment, and the cultural advantages of the so-called Windy City. Looking around him at the traffic, inhaling the stench of a varied and immense population, and hearing the din and racket created by thousands of lives and livelihoods... It all put that notion to rest and spawned an eagerness to return to Riverport.

While not the most modern building in Chicago, Mr. Arbuckle's office was everything Mark hoped to achieve in his own space one day—a light and clean design, up-to-date functionality, and a telephone.

His foot tapped the floor as he waited to see Arbuckle. The secretary eyed him over the top of his spectacles, a wordless request for him to stop the toe music. "Sorry."

A few minutes later, a door opened and a slightly built gentleman shorter than Mark walked out. "Mr. Gregory?"

"Yes, sir."

"Come in." Arbuckle shut the office door behind Mark, then drew his watch from his waistcoat pocket. "I only have a few minutes."

"Yes, sir. I'll be brief."

Arbuckle settled into the chair behind his desk. "What happened to your hand?"

"An accident."

"Is that why I didn't see you last week?"

"Yes, sir, but I'm much better."

Arbuckle's gaze pointed to the package Mark held. "I've already told Mrs. Kingsley that Mr. Lefler will not accept the work of a woman, so I have no idea what you hope to accomplish here today."

"I'm aware of your conversation with her, sir. In fact, she returned from her meeting with you and has now left my employ because she feared doing more damage to my business in the future.

You should know, I don't approve of her decision."

"I am sorry to hear that, but Mr. Lefler has his preferences, and I am bound by them."

"Preferences are one thing, Mr. Arbuckle." Mark pulled the man's original correspondence from his pocket, unfolded the papers, and laid them on his desk. "Rules are another. Please show me where in these instructions it says that a company employing women, or a design prepared by a woman, must withdraw from Harris Lefler's competition."

Arbuckle's lips pinched as though the architect tried not to smile. "You've obviously read the rules, Mr. Gregory. Where do you see that statement?"

Mark blinked, momentarily dazed by the question. He had expected some sniveling excuse. "Nowhere, sir."

"Then what do you propose to do about it?"

Rather than argue, the man handed Mark his opportunity to plead his case. "In the interest of fairness, Mr. Arbuckle, I propose that you accept my design as an entry in the competition."

"Or?"

"I have no 'or,' sir. I didn't come here to threaten or cajole. I came to request a fair chance to submit the work I did in good faith based on the information I was given when invited to compete."

Arbuckle tented his fingers against his mouth. His stare heightened Mark's nerves. Finally, he said, "All right, Mr. Gregory, you may leave your design on that easel."

"Thank you, sir." Mark unwrapped the rendering and placed it on the easel in the corner of the room. That was easier than he'd anticipated.

"In the interest of fairness"—Arbuckle threw his words back at him—"I see your chance to move past the first round of judging as less than one percent."

Claire had mentioned that Arbuckle was impressed with his

design, so Mark assumed that one percent was due to the circumstances—the prejudicial circumstances—not the quality. Still, one percent was higher than zero percent. He would take it.

Mr. Arbuckle rose and escorted Mark to the door of his office. "Expect to be informed of Mr. Lefler's decision on or near July eighth."

"I'll look forward to hearing from you, Mr. Arbuckle."

Mark left the office, his insides doing a merry dance. And to think he owed a competitor his gratitude.

On second thought, he didn't owe Brant. God had shown an interest in Mark's life.

# Chapter Twenty-seven

"Claire, the poor dog has walked that man up and down the street for the last forty-five minutes. With each round they stop in front of the house." Roslyn dropped the parlor curtain back in place. "Why don't you put them both out of their misery?"

Claire glanced up from the book on her lap, some dull tome by a long-dead author she'd never heard of. She'd found it on a bookshelf earlier. Roslyn said it belonged to her husband and Claire was welcome to it, so she'd decided to use it to make herself sleepy. It hadn't worked. Then again, the sun still lit the sky.

She laid the book on the sofa, walked to the window, and peeked outside. Mark did look rather pathetic, but she must remain strong. She left the window before he saw her. "What would you have me do?"

Roslyn's eyebrows arched. "You could go outside and say hello."

Once she'd deliberated long and hard about how she ended things with Mark on Friday, Claire concluded that, as usual, she'd let her self-interest show in her responses to him at the baseball game and in his bedroom. Her face flared with heat over the latter.

She had no right to encourage his feelings for her. She had no right to endanger his business or lead him to believe in the possibility of a future together.

An ache began deep in the pit of her stomach, grinding and stabbing and spreading through every part of her, the burning ache of another loss and more unfulfilled dreams.

SANDRA ARDOIN

There was no satisfaction in knowing he had shown his selfishness. Although she understood the reason for his plan to remove the Kingsley name, it still hurt and implied a reluctance to stand up for her or any woman hoping to work as an architect. She could no longer abide anyone's willingness to toss away the Kingsley name—her name—in favor of pleasing someone like Harris Lefler.

At a knock on the front door, the two women exchanged a glance. The corner of Roslyn's mouth tipped up. "Well?"

"You can tell him I'm not here."

Her friend brushed past her. "I'm sorry. I can't hear you." She rushed up the stairs and disappeared, leaving Claire with her mouth open, afraid to call her back in case Mark heard her shout.

He knocked again. She stood motionless, undecided. Finally, she threw up her hands. This was silly. She was an adult, not a child refusing to play with a neighbor.

Claire opened the door and her heart's erratic beat betrayed her effort to remain indifferent to him, to send him on his way.

Mark smiled, but his eyes conveyed apprehension. "Good evening, Claire."

"Good evening, Mark."

She couldn't look at that little-boy timidity without being tempted to dash onto the porch and kiss away his reserve. To turn back time and see that self-confidence return.

The reminder that nothing had changed between them seared through her once more. It would only make things harder for him...and her.

Bending over, she held her hand out to Cookie, who nudged it until getting the head strokes she demanded. "How are you, sweetheart?"

"Not as well as I'd like to be."

Claire rolled her eyes and unbent. "I was talking to the dog."

"She's a highly empathetic animal, so my answer fits both of us."

"You don't look sick."

He laid the hand with the splinted fingers against his chest. "Sick at heart."

She tried to remain stoic, but like a spy sneaking into an enemy camp, a grin sneaked onto her face.

"Walk with me?"

"Mark—"

"Please?"

Claire glanced both ways down the street, then up at the sinking sun. The afternoon's heat had dulled, removing that excuse, and Cookie whined as if adding her plea to the request. This would be their last time together, and he must know why.

"You won't walk *me* for an hour, will you?"

Mark's face flushed. She meant the question as a joke, but his gaze lowered to the dog. "A few minutes only. I think we're both too weary for much more."

She closed the door behind her, and they strolled down the front walk to the path worn through the grass alongside the street.

They rambled past three houses in silence before Mark said, "I don't even know where to begin to apologize, Claire. You didn't deserve what I tried to do, how I tried to take advantage of you."

At the gasp behind her, Claire glanced over her shoulder at the elderly man who followed close behind them. Clearly, he had misunderstood the meaning behind Mark's apology. *Wonderful.* "It's a nice night, isn't it, Mr. Palmer?"

He toddled in between them, pushing Mark aside. "You should be safe at home, Mrs. Kingsley."

"Yes, sir, I will be as soon as Mr. Gregory and I finish our conversation."

Glaring at Mark, the elderly man addressed Claire. "Want company?"

"Thank you, but that won't be necessary." Claire leaned sideways and lowered her voice. "He's truly harmless." Most of the time.

Mr. Palmer gave Mark the once over. "You sure?"

"I'm sure, but I appreciate your concern for my welfare."

His tense expression continued to exhibit mistrust. "All right. But don't go nowhere private with him. Holler if you need me." He shook a bony finger at Mark. "You behave yourself, young man, do you hear?"

"Yes, sir."

After he toddled away, Mark arched a brow, but those amber flecks in his eyes sparkled like joyful stars, showing off the return of his self-assurance. "Harmless, am I?"

Tingles crawled up Claire's back.

He sobered. "I took the rendering to Mr. Arbuckle yesterday."

Claire's steps slowed.

"It still bears your name, and your name will stay there. I was wrong to suggest otherwise."

*Oh, Mark.* "Did he accept it from you?"

"Only after I pointed out that nothing in the rules prohibits an entry from a firm that employs women."

"I should have thought to say that."

"Why? It never occurred to me until George Brant paid a visit to the office."

Claire's knees locked. "George? What did he want?"

"To see you. We spoke for a few minutes. He presumed that I'd lost the opportunity to submit my design, and on his way out the door, he mentioned the explicitness of the competition rules."

"Odd."

"I thought so, too. So odd that I was curious and reread them." He chuckled. "Brant strikes me as a bully. I don't like bullies, and I didn't like him, but he pointed me in the right direction."

"Why would George help you?"

"I'm not sure he had a choice. Before he arrived, I had quite a talk

252

with God."

In the next few minutes, Mark spoke of his decision to rely on faith rather than himself. Claire saw a side of him she hadn't seen before, one she liked very much.

They reached the end of the block and together turned back toward Roslyn's house. Their talk had cleared the air between them regarding Friday's argument. The hard part—her part—was still to come.

He halted halfway up the path to the front door, drawing Claire to a standstill. "I'm also sorry for bringing up Richard in our discussion. It's no excuse, but I was frantic. You see, I signed for a loan to start the business, and the first payment comes due shortly."

That explained much. "The award for being a finalist would relieve the pressure?"

"Yes." He stopped and turned to her. "You're free to think me foolhardy and irresponsible for putting myself in that position in the first place."

"Few successful companies start without help. Don't they say it takes money to make money?"

"Unfortunately, it's true, but debt is not something I take lightly."

"Sometimes, it's necessary." Not wishing to bring her husband into the conversation again, she didn't tell Mark that Kingsley and Brant began in the same way.

"I've been a pride-filled fool to think I controlled my own destiny. Trusting my future to God feels peculiar, but I'll try to accept whatever comes."

"I'm happy for you, Mark." So happy she hated to ruin the mood. But it was necessary to break ties with him, to disappoint him now, rather than break his heart later.

He led her to the base of the porch. Cookie walked behind them.

She sought the words to tell him of her decision but instead said, "You didn't mention Mr. Arbuckle's reaction."

"Another strange thing. He acted amused. Not in a pompous manner, more as though I'd passed a test. I think he approved of my argument that women weren't specifically prohibited from the competition." Mark paused, then sighed. "Afterward, he informed me that I have less than a one percent chance of my design moving to the next phase."

A bubble of hope for him had expanded inside Claire. His last words burst it. "That proves I was right to stop working for you." She climbed the porch steps. "You're too talented to fail because of me."

"You believe you're responsible for my success or failure?"

"Your work is important to you, Mark. We've already seen what will happen if I'm part of it." She must stay strong. "You're meeting with Mr. Dover on Thursday. Please give him the sketches I've prepared and tell him I thank him for his faith in me."

"Be there and tell him yourself."

"I no longer work for you." She opened the front door. "We need to say goodbye."

He rushed up the steps. His wide-eyed gaze swept her face. "Goodbye? That sounds like more than an 'I quit' or 'I'll see you later.'"

"It's best if our...involvement...ends."

"It's too late to end it." He inched closer. "I love you, Claire."

He loved her? Her steps shuffled backward with the sudden weakness in her knees. "No. You don't." How could he when he didn't know everything?

"You're wrong. I've loved you since the day we met in the store. I can't explain it." Mark grinned with the joy of ignorance. "I don't even understand it, but it's true."

Hadn't she concluded she felt the same about him, even when it was wrong? "There's something I haven't told you about me." She looked away from the entreaty in his expression. "I lost two children during my marriage, Mark."

His brow furrowed, but he reached out and touched her cheek. "I'm sorry."

She jerked from his show of physical sympathy. If he kept touching her, she couldn't say what was needed. She couldn't force herself to make him understand.

"The first time I miscarried, we'd been married a few months. The second time about a year and a half. Afterward, I threw myself into designing, because I hadn't the courage to face the heartache over and over. Richard wanted children, Mark. You want children." The burning ache grew more intense. The ache of empty arms. The ache of loss. She'd learned that not even her work compensated for the guilt of having let her husband down. "I can't... I just can't."

"You don't know that, Claire. It might be different with us."

"The disappointment on your face matches the skepticism in your voice."

He frowned. "I'll admit the news has taken me by surprise. Who wouldn't feel staggered by that announcement? But—"

"There is no 'but' when it comes to my decision."

The sympathy vanished, and Mark's jaw hardened. "Your decision? You'll give me no say in the matter?"

She drove home her point with the force of an arrow to a bullseye. "Don't you understand that this would only cause problems between us?"

"You mean like right now?" He shook his head. "First, you think you're saving me from a business failure. Now you think you're saving me from a childless life? I don't need your salvation, Claire. I need you." His voice had grown fierce with a determination to sway her. "You're the one who told me I'd never live a full life if I continued to assert my control over everything. Aren't you doing the same?"

Was she?

Claire had cost Richard an important project. She had cost him an heir. And, in the end, she had cost him his life. How dare she chance ruining Mark's life, too.

"I can't pretend to understand everything you felt over losing a child." His voice softened. "But I've known couples who have spent many happy decades together never having had children. If I'm willing to trust God for what comes, why can't you?"

Having no reasonable answer for him, Claire entered the house and shut the door before she changed her mind.

"Don't do this. Don't push me aside!" His shout and the pounding of his fist pierced the wood. "Don't push *us* aside."

She pressed her back to the door and glanced up. Roslyn stood on the stairs, pity lining her young face.

Claire whispered past the tight muscles in the canyon of her throat. "It's for his own good."

# Chapter Twenty-eight

C laire trudged to the window and gazed out at a cobalt dawn crowned with gold. Not a cloud hampered the sight of the rising sun, and the warmth promised another day of blistering heat.

Nature imitated her life—lovely to look at, but one couldn't come too close or risk being burned. She'd taught Mark that lesson.

Birds twittered outside her window as she dressed in the gray skirt and white shirtwaist—the uniform she was destined to wear for the rest of her life.

The grit of sleeplessness, abrasive as a pumice stone, scratched the undersides of her eyelids with each blink. For several days, she'd battled against a renegade hope that Mark would try once more to convince her they could be happy with or without children. But she hadn't seen him since Tuesday, not even in passing his house on her way to work.

Claire left Roslyn's house and, a few minutes later, entered her parents' kitchen. It was time to ease their minds. "Good morning, Ma."

Her mother jumped at the sound of Claire's voice and spun around. "My goodness, Claire."

"I'm sorry. I didn't mean to scare you."

Ma waved it off. "What are you doing here so early?"

"If you don't mind, I came for breakfast before heading to the store."

"Of course, I don't mind. You're welcome anytime." Her mother cracked several eggs and dropped them into hot grease in the frying pan.

After tying on an apron, Claire pulled four plates from the shelf above the stove and laid them out on the table. As she worked, she felt her mother's inspection.

"Didn't you sleep well?"

Claire added a fork to each person's place, dreading the upcoming meal. "It wasn't my best night. Actually, I came because I have news."

Her mother paused to stare at her, spatula in her hand. The grease in the fry pan sizzled and popped.

"Ma, the eggs."

She turned back to the stove and flipped the crispy-edged eggs, one by one. "Does...Does this have anything to do with Mr. Gregory?"

The faltering question led Claire to believe her mother still expected a wedding announcement. "Let's wait until the others arrive."

A short time later, Wallace entered the kitchen, followed by Claire's father. Both took their seats at the table.

In the midst of the meal, her father said, "I understand you have something you want to say to us, Clairie."

When had Ma had time to talk to him? She'd only been gone from the kitchen long enough to pick up the milk from the front porch. Then again, how long did it take to say in passing, "Your daughter has something to tell us"?

"Yes, sir. I do." Claire punctured the egg yolk on her plate with a single tine of her fork. The thick yellow insides ran to hide under a small slice of ham, yet Claire had no place to hide from the pleasure she expected to see on the faces of her mother and father.

Pa nodded. "Go ahead."

"I'm no longer working with Mark."

Porcelain rattled as utensils hit the various plates, and her family members exchanged stunned glances.

"No more architecture nonsense?"

"No, Pa."

"It's for the best," her mother said. "You know how worried we've been about you."

"You mean, you've worried I would hurt someone else, someone besides Richard? I'm afraid you were right to be concerned."

Ma's eyes widened. "Now don't go putting words in my mouth. What happened to Richard was an accident. Nothing more."

Her father cocked his head. "Your ma is right. The same applies to Mark's injury. Is there something more to your decision to quit?"

Claire told them of her trip to Chicago. Why she volunteered to go, the reason for Mr. Arbuckle's refusal to accept Mark's design, and Lefler's past rejection of Richard because of her.

"I've never met that Mr. Lefler, but I tell you now, I'll never step foot inside his building." Wallace scowled at his half-eaten breakfast.

Tears pricked Claire's eyes. She told herself it was due to her brother's defense of her, but several sputtering sobs threatened to unleash a torrent of blubbering that had nothing to do with Wallace.

"Because I thought I could return to designing buildings, Mark has lost an important project, one he very much wanted." And needed.

A chair scraped across the floor, and her mother's arms enfolded her. "It will be all right."

How could it? She'd lost her opportunity to work as an architect. Worst, she'd lost her heart to Mark.

She cried on her mother's shoulder until the burn in her tired eyes dried the flow. With a series of sniffles, she wiped her tears on the napkin. Fatigue had gotten the best of her. It was the only explanation for her emotional breakdown.

"I'm expected at the store shortly." Claire backed her chair away from the table and carried her plate to the sink. "I've asked for a couple of days off work in the middle of the month to go to Indianapolis."

Her father pursed his lips. "The anniversary?"

"Yes."

"Would you like us to go with you?"

"No. I'll be fine."

Pa tossed his napkin on his plate and walked over to stand in front of her. He drew her into an embrace that smelled of pipe tobacco and coffee. "If God wants you to work as an architect, Clairie, we will cheer you on."

"John."

"Won't we, Ida?"

Ma hesitated, then nodded.

Though Claire would not seek another architectural position, receiving her parents' support filled her heart with gratitude. "Thank you."

CLAIRE INHALED THE scent of perfume, hair tonic, and cologne as she entered the small theater with Wallace and Roslyn. Ladies and gentlemen, dressed in an assortment of attire from formal to Sunday best, conversed in small gatherings. For this Independence Day celebration, Phoebe had insisted anyone be welcome to her performance, no matter their social or economic status.

The three worked their way down the crowded aisle to empty seats midway from the stage.

"I wish we were able to sit closer." Claire settled into a plush velvet theater chair and tidied the crinkles in the pastel blue silk—the dress she saved for special events.

Next to her, Roslyn craned her neck, looking around. "With this crowd, we should consider ourselves fortunate to have found seats this close."

"Which makes me happy for Phoebe."

Wallace's eyes nearly erupted from their sockets. "I hadn't imagined so many people. There must be more than a hundred here."

"And we're early." Claire's brother acted as their escort, even though he twitched in their father's evening clothes. She suspected he'd agreed to the arrangement solely to see Laurie at the reception in the Newland home after the concert.

Roslyn poked her with an unladylike elbow. "Look who's here." She stared straight ahead but jerked her head the side.

Claire followed the gesture with a subtle glance to her left. Across the aisle and three rows up, Mrs. Grzegorczyk sat with her head turned to speak to the man next to her. Her son. Claire suppressed her first instinct, which was to slump in her seat and hide her face behind a hand.

The harder she tried not to envision Mark dressed in a black tailcoat, white shirt, tie, and waistcoat, the harder it became to rid her mind of the captivating image. Even if it was in her imagination, he wore the look with comfort and composure.

"Why don't you go over and talk to him?"

"What would be the point? Let's just enjoy Phoebe's performance."

Roslyn released a long-suffering sigh. "All right. I'll say nothing else about it."

"If I remember correctly, you've said that before."

A few minutes later, Phoebe walked onto a stage edged in incandescent footlights, a new addition to the theater. She wore a gown of midnight blue, the bodice trimmed with a vee of black lace. Its short train trailed behind as she floated across the floor to the grand piano in the center of the stage. Moving with grace and dignity, her face glowed as applause broke out across the audience.

Throughout the concert, Claire sneaked peeks at the back of

Mark's head as he sat seemingly enthralled by the music. Had it been less than a week since they'd last seen one another? Each day had felt like a year.

When the array of music ended, Phoebe took her bows, then left the stage. The accolades faded, and people began to make their way to the exits.

Rather than hazard meeting Mark and his mother at the aisle, Claire remained in her seat with her head tilted down, and her hands gripping the arms of her companions to keep them seated, too. She let go once Mark and his mother passed by, pleased she'd avoided the awkwardness of being seen by them.

Having been invited by Phoebe to the reception after the concert, Claire and her companions strolled down a street lined with oak trees planted nearly twenty years earlier. They passed the largest residences in Riverport and stopped in front of a two-story, Second Empire house with a limestone exterior and dormer windows dotting its mansard roof. Not quite a mansion, it still impressed.

Lights glowed from the windows and guests drifted inside after a stop at the door to greet their hosts. Phoebe and Spence stood alongside Spence's parents with Phoebe's daughter Maura stationed between the young couple.

"I've walked by this house plenty of times," said Wallace. "I guess I've never taken the Newlands' wealth seriously until now."

At her brother's forlorn statement, Claire said, "It looks grander than it is due to the festivities."

"No, sis. It's grand. Too grand."

"Laurie is simply a person, Wallace, no different from you or me." Should she be encouraging his infatuation with Laurie Newland when she believed he'd only be hurt in the end?

"I think we both know that's not true. She's used to much more than I could ever provide her, no matter how many promotions I receive at the store."

It was the first time Claire had heard him reference the possibility of a future with the girl who was barely seventeen. "You're both still young. Be patient with yourself and her."

At the door, Claire thanked the elder Newlands for the invitation, introduced Roslyn, and hugged Phoebe. "Your performance was excellent tonight."

Phoebe's brown eyes shone in the light from the foyer chandelier. "Thank you. I must admit that it felt good to return to the stage." She glanced up at Spence. "But I won't turn it into a habit."

Six-year-old Maura jumped up and down. "We have a secret."

Claire smoothed a hand over the girl's warm head and studied the flush on Phoebe's face. It matched the alarm widening Spence's eyes. Phoebe drew Maura close and whispered in her daughter's ear. Maura smiled, two teeth missing. "Mama says I can't tell you."

"Then I'll wait." As if Claire couldn't guess.

She and her companions wandered farther into the house to find the few friends they knew among the guests.

Wallace looked over the crowd for that one special person. Claire patted his arm. "Go find her and say hello."

Half an hour later, she and Roslyn stood in the opening between the dining room and drawing room as the elder Spencer Newland—The Second—called for everyone's attention. He and his wife stood in front of the drawing room fireplace and alongside their son, Phoebe, and Maura. When confident he had obtained the ears of the guests, The Second smiled and said, "The Newlands wish to thank all of our friends for their attendance at Mrs. Crain's concert tonight. We hope you enjoyed it." Those scattered throughout the front rooms of the main floor answered with applause.

"You were invited here this evening to celebrate our country's independence and Mrs. Crain's return to the concert stage. However, that isn't all. We also want to announce that—"

"Mama found her prince!" At little Maura's outburst, giggles and guffaws filled the rooms from corner to corner.

Spence picked the girl up and laughed. "I can assure you, I found two lovely princesses." He wrapped an arm around Phoebe's waist and drew her close. "This one has agreed to marry me in the fall." He glanced at Maura. "And this one has agreed to call me Papa."

Almost before the announcement was complete, guests pushed forward to present the entire family with their congratulations. The little girl had the biggest smile of anyone in the room and kept repeating, "Mama found her prince. Mama found her prince."

There was no reason for Mark to have been invited to the reception. He barely knew the couple, but Claire couldn't help herself. She searched her surroundings for her own prince—one with golden flecks in his hazel eyes. The one she'd sent back to his castle to live his life without her.

Breaking ties with Mark had been the right thing to do before she cost him everything. Her heart pounded like a blacksmith's hammer, beating her chest so hard, she was afraid it would crack. She turned to Roslyn. "I need some fresh air."

She hurried outside and bent over the front porch rail, drawing in great gulps of the tepid summer air until her emotions calmed and she stopped trembling. What was wrong with her?

"Is there something I can do for you, Claire?"

She startled at the gentle voice beside her. Somehow, she found her breath. "Verbenia."

The woman stepped alongside her. "That was quite an announcement, yet not a surprise. Aren't you happy for them?"

"Yes, of course. I just..." She just what? Couldn't bring herself to be honest with someone who had shown her friendship? Who had given of her time and life experience to guide a group of women who sometimes seemed lost...as lost as Claire at this moment? "I felt a moment of envy."

"Muffin envy?"

Claire sputtered an overwrought laugh at the reference to their conversation the day they worked on Louisa's house. "This has nothing to do with architecture or performing in front of an audience."

"Mmm-hmm. Then it must be the other thing."

She wouldn't even pretend she didn't know what Verbenia meant. "Have you ever let someone go for that person's good, and then wondered if you'd made the right decision?"

Verbenia stared up at the summer stars, then slapped a mosquito on her arm. "Yes, I have."

Claire waited, silently willing her to explain.

"When I was a young woman, I loved a gentleman who dreamed of going West...Wyoming or some such place. He asked me to go with him." A cheerless grin appeared. "The thought of leaving all I'd known for the unknown terrified me. I'd heard awful stories of hardships on the trail and Indian attacks. But what right did I have to hold him back?

"After many a sleepless night, the time came for us to marry and join one of the wagon trains out of Missouri. At the last minute, I lost the courage and set him free to go alone, unwilling to venture into an uncertain and possibly dangerous life."

"He went without you?"

"I gave him no choice."

As Claire had given Mark no choice. "Do you regret your decision?"

"My husband made me happy. However, for many years, I wondered if fear kept me from a better life—one God had chosen for me and I'd rejected." Verbenia swiveled toward her. "What are you afraid of, Claire?"

*Too much.* "For one thing, repeating the mistakes of the past."

"Such as?"

Gathering her resolve, she shared her story. They discussed

everything from her marriage to Richard to the miscarriages and her guilt over his death to her belief she was a liability to both men. She ended with her reaction to Mark's declaration of love. The more she spoke, the easier it became to pour out her heart.

"I do enjoy architecture, Verbenia. It satisfies a...a creative need in me. Does that make sense?"

"Perfect sense. Gardening is my avenue of creativity."

"That doesn't justify using my work as an excuse to postpone Richard's desire to start a family."

"So you overindulged in your work?"

Claire nodded. "I used it to hide from the possibility of additional pain should I miscarry repeatedly."

The strains of soft, romantic music drifted through the open windows of the Newland home, replacing the jumbled noise from dozens of conversations. Evidently, Phoebe had agreed to give an impromptu concert for the guests.

"It wasn't right, was it?" Claire's voice held a note of desperation.

"Are you asking me, or confirming the answer for yourself?"

"I'm not sure I have any answers. I love Mark, but is it fair to saddle him with someone who may never bear a living child? Is it fair to me should I find I'm expecting a child, only to suffer more loss?"

Verbenia offered another slim smile. "I wish my younger self had understood that God never promises us a life of no hardship. What He does promise is to be with His people through it all. He promises to always go before us and to stand by us in difficulty."

She wrapped an arm around Claire's shoulders and squeezed. "Don't be like me. Be brave. Be faithful. Keep praying for the proper path to take. He will be at your side. He will catch you up in His arms when that path turns rocky and so narrow that you're afraid you'll fall off the edge.

"I don't have the answers to your questions, Claire. I can only point you to the One who does. Follow the path He's laid out and don't ever be afraid to live the life He's chosen for you."

*"You'll never fully live the life He wants for you."*

Claire had advised Mark to leave his problems in God's hands and commit to faith in Him even through the storms of life. She was a fine one to speak, wasn't she? When had she turned her problems over to him? When had she given Him control of her guilt, her future, her decisions...her fear?

Verbenia slapped another mosquito. "I'm going inside. Coming?"

"In a minute." Claire watched as her friend—her wise mentor—opened the door. "Verbenia, did you ever get your answer? Had you passed up the better trail?"

"It doesn't matter, does it? Your path isn't dependent on mine." Verbenia slipped inside, leaving Claire alone on the porch with her thoughts and the mosquitos.

Claire pulled off her glove and held out her left hand. Moonlight glinted on the gold ring, sparkling with amber flecks.

What did God want for her? Where would He lead her if she asked?

# Chapter Twenty-nine

A s he walked away from the post office, Mark shuffled through the three pieces of mail he'd picked up on his way home. His gut clenched when he saw the envelope from Chicago, the familiar crown design embossed on the front. Arbuckle's envelope with Mark's prospects stuffed inside. A letter only. No rendering returned. Was that good news?

After placing all three pieces of mail on the dining room table, he went to the kitchen for a cup of coffee to brace himself. Every day, he had prayed for God to give him the strength to accept an adverse response and, if that were the case, an answer to the problem of his loan.

The other day, feeling the old urge to act instead of trust, Mark had walked into the church with the cross that rose higher than the roofs around it. He'd spoken with the pastor, who gave him a Bible and pointed him to a special verse. Mark had committed it to memory. He murmured it again. "Trust in the Lord with all thine heart; and lean not unto thine own understanding."

In the past, he'd leaned so hard on his own understanding that he'd toppled over.

His mother stood at the stove, stirring their supper. It smelled good, but he'd had little appetite since Claire shut the door on him...on their future. It was one more part of his life he'd put in God's hands but had to admit to almost snatching it back the night of Mrs. Crain's concert. During the entire performance, Mark stared at Phoebe Crain, but Claire occupied his thoughts.

Since the pianist was a close friend, he had expected Claire to attend. To his dying day, he'd declare that the skin on the back of his neck bristled, alerting him when she entered the theater.

He'd shifted in his seat only so far as to watch her walk down the aisle, her beauty enhanced by the dress that matched her eyes. Afterward, he kept his gaze forward, not wishing to make either of them uncomfortable.

The way she remained in her seat, refusing to look at him while everyone else filed out of the theater demonstrated her lack of a change of heart regarding them.

Yes, he wanted children, but he wanted Claire more.

Mark missed her more than he'd ever supposed possible. He'd asked God to show him a way to convince her that they belonged together, that she needn't be afraid of the future, because he believed in the two of them with his whole heart. He believed God brought them together and, when the time was right, would let Mark know to act.

Until then...

This trust business was one of the hardest things he'd ever attempted.

Mark grabbed a cup and saucer from the shelf. "Where's Mr. Olesky?"

Having a boarder—this one in particular—still vexed him. Maybe his continued apprehension over the man was due to his mother, who remained a handsome woman for her age.

Did he really want a stepfather after all these years? Did he have a right to object to Mama's interest in a man when he'd despised her objection to Claire?

Then again, maybe he imagined something between the older couple that didn't exist.

"He said to eat without him. He planned to return later this evening."

Good. Mark filled his coffee cup, topping it with a bit of cream from the icebox. Thoughts of the envelope from Chicago intruded as he stirred the brew into a mellow tan color. Putting off bad news wouldn't change it.

He placed his coffee cup on the dining room table and picked up the mail, then opened the envelopes one-by-one, saving the best—or worst—for last. The first was a bill from the grocer, the second a bill from the mercantile, and the third...

Mark slit the top with his finger and pulled out a single sheet of paper. He skimmed the words in two short paragraphs, then tossed the letter onto the table. His hand hit the cup. He tried to catch it but missed, and it crashed to the floor. Coffee puddled around the splintered pieces, leaving them looking like islands in the middle of a river.

At the noise, his mother rushed in from the kitchen. "What was that? Did you drop something?"

"I'm sorry. I broke the cup."

She rushed back to the kitchen and grabbed a towel to sop up the coffee, while he picked up the porcelain pieces.

When they'd finished the cleanup, she tilted her head, observing him. "What is wrong, Marek?"

May as well tell her the truth—the full truth—since it might mean uprooting her again for a return to Chicago. He pulled out a chair. "Please, sit down."

She wiped her hands on the apron she wore and sat in the seat he'd provided. "What is it?"

Mark sat catty-corner to her. "I did something foolish. I let my ambition and arrogance overrule my common sense."

"My son is not foolish."

He clasped his hands together on the top of the table. "I was this time, Mama. I took out a loan last winter and assumed my business would be more successful by now, that I would easily make the first payment and interest when it came due at the end of this month. Unfortunately, it looks as if that won't happen."

She frowned. "But you have been successful. You have received projects."

"Yes, but not enough to apply to the loan payment and pay my other bills." To ensure she understood the gravity of the situation, he gave her the details of what he owed and what he still lacked. "You should be prepared for the possibility of a move back to Chicago."

Mark waited for her to show glee. Instead, she pointed to the letter from Arbuckle. "Does this talk of moving back to Chicago have something to do with that paper?"

He picked up the letter. "This informs me that my project was not chosen to proceed to the next stage in the competition."

"Because Mrs. Kingsley worked on it?"

The last thing he wanted was to give his mother more ammunition to dislike Claire. He still held out hope that the woman he loved would see reason. Of course, he had no idea how that would happen if he didn't remain in Riverport. "It's a consequence of thinking that I alone had power over my success or failure. God...and Claire...have taught me differently."

"I am sorry for your trouble, *mój słodki chłopcze*. Will you return to your position in Mr. Burnham's office?"

Would he lay aside his pride, his push for respect, to support them?

In the past few days, he'd learned of the recklessness in letting a years-old anger keep him from reliance on God. The reminder of that lesson removed some of the sting of Lefler's rejection and the loss of his pride.

"Right now, Mama, I'm living on the faith that everything will work out as it should."

"I am sure it will." She rose from her seat and patted his shoulder as she passed behind his chair. "I will be back in a moment."

When she returned, she opened his hand and laid a stack of bills on his palm. A significant stack.

"What is this?"

"It is for your loan payment."

He shoved the money back at her. "Mama, I won't take money from you."

"And why not? Is it not good enough?"

"It has nothing to do with being good enough, but only a shiftless son takes money from his mother." He might be foolish, but he wasn't shiftless. "Where did you get all this, anyway? How much are you charging Mr. Olesky?"

"It is not from Mr. Olesky. It is my hat money."

He quickly counted the bills and his jaw tensed. "Are you telling me you've saved all this for purchasing hats?"

His mother shook her head. "Not for purchase. This is from sales."

Mark scratched his forehead, totally confused. "You sold your old hats for ninety-eight dollars?" Already-worn pieces of fluff and feathers?

She patted his cheek, but he sensed she restrained a desire to slap some sense into him. "This is money saved from hats I have made and sold over the years."

He fanned the bills. She had made the headpieces as a hobby and for friends, or so he'd thought. This was the first he'd heard of her selling them. "Are you telling me you've had a business all this time?"

"A relatively prosperous business. At first, I used it to get over my grief when your *tata* died. Then, my friends praised my hats to others, and those people began to ask for their own. I thought, why not? We must eat, must we not?"

Mark hung his head, wagging it in amazement. What else didn't he know about his mother? "Why didn't you tell me?"

"You were determined to take care of us both, Marek. After your father died, you felt a responsibility to me—a responsibility no young child should undertake. How could I tell you that it was my hat money that paid the mortgage when you were so proud and worked so hard to do everything yourself?"

Maybe if she had told him when he was a child that he couldn't do everything by himself, that nothing rested solely on his shoulders, he would have saved himself a painful lesson as an adult. But he couldn't—wouldn't—blame his mother for his arrogant folly.

He pressed the money into her hand. Should he fail to pay the loan, she would need her savings to purchase another house in Chicago. Neither of them could stay in Riverport after people learned he was an unreliable deadbeat. Who would hire him for architectural services? And how would he face Claire?

He was tempted to snatch the bills back. With his mother's money, along with what he'd already saved, he could pay the first installment on the loan.

*Trust.*

"This belongs to you, Mama. There will be another way." God would show him the way. And if He wanted them in Riverport, they would stay. Somehow.

"I know, *mój słodki chłopcze.*" Again, she patted his cheek, this time with the gentleness of a loving mother. "You are a good son and a fine man. You deserve..." Her voice broke, and she cleared her throat. "You deserve to be happy. But moving back to Chicago will not bring the happiness you seek, the happiness I have seen in you since coming here."

"Mama—"

"All these years, I have expressed my discontentment to everyone. I have given in to my selfishness and pride, unwilling to accumulate to life—"

"Acclimate." When she tilted her head, he smiled. "I assume the word you want is acclimate."

"Do not correct your mother." She waved a hand through the air. "What difference does it make? I am trying to say it was wrong to bring misery to those around me."

"What caused this change?"

"I received a letter from Nadia the other day."

A chill rolled over Mark. "Mr. Kowalski?"

"He is as well as can be expected. Did you know Paulina attended classes at the Chicago Evangelization Society?"

"Mr. Moody's institute. She told me. What about it?"

"Nadia said that as soon as her daughter's friends from the Institute learned of her father's poor health, they began to bring meals and sit with him to allow the women time for chores and necessary shopping. They have cooked and cleaned, prayed for the family, and calmed their fears. Paulina's beau, Frederick, has proven himself to her parents. They have given their blessing to a marriage."

"I'm glad."

"None of Paulina's friends are Polish or Catholic, you know, but they have been compassionate and accepting, unlike Nadia and me.

"I am ashamed of my claim that no one could care for our people like other Poles. I was too stubborn to admit that I have met many in Riverport—in my life—who are thoughtful, including Mrs. Kingsley. She saved my precious Cookie and did her best to help you with the project for Mr. Lefler. She has a kind heart, Marek, and I see she has made you happy."

Even in those times when Claire became irrational, she made him happy.

"I met Mrs. Malone at Newland's earlier today."

His mother sprang one surprise after another on him. "You spoke to Roslyn Malone?"

"We had a nice visit. She is too direct for my taste, but young and not unlikeable."

To others, it might seem Mama had gone off topic, but Mark knew otherwise. "What did she say?"

"For one thing, she said Mrs. Kingsley left this afternoon for Indianapolis."

Left Riverport? "Did Mrs. Malone say when she'll be back?"

"Perhaps she will not come back."

"She said that?"

"I said that. You called yourself a foolish man. I will agree that you are foolish if you let Claire get away with saying she is no good for you."

These words came from his mother?

She turned her earlier remorse into a sharp reprimand. "Do not just stand there, Marek. I mean Mark." The name stumbled from her lips. "Go find her and bring her home, *mój słodki chłopcze*."

He'd begun to fathom enough about God over the past couple of weeks to be ninety-percent certain He wouldn't lead him into a position of harm...if this was God's leading.

But was this God's leading?

Where was the proof of Claire's feelings for him when she still wore her wedding ring? When she'd turned away from him at the concert and returned to Indianapolis without a word for him?

"I'm not sure Claire is ready to see me."

"Bah! Make arrangements to go get her and bring her back."

Mark hadn't the first notion where to look for Claire in Indianapolis, but he kissed his mother's cheek. "Thank you, Mama, and for you, I will always answer to Marek."

Twenty minutes later, Mark knocked on the door of the Pittman house. When Claire's father answered, Mark said, "May I speak with you, sir?"

The man cracked a half-smile. "What took you so long?"

# Chapter Thirty

C laire had arrived in the city last evening, too late to pay this visit. Now, as she entered the Crown Hill Cemetery through the arched entrance, she carried with her less guilt and grief than in the past.

With the death of their first child, she and Richard had purchased plots on this high point, or "crown," overlooking the center of Indianapolis to the south. Though only the bones of her husband occupied the tiny plot of ground, it seemed fitting for him to be in a spot that would face the type of buildings he'd dreamed of designing.

Only days ago, she would have followed that thought with "but never had a chance because of her." Yes, she'd let hurt distract her from realizing the danger the day he died. However, the voice of blame no longer haunted her to the extent she'd allowed it to for two years. All that was left was a sadness in knowing her last words to Richard were said in anger.

Claire had learned her lesson the hard way and prayed that, once she returned to Riverport, Mark would be willing to see the change in her. Until then, she must say goodbye to her old life, her old fear.

While wandering down the path toward her destination—an open area that held rows of headstones and small monuments to loved ones—she focused on the sounds of the birds chirping in nearby trees and relished the warm, soft breeze that danced across her face. The cheerfulness of nature kept her mind off the somberness of the occasion.

Past visits had never failed to wrench every ounce of emotion from her and wring her dry of tears. Today, a sense of serenity replaced the impulse toward melancholy—a hard-fought-for serenity, but one that assured her that she'd begun her life's next journey on the right path. What lay ahead, whether comfort or distress, she had no idea, but she'd walk with the courage of knowing that God, not fear, accompanied her.

Claire encountered numerous people out for a stroll through the park-like setting, people who might not have anyone interred here, but who enjoyed the lovely surroundings.

The section where Richard was buried came into view, as did the gentleman standing at his gravesite. She squinted to identify him, and her stomach dropped. George. Why had he picked now to pay his respects? In fact, why pay his respects at all to someone he'd elected to forget?

She thought about turning around and coming back later but trudged through the grass to stand beside George, her attention on her husband's headstone. The once-pristine sandstone marker was soiled by two years of dust and dirt.

On either side of the grave, two smaller headstones poked from the ground. Headstones planted in memory of lives never lived.

"Claire."

"George."

At the end of the curt greeting, they stood mute. Claire struggled for something to say. An apology might be in order. Yet...

Finally, George filled the awkwardness. "Do you remember the time Richard and I inspected the abandoned Cascade Hotel?"

The memory of the decrepit building in a small town north of here brought a reluctant smile to her lips. "You looked it over in order to prepare plans to renovate it."

"We examined every corner."

"That's when Richard caught a glimpse of a 'cat' slipping around a corner."

George chuckled. "He insisted it be safely removed from the building before any work began, so we set off to chase it down."

The memory widened her smile. "I burned his clothing and made him sleep outside that night."

"You burned mine, too." George laughed. "I still can't understand how he mistook a skunk for a cat. From then on, I never let him forget his spectacles."

Claire joined him in laughter. "Poor Richard. I'd never seen him more embarrassed."

The merriment over the story died off. "Did you know he lost a project with Harris Lefler because of me?"

George's chin dipped to meet his chest, and he didn't respond for several moments. "Did he?"

Of course, he knew, but she accepted his answer as a kindness.

"No matter what you think, I really did care about Richard. He was my best friend." He turned to face her. "I'd like to put aside our differences and be your friend, too."

Claire crouched and, after removing a glove, pulled the stem of a dandelion from the base of the headstone. She blew on what was left of the fluff, sending it floating on currents of air, and taking the time to think about George's request.

"I very much wish to remain angry with you, George. I wish to, but I can't. Richard wouldn't want us at odds, because you were *his* best friend, too." She slipped the glove on, and he helped her to stand. "That was a nice thing you did for Mr. Gregory."

"I didn't do it for him, though I'll admit to being sorry he didn't make it to the next round in the competition. I wouldn't have minded defeating him in the end."

As anticipated, Mark's design was rejected. For once, Claire felt no self-reproach. Sadness, yes, but she wasn't responsible for the bigotries of others, only her own.

They both reached out and touched the headstone a final time before George walked Claire back to the cemetery's entrance. Without giving it a second thought, she kicked her resentment of him into the past where it belonged. She laid a hand on his arm and gave a gentle squeeze. "Goodbye for now, George."

"Goodbye, Claire." George's brow furrowed, his attention behind her. "You came with him?"

She turned toward the man pacing within the arched gateway into the cemetery twenty yards away. "No."

Not long ago, she would have considered Mark's presence here an insensitive intrusion. Today, her heart sang with delight.

"Clearly, someone else waits to take Richard's place." George grinned and walked away.

Claire shook her head. That was the George she remembered.

Before meeting with Mark, she paused to observe him. Hope rose like those dandelion seeds on the air currents. Surely, he had come for one reason. For her.

WAITING AT THE GATE, Mark paced while Claire talked to George Brant. Would she be outraged that he'd come, that he'd intruded on her time of remembrance?

Had it not been for her father's recommendation and blessing, he'd have remained in Riverport and met her at the train station on her return. However, Mr. Pittman believed his daughter needed him—today and in the future.

Now what was he to do? He hadn't expected to see her with Brant, much less see her touching him.

Brant noticed Mark and said something to Claire. When she turned, Mark searched her expression for pleasure or dismay. She had mastered neutrality.

Brant crossed the lawn toward him. "I cannot say I'm surprised to see you." Then he walked away before Mark could respond.

Mark put one foot in front of the other, his gaze locked on Claire. She met him halfway. He'd prepared himself for the awkward meeting given the circumstances of their parting.

He was here, beside her, even though it eluded him as to where to begin. "This is a beautiful place." He was content to speak of the trivial until their feet landed on a more important topic.

"Yes." She glanced around. "How did you find me here?"

"Your father."

"Pa?"

"We talked for some time last night. He told me where you went...and why. I think I'm growing on him."

"He isn't as severe as he came across the first time you met or the day of my move." Claire walked toward the entrance gate, her steps slow and precise, and he followed. "I'm sorry about the Lefler competition."

"How did you know?"

"George."

Mark eyed the man as he climbed into a waiting carriage. How had he discovered it? It didn't matter. "The whole thing was my fault. I'd heard the rumors when it came to his opinion of working women. I should never have put you in the position of dealing with Mr. Arbuckle."

"You had no one else."

"I could have sent my mother."

"As I recall, you did."

"To be honest, besides providing a chaperone for you, I'd hoped that, in traveling together, you and my mother would discover some common ground."

"We found a little. I'm not sure she'll ever see me as worthy of..." Claire pressed her lips together.

Worthy of him? Worthy of being his wife?

"She's come around, Claire...about you, about her circumstances." He explained the letter from Nadia Kowalski and his mother's change of heart.

"Poor Paulina. Although, I am happy for your mother." She clenched her hands behind her back. "How is the Dover design coming?"

"I met with the couple and showed them the preliminary plan. They liked it very much, especially your ideas for the interior." Mark kicked aside an old, broken acorn. "Dover was disappointed that you wouldn't be moving forward on the project."

"He won't change his mind about working with you, will he?"

"No. He'll keep his word."

With his hand at her elbow, Mark led Claire in the direction of his hired carriage. He hadn't planned to lay this out here, but she seemed to be waiting for him to say something. "Dover isn't the only one disappointed that we won't be working together."

She voiced no objection. In fact, it appeared she wished to hear more.

"Be my partner, Claire. We'll rename the business Gregory and Kingsley Architects."

Her face fell. "Gregory and Kingsley."

He'd thought she'd be happy to be offered an important role in his company, the kind she'd once wanted. Instead, she looked as if he had stolen her stick candy and run off before she could stop him.

She arched a thin eyebrow. "You came here to talk me into a partnership with you?"

"No." Not that kind of partnership. "Well, yes, but—"

"Mark, there's something you should know. I urged you to go after the Lefler invitation to get back at George for erasing the Kingsley name from his company. My reason for working with you was to see that name on a final plan."

"To keep his memory alive?"

"As penance for my role in his death." She shook her head. "After a while, I just wanted it for me."

He appreciated her honesty. He welcomed learning everything about her, even her less-flattering secrets.

Mark drummed his uninjured fingers on his thigh. He might as well get said what he'd traveled all these miles to say, what her father had encouraged him to say. "I want that for you, too, Claire. I want you as a partner in my company, but that isn't the reason I came to Indianapolis."

"Then why?"

He captured her left hand and paused a moment to be sure she wouldn't pull away. To his delight, she didn't. Nerves heightened by what he was about to say, his thumb brushed the top of her fingers and froze with an awareness that something was different.

He pulled off her glove. "You removed the ring." Richard's ring.

She glanced at her finger as though its nakedness held no significance. "It was time. Why look back years from now and wonder if I chose poorly?"

Bewildered, Mark's brow creased. Chose poorly? What did it matter what she meant when it fostered his optimism?

Her fingers—her bare finger—curled around his. "You were about to tell me why you traveled to Indianapolis. Was it to escort me home?"

Home? Mark liked the sound of it, because Riverport was home. God led him there, and Mark trusted that was where He wished him to stay. Somehow.

"Yes, I wish to escort you home. Even that isn't why I'm here. Our last conversation didn't go as I'd planned. I didn't ask you what I wanted desperately to know."

"Which was?"

He drew in a deep breath. "Claire Pittman Kingsley, will you marry me?"

She stared up the road in the direction of the city, killing him with her silence. Finally, she faced him and smiled. "That's not a trivial question, Mr. Gregory."

"It wasn't meant to be." Her answer wasn't a rejection. Still... "What's wrong?"

"We haven't settled our biggest problem, Mark. You want children. What if—"

He sighed. "Darling, we talked about Lizzie O'Keefe losing three children. I should have told you the rest of their story. They went on to have two more healthy babies. This next child will be their third. Yes, they're prepared should the worst happen, but they aren't letting it take away their enthusiasm over this baby."

"Are you being truthful? You're not trying to convince me?"

"I am trying to convince you...with the truth."

She peered up at him through those long lashes. "That doesn't mean we'll be as fortunate."

"No, it doesn't. But as long as your health isn't endangered and you're willing to take the chance, we'll face that 'what if' together and pray that God blesses us with children of our own. If not, there's a big orphanage outside of Riverport filled with children who need a family." He winked. "We might even find a Polish child to adopt."

She laughed. "Wouldn't that please your mother."

"Immensely."

Her mirth wavered, replaced by deep lines between her eyes. "Are you sure you're willing to risk—"

He growled. "Claire, I'm willing. Are you?"

He passed through what seemed an eternity, waiting for her response. Then...

An inviting smile graced her lips. She held out her arms. "They're open whenever you're ready to walk into them for all time."

Mark ran her answer over in his mind, worried he'd merely heard the words he yearned to hear.

"Well, Mr. Gregory?"

He conquered the empty inches standing between them and stepped into her arms. "I'm ready. I'm more than ready, Mrs. Kingsley."

# Chapter Thirty-one

C laire entered the office carrying the mail she'd picked up from the post office. Mark stood by the desk wearing that special grin that warmed her all over. He swept her up in his arms, knocking the mail from her hands. After twirling her until the room spun, he stole a quick but luscious kiss and set her back on her feet.

She fought dizziness—from the motion, from the happiness. "Does that mean you missed me?"

"Maybe." His second kiss, not as quick as the first, left her grasping for a full breath. "I didn't think you'd ever get here."

"Since it was my last day at Newland's, I said goodbye to everyone."

He pulled back to see into her face. "I couldn't bear it if you ever said goodbye to me, Claire."

"Never."

"Remember that." He let her go and picked up the envelopes scattered across the floor, scrutinizing each. "This looks like a letter from Paulina to you."

She snatched the one he held out, tore it open, and scanned the contents. "She's asking us to ship Bella to her. Do you think the puppy will be all right in the baggage compartment of a train by herself?"

"If you're worried, why don't you and my mother take Bella to her?"

Claire kissed his cheek, eager to see her friend again, not

minding the trip with her future mother-in-law. "I'll do that." Perhaps she'd meet Frederick while she was in Chicago.

How grateful she was that her efforts to bring Mark and Paulina together had failed.

"How is her father?"

She frowned at reading Paulina's words. "The same. She wants to cheer him in his last days and thinks having the puppy around will make him smile."

"I hope so." Mark clutched another envelope. "That reminds me. Mrs. Dover's birthday is coming up next month. Guess who's claimed the largest puppy as a gift for her."

"Mr. Dover? Really? How sweet of him." The older couple had grown into more than clients to Mark and Claire. They were quickly becoming dear friends, and she would gladly see the pup grow up and run free on their new property.

Mark asked, "What do you think of us keeping our miracle pup?"

Only two weeks had passed since he'd proposed, but their plans had moved forward with the speed of a pitcher's fastball. Their wedding was scheduled for the end of October, a week after Phoebe and Spence would marry.

If Mrs. Grzegorczyk had her way, it would be tomorrow. Not that Mark's mother was eager for a new, non-Polish daughter-in-law, but she viewed as indecent an engaged couple working alone together all day without the legalities of marriage.

They had given Mr. Olesky notification that he must find another place to live by the end of September. The strange man disappeared sometime during the middle of that night. Although none of them were sorry to see him go, their inquiries only revealed that no one had heard of a man named Alec Olesky. Strange, indeed.

"Claire?"

"Hmm?"

"The puppy?"

"Let's keep him."

"He started out a trouble-maker, and he's growing into a greater one. Are you sure?"

The pup they had saved found a way to get into everything. Curious and cute as could be, she wouldn't think of sending him to a new home. "I'm sure."

"We'll also need to find a house of our own." He paused, then said, "If you're agreeable, I'd like us to consider your design, the one you and Richard drew."

"That's an old dream, Mark."

"We can revive it."

She shook her head. "No. It's the past. From now on, we make new dreams. Dreams that will endure for the rest of our lives."

He kissed the tip of her nose. "I like that idea."

Mark flipped from front to back the envelope still clutched in his hand. "Do you know an Edward Trent?"

"I don't think so."

"The name is familiar, but I can't place him."

Claire thumped the envelope. "Well, as Wallace once pointed out to me, there is a way to find out who he is and what he wants."

He slit open the envelope and pulled out a single sheet of paper. After a few seconds of reading silently, a smile crept onto his face. It grew wider and wider. "Now I remember where I've heard the name. He's almost as prosperous a businessman as Harris Lefler."

"What does he want?"

Mark released one of those shrill whistles as he'd done at the baseball park and handed her the letter. "Read this."

The more Claire read, the greater her astonishment. "No wonder Mr. Arbuckle took a long time in sending your rendering back."

"Sly dog, isn't he?"

"And surprising."

Who would have imagined that the crotchety man would show the rendering to someone who would choose to hire their firm and build Mark's design, despite his association with Claire?

Rather than rename their partnership Gregory and Kingsley Architects, they chose to keep the original business name. After all, Mark had worked hard for it, and if God blessed them with children in their marriage, her responsibilities and priorities would change.

As long she continued to seek God's direction, if He said no to future babies, she would trust that He'd give her the courage and faith to accept her path—however rocky, however painful.

Mark pulled a bank draft from the envelope and held it up. "Mr. Trent included a partial payment. It covers the balance of the loan plus an additional five dollars." Awe filled his voice. "This was not how I pictured the Lefler design satisfying my obligation to the bank."

Claire had offered the money she'd received from George—enough to pay the loan in full, not just this month's installment. Mark turned her down. She almost insisted, not for her own glory or because she had no faith in him, not from remorse or a duty to Richard. She wanted to insist because she believed in Mark and in their dreams, whichever ones came true, and however God chose to accomplish them. Now she was glad she hadn't insisted, because she would have interfered in God's plan and the growth of Mark's faith.

He waved the paper in front of her. "Never think God isn't interested in our lives, Mrs. Kingsley."

She plopped her hands on her hips in mock exasperation. "I believe I said that first, Mr. Gregory."

"So you did, and you were right." Mark stuffed the bank draft back in the envelope. "We have work to do."

She snatched the envelope and dropped it on the desk. "Tomorrow. Tonight, we have a baseball game to attend."

Mark wrapped an arm around her waist and pulled her close. "I have an idea. Let's postpone our arrival until the middle of the seventh inning."

Claire laughed. October *was* too long to wait.

# *Acknowledging...*

*Lord, like Mark and Claire, I need your guidance every day and in all I do, even and especially when writing a book. You provide that knowledge and understanding so available for me to lean on. Thank you.*

A special way in which God provides wisdom is through others. I'm thankful to each person listed below.

Brainstorming is a big part of ferreting out the plot, and these ladies help me do just that: Angie Arndt, Marie Coutu, and Jerusha Agen.

Next, I'd be nowhere without someone I can depend on to tell me when my story goes off track and suggests ways to deepen the writing, as well as someone who boosts and encourages me. That person is my go-to, amazing writer friend Heidi Chiavaroli.

Lynne Tagawa provided the editing for this book. She was awesome at (and insistent upon) keeping me rooted in the era regarding word usage, so important in historicals.

The name Paulina gave her puppy was chosen by a couple of ladies from my Love and Faith in Fiction newsletter community. Their suggestion is much appreciated.

And, of course, my family always deserves much in the way of thanks and credit for all their support.

# *Don't Miss Unwrapping Hope*

### *She's a mystery his heart longs to unravel.*

Phoebe Crain, once a lauded concert pianist, lives in anonymity after being disgraced by a wealthy man. For her daughter's sake, Phoebe can't afford a second mistake in love, yet each day brings a struggle to resist trusting in the integrity of a department store owner's heir...another man of wealth.

Spence Newland has fought for years to prove his worthiness to take over the family business. But store scandals and his own insecurity threaten everything he has worked to achieve, even the future he's come to envision with Phoebe.

Will they give in to their greatest fears or conquer them and unwrap the gift of a forever together?

*Travel back to 1896 for a story one reviewer labeled "a lovely tale of the heart."*

SANDRA ARDOIN

# *A Word to Readers*

Thank you for reading *Enduring Dreams*. So, did you enjoy it? I hope so. I also hope you took something from the story that you can apply to your own life.

Let me make one historical clarification. At the beginning of the book, I included an inspiring quote by Daniel Burnham. While there's speculation that it isn't a word-for-word quotation (no one knows for certain), it is widely attributed to him based on a speech he made in 1910. A partner in his firm made it famous when he put it on a 1912 Christmas card with Burnham's name.

Please consider leaving a short, honest review on a retail site that carries the book. Believe it or not, the number of reviews a book has is crucial to its visibility, which means it's crucial to another reader's opportunity to find it. No need to get fancy. A couple of sentences without spoilers will do.

Don't forget to look for the second novel in the Widow's Might Series soon. To learn of its release or about upcoming specials, subscribe to my Love and Faith in Fiction newsletter at www.sandraardoin.com/newsletter.

ENDURING DREAMS

# *Historical Romances by Sandra Ardoin*

## Widow's Might Series

*Enduring Dreams*, Book One
*Unwrapping Hope*, Novella

## Additional Novels and Novellas

*A Love Most Worthy*
*A Reluctant Melody*
*The Yuletide Angel*

# *About the Author*

AS AN AUTHOR OF HEARTWARMING and award-winning historical romance, Sandra Ardoin engages readers with page-turning stories of love and faith. Rarely out of reach of a book, she's also an armchair sports enthusiast, country music listener, and seldom says no to eating out. Visit her at www.sandraardoin.com. Connect with her on BookBub, Facebook, Twitter, Goodreads, and Pinterest.

# Don't miss out!

Visit the website below and you can sign up to receive emails whenever Sandra Ardoin publishes a new book. There's no charge and no obligation.

https://books2read.com/r/B-A-IRCH-QGJGB

**BOOKS 2 READ**

Connecting independent readers to independent writers.

www.ingramcontent.com/pod-product-compliance
Lightning Source LLC
Chambersburg PA
CBHW020413260626
47156CB00007B/2363